EKKO

Book I

White Limousine

———

Johnny Walker

EKKO

Book I: White Limousine

Third Edition (E12-12)
ISBN: 978-0-9889944-0-9
ISBN10:   0-9889-9440-2
© 2014
1 2 3 4 5 6 7 8 9 10 11 13

For information address CIC Publishing, NY, NY.

Some characters and/or places appearing in this work are fictitious, or public domain. Any fictitious resemblance to real persons, living or dead, is purely coincidental.

All copyrights and works are owned by the author.

Replaces Second Edition
© 2011
ISBN 1-4507-7456-7
Replaces First Edition
© 2006
ISBN 1-4241-5394-8

PUBLISHED BY CIC PUBLISHING

Printed in the United States of America

Dedicated to Anita

Table of Contents

EKKO...2

CJ..7

The Hayson...16

Dead Bear...43

Sliced..65

The Settlement...74

Deals...101

New Orleans..114

Clarise...132

E..150

Sound Check...167

Frederick...176

Milo...192

Nathan Juju...203

The Landlers..231

It's a Boy..240

White Limousine..245

Savannah...266

Mr. 5008..284

Back Pages Content.....................................301

Black Coffee Excerpt (Book II).....................306

EKKO

Just one bolt—that's all. One measly, stubborn little piece of iron had brought the job to a screeching halt. It didn't seem rusted, or bent. There weren't any damaged threads.

'*What the hell?*'

The repairs had gone without a hitch so far, but this puppy wasn't budging. That left CJ with two options: either grab a hacksaw, or beat the living crap out of it. He had to get it out soon, though; the late-night hour was right around the corner.

CJ slammed the bolt with a hammer, a massive blow, manly enough to rock the mounting. The tiny fastener flew through the air and the speaker plopped down on his shoulder. CJ steadied it best he could to carry it down the ladder.

Something scurried across the ceiling. He saw it from the corner of his eye. He looked to the wall of mirrors—on the far side of the showroom. There was a ghostly semblance of a man standing below him, casually resting his hand on the ladder.

"Dammit!" CJ muttered and then sighed. "Never … look … in the mirrors."

A freezing draft whisked against his body. It rustled the hair on his forearms and shook his sense of balance. He hurried down the ladder with the loudspeaker, nothing new—until the ghost grabbed his shin with an ice-cold grip. A freezing pain rushed through CJ's bones and he flinched. The ladder shook. The speaker leaned to one side just as the banshee bellowed a high-octave shriek—a piercing, painful scream. The lights flickered and CJ missed the next step, sending the speaker, and him, tumbling to the ground.

The semblance went to CJ and stood above him. No doubt pleased with his prank, he put his hands to his stomach and threw his head back, flashing his pearly whites. It was a wicked laugh. Not cool.

CJ tried to roll away, but the semblance stomped the ground, blocking CJ's move. He leaned over CJ and opened his jaw in slow motion, stretching his face more than humanly possible, and with one quick blink, the canines shattered from his mouth and showered CJ with a cold white dust. One step closer and the ghost's hair started falling from his head. Weightless and air-like, the locks piled onto CJ's legs.

Two beats later the ghost was an inch from CJ's face, still boasting. His skin withered, and his black lips shriveled, then his gray hide tightened and formed to his bony skull. He held CJ's attention with his blackened stare while his skeletal fingers reached for the amulet hanging from CJ's neck.

CJ knocked the hand away and shuffled backward, but the semblance was suddenly standing behind him, peering down at CJ with a set of lifeless eyes. "Hear me now," a growling voice said, as the ghost slashed his bony fingers across CJ's cheek, piercing his face with a freezing, inhuman pain.

It was on …

CJ leapt to his feet and took a swing.

The phantom made a dash for the lounge.

"Not the lobby!" CJ said. "Crap."

He had to follow, knowing the semblance could be ruthless … but even worse, there was no way of warning the patrons at the bar.

CJ went through the double doors and maneuvered through the crowded lounge, treading with caution under the sapphire-colored lights. He searched the bar with an eagle eye, trying not to confuse the ice-blue silhouettes of humans with the inhuman glow of the ghost. The semblance was hiding somewhere in the translucent haze, slithering through the sea of necklaces and pinstriped suits. CJ crept through the crowd. Nickel barstools and silver sconces popped in and out of sight as people stirred about.

The semblance, meanwhile, had planted himself at the far corner of the bar, where he stood lifeless … his dark presence blending with the shadowed walls behind him. He remained unnoticed for the most part, lingering in an area that received little to no light—until a few patrons at the bar began to sense his menacing stare.

As customers turned toward the stranger, their pleasant expressions took flight. Faces became cold and unresponsive. Others in the bar picked up on the distraction and they, too, stopped socializing to look his way, enticed by his mysterious confidence. The chain reaction spread through the lounge like a virus, and the patrons quietly gathered together. And there they stood, collectively staring at the shadowed man, anticipating his next move.

A surge of dark frequencies rippled through the airwaves just then, killing every last timbre of sound with one smothering pass. On the tail of the wave came a steady flow of hypnotic sound waves, pulsing up through the floor, driving the rhythmic vibration into the bones of the patrons.

Seized by the pulsating grip, the crowd became hysterical, facing each other and bursting with laughter. Within a few beats the tonal enchantment had the men and women dancing in circles, arms held high, cheering as though the Berlin Wall had just come crashing down. It only took a few measures for the crowd to reach a state of ecstasy, an almost orgasmic peak, when suddenly the pulsating rhythm stopped.

The cheerful arms dropped flat. Heads became sluggish, leaning forward, and backward, and some even sideways. Knees buckled, and one by one the customers started collapsing.

The phantom watched CJ from across the room, maintaining his devious poise until the last few club-goers had plunged to the ground. It was then that CJ had a clear view across the bar. As he zeroed in on the spirit's face, CJ's legs went weak … and the room started spinning.

CJ

In a New York City apartment on West 28th Street, a cell phone rang.

CJ sprung from bed and looked around, lost at first, but as soon as he saw his tool bag he plopped back down on the covers.

It was the end of spring, but not quite summer in the city. A muggy dampness had invaded the room. CJ grabbed the edge of his bedsheet and wiped the sweat from his face. The phone kept ringing. He rubbed his eyes, wondering how he'd got home. As he reached for the phone, he eyeballed the window and grabbed a pillow. Nestling the phone and bedding, he answered.

"Yep."

"The stand-by list has reached two hundred for Friday night, CJ. You want me to close it?"

"Good morning."

"It's not morning, CJ. I've been in this broom closet for hours already."

"Ahh, Radine. How could I not recognize that Brooklyn whine?"

"Screw you, CJ. You love me. So what do I do?"

"Which band are we talking about?"

"Nathan Juju … but there's a backup band this time."

"Go to three hundred before you kill it, Radine; they won't all show up. What time, 7:00?"

Radine cupped the receiver to her shoulder and stared in a compact mirror, meticulously arranging her burgundy-colored hair, most definitely garnishing her bounty of cleavage. "CJ … the shows are always at 8:00 on the weekends. *You know that*."

"Yep. Sound check at 5:00, right?"

"Hey, some members of the backup band have been calling. The musicians want to get in the showroom early on Friday. Do I let 'em in?"

"No!" CJ sat up and threw his pillow aside. "No, no … don't do that. Tell them the room is booked until 4:00. They can load in after that. It's in their contract so they won't give you any shit. Capisce?"

"Got it, CJ. What time will you be here?"

"Should be around 1:00, Radine. I'll call you when I hit Logan."

"Logan?"

"Yeah, Radine. See … that's an airport in Boston, where planes land."

"You're such a smart ass. I was going to send a car, but gee wiz, I seem to have lost the phone number of the car service. Guess you'll have to walk now."

Still wearing work clothes from the night before, CJ lay on top of the bed, staring at his tool bag. It was sitting where he'd dropped it the minute he walked in the door.

At thirty-four years old, he'd been involved with music and sound—in one aspect or another—for over twenty-five years … starting with violin lessons at the age of eight. By fifteen, he'd already rewired every tavern and bar within a fifty-mile radius of his hometown.

His childhood bedroom had been the testing ground for his experiments. Rows of car batteries had been lined along one shelf with clamps and cables running in all directions. The closet door had been rigged to open with a homemade remote. Then there were the thin strips of mirror, long rows of them mounted like molding at the top of the walls, methodically aligned to send a bright-blue laser beam bouncing across the ceiling. It was ten-fold brighter than a standard light fixture could provide. By the age of seventeen, he'd needed a bigger play-ground.

Other than having to work for anything he wanted, he'd had it smooth growing up in the mountains near Lake Tahoe. Home was the number one priority, a principle his parents nurtured with love and respect. But deep inside he knew there was more. Most boys his age had posters of Farah Fawcett hanging by the bed, but CJ's walls were covered with mural-sized maps. He'd highlighted major highways, and drawn circles around different towns with black magic-marker. Some cities had been flagged with Post-its and magazine clippings. He had to find these places. They wouldn't come to him.

Leaving home at such a young age was met with opposition by his parents, who had made it clear he was to inherit the business his father had spent so many years building. But his departure came without notice one evening, unplanned and messy. CJ honored the request of a band—instead of his family. It broke his mother's heart. Bad words were said. Emotions flared. He knew it would smooth over in time.

After a few weeks of touring the northwest with a small band, he got a call from the Lake Tahoe Police Department. They'd been trying to track him down. The house he'd called home had gone up in a blaze a few weeks back—burned to the ground in the middle of the night, his parents along with it.

He couldn't help but wonder if he'd caused the fire, if one of his experiments had overloaded the circuits, or if his wiring playground had created a technical graveyard. Whether he was, or wasn't, to blame, there was nothing to go back to. At seventeen, the road became his home.

"CJ, you had a delivery this morning. I don't know what it was, but I sent it to the back door."

"Call the kitchen when we're done, Radine. Last

time you did that, the porter stuck my gear in the freezer. Follow up on that, will ya?"

His job is to oversee live performances, technically, and it often sends him rushing down several flights of stairs and bolting to the back of a stage. From there, he'll crawl in between musicians and their equipment to switch cables in the SNAKE—a wicked-long, sound-based extension cord connecting the stage to the soundboard, giving the soundman full control of every instrument and microphone plugged in to it—then he'll soar up the stairs and back to the sound booth before the song has ended. In venues where he'd worked on a regular basis, specific tools had been hidden on top of girders, or inside cubbyholes, to repair nearby equipment on the fly.

Artists who can afford to fly someone around the country often request CJ, because he insists on each job being as flawless as possible—for the artist first, then the club owner. That's the real world to CJ, and that's what's kept him working year-round. He's traveled by every means possible and made it through some hard-hitting road tours.

Over the years he'd also come across a number of dead bodies—more than most would see in a lifetime. Strangers for the most part. Victims of the nightlife.

"CJ, there's a guy here named Dirk. He says he has some microphones for you. Should I sign for them?"

"No, no ... those mics belong to the French Conservatory, Carnegie Hall, thirteenth floor. Ask him to ship those for me and I'll cover the cost."

Radine giggled and turned away from the ticket window. "Isn't Dirk the name of a porn star?"

"Is that what you do in the booth all day?"

Driven by a hunger for the unknown, CJ's passion for music has allowed him to travel the world, and that's a playing field big enough to provide a steady flow of adventure. Whether in Atlanta, Georgia, or Banff, Canada, he'd looked for places to snoop around, such as abandoned shacks in the middle of overgrown meadows, or ancient crawl spaces rotting away in suburban theaters. He'd even spent the night in an abandoned prison right outside of New York City—just for grins. After many years of traveling with projects and jumping into precarious situations, he'd somehow survived the perilous odds.

The shit-happens factor had come around plenty of times, but it hadn't taken him down.

"A girl named Tina called. She wasn't very nice to me, CJ. I couldn't get any information out of her, but she wanted to know when you'd be here."

"If it's important, she'll call back. If she's nasty, put her on hold and leave her there."

"Oh, look. I found the number for the car service."

"Use it for your next blind date. I'll jump in a cab.

See ya Friday."

"I love youuu, CJ," Radine whined and hung up the phone.

CJ set his phone down and lay on the covers, thinking, listening to the hypnotic trickling of his oversized fish tank, rubbing the amulet around his neck. As though a door to the past had just opened wide, the ghostly encounter last night triggered some flashbacks about bizarre encounters from his childhood, such as bending sound waves and talking with spirits in his father's shop. It was easy to bring the apparitions around by adjusting frequencies on the old radio—his grandfather's radio. No big deal. The spirits that spoke would even cross over and enter his playground, and from what he could remember it was fun, except when he got scolded for something they did, such as knock over appliances, or shred a pile of boxes. Maybe he stopped trying, or maybe the apparitions got bored, but at some point the spirits seemed to stop talking and the game lost its appeal. Even so, they'd continued to reveal themselves, mostly when he manipulated sound frequencies, and it seemed as natural as the sun coming through the window.

He'd always thought he was like other people he'd heard about. People with a certain sensitivity. Even as he got older, the apparitions kept appearing in music venues and old theaters. Why hadn't he ever explored the subject, or dug deeper?

But the episode last night wasn't from a vaudeville ghost that died from a heart attack onstage, or a drunken techie who'd fallen off a catwalk. This one was different. It seemed to be … hunting him down … looking for something. And why did it want the amulet around his neck?

Come to think of it, where did the amulet first come from? He'd had it so long he couldn't remember. It was the only thing he'd found when he dug through the ashes of his childhood home. It was right where he'd left it: jammed into one of the fuse sockets in the circuit breaker. In fact, he'd gone straight to it. Why did he—

The phone rang and CJ twitched. He patted the covers, searching for his phone.

"Tell me some good news," CJ said.

"Doesn't get any better," said a man with a British accent.

"Heard that before."

"This is Dean Autry, with Intertwine Artists. Am I speaking with CJ?"

CJ sprung up on one elbow. He'd worked with bands managed by Intertwine in the past. The gigs had been dream jobs. Intertwine wasn't in the habit of leaving people stranded with crappy vans and sloppy schedules. Not only did every provision match each employee's itinerary, but the cars arrived on time, and all flights had actually been reserved—ahead of time. Intertwine was reliable; this company took care of the essentials, the time-consuming details that made traveling a pain in the ass.

"Hi, Dean. What's up?"

"Well, you are frank; I like it. Let's get to the gen, CJ. We have an unpleasant situation with a tour. It's launching next Tuesday, and we don't have audio locked down."

"That's one week away, Dean. I'm not sure—"

"It's a three-month tour. North America only; I give you my word. How soon are you available to come in? I'd like to discuss the contract with you. It's quite attractive."

"I don't think I can take the job, Dean, as great as it sounds."

"What say 6:00 P.M. tonight?"

"I'm working tonight."

"And the following morning?"

"Not good either. I'm going to New Hampshire tonight, right after work. Back on Thursday, then up to Boston on Friday. What about Saturday?"

Dean chuckled. "As it turns out, I'll be in Boston on Friday night, as well, with Nathan Juju. It's merely a dry run to determine how much dust has gathered during their absence."

"Yeah, I know them. Good band. Straight ahead rock-n-roll. I'm going up for that gig. But I guess you knew that."

"We may bump shoulders Friday, but we won't have a chance to discuss business. Saturday is splendid. We're at 141 East 41st Street, Suite 1753. What say 2:00 P.M.?

"Great. See you then."

The Hayson

CJ wrapped up a tech rehearsal and locked the sound booth around 8:00 P.M. It was an easy night, one singer and a band prepping for a show that would soon follow. He left the rock club on 14th Street, then slung his backpack over his shoulder and headed for the parking garage. When the attendant screeched up with his truck, he tossed his bag in the back and hit the open highway. Around 2:00 A.M. his phone rang.

"Hey, DeBussey. Thanks for calling me back. I need a huge favor. Check in on Larry at the Dark Star, will you? There was some major chaos in there last night. I sorta left him hanging."

"What happened?"

"I'm not sure. It was one of those full moon nights, ya know? Strange stuff going on. Things were outta whack—big time."

"Sounds like selective memory to me," DeBussey told him. "What are you getting me involved in, CJ?"

"Just a new speaker. Should arrive tomorrow. Chris can install it but I need you to help him EQ the room."

"Can't it wait till you get back?"

"Maybe, but I want to head Larry off at the pass. I know he's gonna call. Can you give me a few hours of your time?"

"Sure, CJ. Piece of cake. I'm staying at your place for a couple of days. We'll call it a barter. So where is this cabin you're heading up to? New Hampshire?"

"Yeah. It's up in the White Mountains."

"What's the occasion?"

"No occasion—except I just got another bill for the taxes. It's been mine since I was a kid, and it used to be cheap so I never worried about it. Fast-forward fifteen years, or so, and it's getting expensive. Real expensive, like, the taxes just tripled. It's time to decide whether I should keep it or not. Maybe I should sell it. I definitely don't use it."

"Always on some crazy adventure. I admire you, CJ. You got a brass set. I'd be scared shitless going up there by myself."

"I'm expecting to find an old pile of wood. My grandfather bought it a hundred years ago but no one's been there since he died. I've never seen the place. I'll probably have to stay at a hotel close by."

"Wait … you've never been there?"

"No, I didn't even know this place existed till my parents died. I inherited it from my dad, but he never talked about it, which is why I guess I never had much of an interest in the place. I'm sure it's rotted and grown over, but maybe the land is worth something. Either way, I need to take a look and make a decision."

"I thought your family was out west."

"They are, well, were. I never knew my grandfather. He died when I was one. My dad never talked about him, either, except that he was a musician. I heard he was kinda kooky."

"So that's where you get it from."

CJ saw a sign on the side of the road, peeking out from behind some trees. "I think this is it. I'll talk to you soon. Thanks for taking care of Dog."

CJ pulled off Kancamagus Highway, onto a dirt road jam-packed with massive tree branches, most hanging low to the ground. He squeezed through, pushing the limbs aside with the windshield as he maneuvered through what soon became a small trail.

As he bounced along the path, he started thinking about his parents. After all these years the guilt had never gone away. Would he ever know if he'd caused the fire? Was he technically a murder—

Bam!

The truck hit a hole and the amulet bounced to his chin. He stopped the truck and clutched the amulet, rubbing it in his fingers, thumping it with the scar on his thumb … thinking. He held the amulet to his face.

'*Holy shit … this amulet had a purpose. Some meaning. Why else would a spirit want it?*'

He put the truck in drive and went farther down the

trail, questions still racing through his mind. Why had everyone disregarded the cabin? Would he find spirits there? What if he came across his parents?

'*Okay, that's just crazy.*'

Or was it? Would finding them in the spirit world bring it all back? Would he ever stop wishing he could see them one more time? He'd run the scenario through his mind a thousand times, the way they died, the way he'd run out on them, the way he'd jerry-rigged the circuit breaker to get more juice.

Twenty minutes later he came around a bend and his truck rolled into an open field. The sudden brightness of the stars startled CJ and he hit the brakes, and there he sat, observing the pasture. The massive moon shined down like a giant stage light, defining the shape of the meadow. At the far end of the field sat a dark structure, shadowed by the majestic tree line.

CJ drove closer, gently bouncing through the field until he was thirty feet from the outline, then he switched his headlights to high and illuminated an old shack of a cabin, shelled in weather-beaten planks and gray porous logs.

An old padlock was intact and dangling on the door, but it was worthless because the entire lock strut had been yanked from the wooden frame, coinciding with a floor-to-ceiling crack in the door, kicked in by someone. One gentle shove with his foot and the door swung wide open. He reached inside and felt for the light switch, flipping it up and down.

No lights came on.

CJ went to his truck and leaned the seat back, then called it a night.

"Thanks for calling The Settlement. Radine here. What's up?"

"And a pleasant evening to you, Nadine. Is your manager on the premises?"

"It's Radine, with an R. Who's calling?"

"Name is Dean Autry. I apologize for calling so late."

"No problem. We're open till four but only serve soda after two. No exceptions and yes, you need ID," she recited.

"Truth be told, I'm requesting a work reference on CJ Singleton."

"Yep, CJ's one of ours, but the manager is tied up right now. I can take your number."

"Perhaps you can assist me if you have a moment."

"CJ better not be looking for a job. I'll kill him. And if you're trying to take him away, I'll say horrible and nasty things about him."

"Even if they're not true?"

"That's right. Don't even think about taking CJ away from us."

Dean chuckled. "I'll only request him for a short amount of time. I assure you. So tell me, what's your general opinion of CJ? I have to say I'm already sold on

20

the lad but, tell me; how does he get on with others in the crew?"

"He runs the shows, but he works alone a lot, too. In here all night sometimes. That's so creepy. I know he's had gangsters try to slice him with stemware, and he's had run-ins with knives. He's a tough one, that CJ. He always walks away unharmed."

"Well, that's good to know I suppose, however, I'm not too interested in his—"

"Oh … and one night, someone pulled a gun on him. We thought he was being robbed, but it was a jealous boyfriend."

"Are there often conflicts between his work and the birds?"

"Birds?"

"Is he a ladies' man?"

"Oh, *birds* … that's so funny. Actually it's kinda the opposite. He's kinda shy. From what I can tell, he doesn't get too close to anyone. It took me a few years to get to know him. Personally, I think he'd rather fix old stereos than get to know people, but I guess I understand. He's lost a lot of friends. Close friends. Then his girl-friend, Simone, died. He really clammed up after that."

"I'm sorry to hear that, but again, I'm trying to gather a feel for who he is, professionally … at his trade."

"Let's see. He's tough but cool. Funny but dependa-ble. Everyone trusts him. The ladies love him but he's a mess—like, a clean mess, 'cause he always smells good—like, showered … but still a mess. I wish he'd buy a mirror, or just use one once in a while. But then I'm into fashion, and *personally*, I love his scruffy brown hair. I straighten him up when he gets here. I can only imagine CJ in an Armani suit. That would be so hot."

Dean rolled his eyes. "Has he ever missed an appearance?"

"Appearance? He's the soundman. He doesn't do appearances. At least not here anyway."

"I see. Let's try this. Has he ever *not* arrived for a scheduled function?"

"Oh, no. Not CJ. Nope. Sometimes we can't find him, but that's usually when he's crawling in between walls and floors. Says he's running wires. I think he likes getting dirty."

"Thank you, now. You've been most helpful."

"Okay but you've been warned. Don't take—"

"Good night, Nadine."

"It's *Radine*, with an R!"

CJ woke to a loud banging noise.

The sun was blinding, but he could see a blurry figure through the dirty windshield. He leaned forward and peeked through a clean spot. An older woman with a pitchfork was pounding on the side of his truck.

CJ got out.

She tucked a few strands of gray hair behind one ear. "Who are you, and what are you doin' up here?"

"I'm CJ. This is my family's place. I came up to check it out."

"Then you're a Fitzgerald young 'un—aintcha?"

"No … Singleton."

She lowered the pitchfork. "Right answer. I live up there by the highway. I saw your headlights a few hours ago. Just checking on things."

"Sorry if I woke you. I didn't see any houses."

"Don't nobody see it. Hidden by trees." She wiped a bandana across her face. "You picked a good time for a visit. Already hot and it ain't even eleven."

CJ eyeballed two big dogs standing beside her. "Friends of yours?"

"If need be."

He shut the truck door and said, "This was my grandfather's place. I inherited it when I was a kid. Didn't know what to expect." He faced the forest. "I had no idea it was so tucked away."

"Ain't never been here before?"

"No, never have."

"Any family members come up lately?"

"I'm the last one left. But then, I didn't know about this cabin till my dad died. So … I guess you never know."

The woman squinted and gave CJ a troubled look just then, as if he'd pissed his pants and hadn't known.

"What?" CJ asked her, rolling his eyes down.

"You look like him," she said in a softer tone.

"Who? My grandfather?"

As if she'd been caught being tender, her back stiffened and she went back to being a hard-ass farmwoman. "You might want to be careful. I seen some strange lights comin' from up in here. I reckon kids use this old place to fool around. They might be back. Best leave some lights on."

"There's no power."

"Foller me."

She took CJ through some hanging tree limbs to a small wooden shed. "Cottage was robbed near 'bout thirty years ago," she said over her shoulder, as she opened the door and stepped inside. "No one came to check on the place, though."

CJ poked his head in the shack.

"Ain't a soul been here since, of your kin anyways." She opened a rusty panel and flipped some switches. "That should do 'er."

CJ backed away so she could step out.

"You come see me if ya need anything. I'm in the old gray house by the highway."

"The one hidden by trees. Got it."

As she drove away in her pickup, CJ looked around. This was as isolated as he'd been in years. Gigantic White Pines grew four feet in diameter along the edge of the field, supporting building-sized trees that soared high in the sky.

CJ walked along the outside walls of the cabin, and then to the back, where the field sloped and vanished into the dark woods. The forest was beginning to wake for the new spring and summer ahead, and the melting snow had begun to create little streams on the slanted hill. As he stood listening, it sounded as though the forest was breathing on its own, with snow crackling in waves every time a strong breeze swept through the hills. He went to the fringe of the thick woods. There was a clearing in one spot, like a path had once existed. Trees had been chopped down with an axe. There were five boulders next to one trunk, barely visible underneath the wild shrubs.

Slow drips of melting snow were rolling off low-hanging branches and hitting the ground *mezzo forte*, where they raced downhill and dampened the lifeless streambeds. In other places, rapid trickles sang out as they dribbled into small pools of water that had already formed from just a few hours of hot sun; their volume diminished, or augmented by the depth of the puddle below. Beads of water sailed down from high in the trees, each plummeting to the earth after a windblown, oscillating flight.

Given the amount of trees in the dense forest, the overall sound of winter's exodus resembled that of an orchestra. The slower, heavy droplets provided a foundation for the ensemble as they beat down like the steady thumping of a bass, while the invigorating, fast-flowing trickles bellowed through the trees with the same passion and vigor as a section of violins. Sporadic discharges of melting snow filled in the midsection, pouring down at random as accumulating pockets of water eventually outweighed their supporting limbs. Topping off the ensemble were the cracking branches and large clumps of falling snow—the impromptu crashing sounds of a percussion section. He wondered if this type of setting had an influence on early composers, or if someone like Schubert wrote *Die Winterreise* in a forest like this.

After a quick survey of the cabin's interior, he decided to make use of daylight. The old bungalow and all its mess inside could wait until nightfall.

Around 1:00 P.M., he was ready for something fun, something stimulating, something he hadn't done in years, and that something was a hike through the forest.

He knew of several ways to prevent getting lost in a place this desolate, one of which was to simply follow a stream. Otherwise it could be days before a person might find his way back.

Some ten yards into the forest, a tiny brook had just begun to carve a twisting path down the hill. He put on some wading boots he'd found in the cabin and set out on his hike, following the little stream.

After a hundred feet or so, the little water trail merged with a small river flowing down the center of a dried-up riverbed. Since the mountains had barely begun to thaw, the river was only one foot deep, but the eroded embankments on each side rose higher than his waist. The soothing water swirling around a few large boulders would soon be a powerful cascade of roaring rapids. His timing was perfect; he could wade through the center of the little river with ease.

It was hard to believe there was a place more detached from the world than the cabin, but within a few hours, he'd found it; a tiny section of the globe lucky enough to have never seen a Coke can. He'd placed markers along the way: five rocks in a straight line, to his left—no more than thirty minutes from the last set of stones. He'd learned that trick from his father, who must have learned it from his father, obvious by other rocks placed five in a row here and there, just like the stones that led him this far. He felt a sense of familiarity just then, as though his dad were with him. The older stones were weather-beaten, even sunken down from decades of a harsh environment.

Over an hour later, CJ came to an enormous boulder in the middle of the stream. He climbed up and took a break from schlepping through the water. The sounds of the woods seemed to come alive while he sat there. Snapping branches and distant, hollow birdcalls began to echo through the hills. Except for the lack of Squaw Carpet, the forest seemed remarkably similar to the mountains in Lake Tahoe. Then he noticed the misty rays of sunlight shooting down through the trees, creating a maze of neon shapes on the forest floor, much like gobos on a well-lit stage.

Even more impressive were the protruding shelves of snow lining the jagged edges of the riverbed, exposing a network of unseen water veins that had secretly traveled down the mountainside, hidden under a blanket of snow.

He began to hear something that didn't resemble nature, though. It sounded more like someone hammering tin, or banging on metal.

"No way anyone lives up here."

He jumped off the boulder and followed the sound upstream, where he came around a bend and caught his first glimpse of a white-tailed deer standing in the middle of a sandbank, its back to CJ. The animal sensed his presence and raised its head, as cautious as he was—if not more, being that both were deep in the wilderness at the very beginning of spring, where hungry animals were lurking: creatures with big claws, and sharp fangs.

The grass-eater stood on guard with bent knees, ready to leap away. CJ ducked below some tree roots, waiting for the doe to relax. The animal started digging again, pitching sand and snow aside as it scraped the riverbed in search of foliage. With every stroke of its hoof, the deer connected with something metal.

A hefty clump of snow fell in the stream behind CJ. A thunderous, cannonball splash went high in the air. It scared CJ. It startled the doe.

When CJ looked back to the deer, it had vanished. He waded through the water to the raised sandbank.

He saw something silver in the sand, as though a shiny coin was peeking through the snow. When he reached down to grab it, he discovered it was something larger. He scraped dirt and snow away and soon uncovered a square box. He tried to pull it from the sand but it wouldn't budge. He gouged out a square trench with a stick—deep enough to grab the bottom edges.

One good tug and the silver case broke free from the mud. He was suddenly holding a strange box the size of a VCR. He dipped the box in the stream and the sandy pebbles swished away without resistance—as though the item had been coated with a protective sheen.

He had uncovered a shiny, silver box in the middle of the wilderness, with no signs of rust or age. As he searched for a way to open his new toy, his mind began to race.

'*Maybe it fell from a plane. Maybe it's full of money. Shit … maybe it's an old bomb.*'

He gripped the box with both hands and held it to his face, tilting it, spinning it, studying the object from all angles. That's when he saw a round indentation above the handle. A smaller circle of metal was protruding from the center of the groove. He raised an eyebrow, then untied the amulet hanging from his neck. He held it next to the case. The amulet was the exact size of the notch in the silver case.

"What the hell?"

It wasn't a question of who, or why, or what; it was a matter of how soon he could satisfy his curiosity, and since the ball was in his court, he placed the amulet in the indent.

There was a clicking sound.

A metal pin emerged from the case and rose through the center hole in the amulet. He pressed on the pin and the front panel of the silver box opened with a slow and smooth, hydraulic motion, exposing four shiny discs inside.

The objects had an even amount of space between them. The casing had been designed that way; to secure them in a specific direction, obvious by the thin wedge of metal protruding from the side of each round object, pointing north, south, east, and west. He turned the box upside down to shake the discs out, but they wouldn't move. He tried pulling them out, but he couldn't get a firm grip.

While fumbling around, he pressed down on one of the glimmering circles and it rose upward half an inch … just enough to grip it with his fingertips.

As he pulled, a shiny cylinder the size of a can of spray paint slid from the casing. He set the case down and rolled the cylinder in his hands, looking for a label. There were no markings anywhere. The protruding metal bar ran the length of the cylinder, from one end to the other, rising not quite a quarter-inch, but still noticeable. The object seemed featherlike for its size, yet sturdy.

He touched the raised piece of metal but it didn't move, so he pressed a bit harder, enough to feel it was firm. Then he slammed the metal bar with his wrist. One half went even with the cylinder. The other half of the thin bar stayed above the surface—as a light switch would do.

Then the cylinder made a humming noise and seemed to come alive in his hand. He tossed it on the sandbank and took a few steps back.

Thinking the cylinder might actually be an old bomb, he jumped behind a dead tree that had toppled into the riverbed, and there he covered his head and clinched his teeth, coiled in a tight ball. With every passing second CJ tightened his muscles and squeezed his eyes, waiting for the bang.

Instead of an explosion, he heard a crackling sound, as if the bomb had lost its bang.

He peeked over the tree expecting to see a string of sparks, or maybe sizzling gunpowder, but instead, he saw a surge of neon-blue lights streaming out from one end of the cylinder, flashing seven feet high, in ten different directions—crisscrossing through the air as if they had a mind of their own. Maybe he was tired, or maybe he'd overworked his ears lately, but he could have sworn he heard the slightest ringing of a tone.

CJ stayed behind the tree and watched the streaks of light spin, and zip, and twist around, when all of a sudden the lights began to come together and gather as a group. Within a few beats, the bright spectacle had taken the shape of a person.

CJ's heartbeat raced.

After forming into a figure, the strange lights started to stir—from within, until the blue energy had finished some type of transformation. Before he knew it the lights had faded, leaving a man standing on the sandbank.

'*Holy fucking crap.*'

The man was foggy white from head to toe, wearing deerskin boots. His fluffy, untailored pants were fastened to his waist with twine. The stranger had a string-tied vest around his chest, and he wore an old moss hat with a long feather in one side, also milky white in color. In his cloudy hand was a wooden flute, or windpipe.

CJ recognized the faded white glow. It was the same color as every semblance he'd ever seen, but of all of the times a ghost had appeared before him, this was the best one yet. He seemed ancient.

But CJ wasn't in a nightclub, or a familiar setting where he knew how to get away. There was no radio to unplug, or frequencies to kill, and that was enough to make this apparition more frightening than the others.

The ghostly man stood on the sandbank with his arms by his side, looking straight ahead. He was motionless, like a cement statue, void of the slightest expression.

A terrifying growl roared through the trees just then, deep within the forest. Branches snapped and a flapping thunder filled the air as hundreds of birds flew over his head. It had to come from a bear, or a mountain lion, or God knows what at this point.

"Hayson," said a voice.

CJ spun around to look at the semblance, who was pointing toward the silver box, but staring at CJ. Goose bumps flashed across CJ's skin.

The sound of crunching snow and snapping twigs grew louder.

"Hayson," the ghost repeated.

"Shh!" CJ put his finger to his lips and looked to the

forest, then back at the semblance, and then back at the forest—unable to decide which scenario was more frightening: a growl from a hungry animal … or a ghost that came from a shiny cylinder.

CJ ducked in between the riverbed wall and the fallen tree. He stayed low; the veins in his neck thumping like a pounding drum.

The semblance stood calm in the middle of the raised sandbank.

Another grisly roar echoed through the hills. The animal was getting closer.

"Dammit!" CJ looked around for a tree to climb, or a better place to hide. Then he remembered a show about a hiker who'd detoured a wild animal by banging rocks together. CJ glanced around for some large stones, but there were only tiny pebbles at his feet. He poked his head over the tree and saw the silver box, the cylinder lying next to it. CJ leapt over the tree, grabbed the cylinder, and jumped back to his hiding spot.

The semblance seemed fearless, even peaceful as he watched CJ leap here and there, but then the ghostly man pointed in the direction of the growl and repeated the word: "Hayson."

CJ poked his head over the tree and said, "*Stop it.*" Then he ducked down.

In the blink of an eye CJ heard a tree rustling, followed by an enormous splash. He crept his head up to see a massive bear tromping through the shallow river. It had the power of a large truck, crushing everything in its path, splashing water above the walls of the riverbed. The animal was on a direct course for the white ghost. In a matter of seconds the beast would be in his face.

When the bear got within ten feet of the sandbank, CJ snapped a branch from the dead tree. He stood and hollered, beating the limb against the cylinder.

But banging on the silver object only slammed the other end of the side-switch into the cylinder—the end that had remained above the surface—and without knowing what he'd done, the cylinder made a loud crackling noise. Another multitude of aggressive blue lights came flying from the cylinder.

CJ assumed another semblance would appear, but this time the blue streaks attacked the bear with a flurry of cobalt-colored electric veins, stopping the mammal dead in its tracks. The bear plummeted facedown and slid forward on its chin, thrusting the back half of its body over its head. Waves gushed over the sandbank when the massive bear fell on its side and slammed the earth with a ground-shaking thud. And there went that slight tone again.

All of a sudden the bear lay silent on the sand bank, only three feet away; its thick fur matted with mud and small twigs, reeking of dung and soil. The silent beast rose up to CJ's waist, with hundreds of blue lights streaming and crisscrossing, containing the massive animal in a tight-knit web.

He'd never been this close to a bear—not to mention one seized by a swarm of lights. His knees began to shake.

This was a first.

CJ stayed behind the tree, anticipating the next move, spellbound by the beautiful blue lights, yet frightened by their fury. Then another loud crackling noise sounded off, followed by a bright flash. The netting started streaming back toward CJ. He dropped the silver tube and jumped back, but that didn't stop the lights from circling over the tree trunk and finding the cylinder. After the netting had apparently vanished into thin air, CJ looked around, at the sand bank where the bear had fallen, at the semblance—still standing calm, at the silver cylinder by his feet. That's when he noticed both ends of the side-switch were once again raised above the surface of the cylinder. It was tough to swallow what had happened; that the bear hadn't walked away, it didn't roll over and run, and it hadn't climbed out of the riverbed and tromped through the snow. The bear had vanished with the blue lights—back into the cylinder.

"Hayson," the ghost said again, a grin on his face. The semblance then let out a trifling, steady chuckle, hardly loud enough to hear. But CJ heard him, and as he continued to laugh he began to cross over and enter CJ's world. His teeth looked real now, and his hair had become black in color. The multicolored feather in his hat complimented his deerskin clothing, and he suddenly appeared as real as any person on the street —excluding the garb.

CJ jumped over the tree and approached the semblance. He raised the cylinder and asked, "This is a Hayson?"

The ghost smirked.

CJ lifted the silver case and pointed to the other cylinders. "Then what are these?"

"Hayson," the ghost told him.

"No, *this* ..." said CJ, shaking the cylinder in his hand, "... is a Hayson." Then he went down the row of cylinders in the case, pointing at each one. "What are these?

The ghost nodded.

CJ cocked his head. "Each one is a Hayson?"

The ghost started walking away.

"Wait! Tell me more."

The semblance went to the embankment and climbed up to the forest, where he crunched through the snow, waning in and out of sight as he went deeper into the trees.

CJ held the silver case and looked around, still a bit shell-shocked by what had just happened, but then he saw something familiar. There were five boulders the size of beach balls sitting on the edge of the riverbed. They'd been positioned in a straight line.

DeBussey cupped the phone to his shoulder and held a plastic bag over CJ's aquarium. He poured live guppies into the tank and said, "I don't know if he wants me on that job, Radine. He hasn't made it clear, and CJ makes everything clear."

"Well, he hasn't put you on the schedule. Maybe he's okay, but I can't reach him and I need to know who's coming in to run the sound."

"If he wanted me, he would have let me know by now." DeBussey looked around the apartment. "I feel like I'm in a supply room. Does he really live here?"

"Do you see any porn?"

"What? I'm not digging through his shit! I'm just feeding Dog while he's away."

"*His* dog, DeBussey. It's *his* dog."

"No … it's 'Dog.' *Dog* is a *fish*."

"I love him to death but that's just weird."

"You think that's weird? Check this out. Dog likes to be scratched on the head with a wooden cooking spoon. Yeah, yeah … CJ told me about this, but I didn't believe him."

"What?"

"I'm serious. The tank holds like a gamillion gallons of water and the fish is about a foot long." DeBussey dipped a wooden spoon in the tank and Dog swam to it, then curled its body and swam in tight circles around the spoon. DeBussey rubbed the spoon over Dog's nose and said, "Good-looking thing—bright yellow with black squares. It follows you around the room. Kinda watches you. A little creepy, if you ask me. There's even a dog tag on the tank." DeBussey leaned in close. "It says 'DOG,' with CJ's address and phone number on it."

"If that story gets out, they'll lock him up. Let's keep this between you and me."

"Actually it's pretty cool. Sounds like there's a flowing creek in here."

"I don't care about his fish. Look through his stuff, DeBussey. Tell me what you see."

"I'm not spying on CJ. No way."

"You can and you will."

"No, Radine. I won't."

"Fine. Next time you and your friends want to see a free show, don't come to me cause I'll charge you for every ticket, every drink, every piss you take from this day on."

"That's bribery, you bitch."

"That's life—and with a capital B, thank you."

DeBussey paused. "I don't know. Maybe he doesn't live here. It's more like a warehouse than an apartment. There's totally rows and rows of gear and speakers and… like… tons of shit piled up on shelves." DeBussey went to a wall unit full of small canisters. He opened one tiny bin. "Bolts. Now I know where he gets all his gear. He could open a hardware store."

"No dresser? No closet?"

"Here's a closet." DeBussey swung the door open. "Ha!"

"What? What is it? Tell me!"

"More shelves, all filled with *Rolling Stone* magazines. There must be twenty or thirty years of magazines in here. They're logged and organized. I'm impressed."

"I'm not. I want some dirt. No leather harness? No whips and chains?"

"Nothing. I see a few pairs of jeans and a pile of T-shirts. Wait ... I see a suitcase." DeBussey slid a piece of luggage from the top shelf and balanced it on one raised knee. "Wow!"

"Stop it, you asshole! Tell me what you found!"

"The whole suitcase is filled with airline tickets! Hundreds of—"

"How dull. Don't touch anything. If he's that orga-nized, he'll know you got nosy and went through his things. That was shady of you, DeBussey. Pure shady."

"Me? This was your idea."

"Whatever. Enough with the report on Boringville. Are you coming in?"

"I don't know," said DeBussey, backing out of the closet. There was a Motel key cabinet hanging above the oversized table, and DeBussey went to it. "I'm scheduled at Sublines that night." He took a set of keys from a hook inside. "But I'd do anything to get out of that gig. That place is haunted—big time."

"Eww ... I've heard. I wish a big Indian spirit would come after me in the middle of the night." Radine moaned and said, "Me and Sitting Bull? Can you imag-ine? That is so hot!"

"Call me if you don't hear from Sitting Bull—I mean CJ, okay? I'll come in."

"You da man, DeBussey. And stay out of his shit, you snoop."

CJ got back to the cabin just after the sun had gone down. The temperature had taken a dive so he lit a fire and started putting the ransacked cabin back together. He set tables back to an upright position and hung old pots and pans back on the walls. The broken door was an easy fix, and once it was secure, he placed a tin bucket in front of it, as an alarm for intruders, or possibly more bears.

There were pictures on the floor, some still leaning against the log wall they'd slid down from. He stared at one and noticed the man in the photograph looked familiar. The man also had CJ's amulet hanging around his neck. The glass covering the photo was already broken, so it didn't take much to pull the shards from the frame. He held the picture to his face and looked even closer, at the warmth in the man's eyes, at the cabin in the background, at the amulet around his neck.

CJ turned to ask a question, as if someone were standing beside him, but no one was there. He knew so. He was only hoping, wishing he could turn to his father and ask, *is that him? Did he give me the amulet? Is he my grandfather?* It took all he had not to get emotional, not to relive his parents funeral. "Why did everyone leave me?" He stared at the picture, then placed it in his bag.

Piles of paper had been strewn about, now lying on the floor under an even layer of soot. He tossed them in a box. He swept the floor and tidied up a bit, then threw more wood on the fire. When it came time to wind down, he pulled a few documents from the box of papers and sat back in a rocking chair, listening to the crackling fire while he read about his family.

A wavering circle of light caught his eye, dancing on the cabin wall. He looked at the fireplace and saw a bright yellow spot in the mantle, high above the flames. He went to the fire and looked closer. A small circle had been cut into the metal frame.

His eyes narrowed as he gazed at the yellow flames through the open circle, rubbing the amulet on his neck. He remembered then, how he wondered if there were secrets in this cabin.

He removed the amulet from his neck and placed it in the hole. It was a perfect fit. He turned back to the wall. The circle of light had got smaller and more stable, now shining on one log close to the ceiling. CJ climbed to the spot of light and placed his hand on it. The log wobbled and moved in half an inch. After he'd pulled the log from the wall, he peeked inside, then he stuck his hand in the dark opening and felt around. He nudged something and jerked his hand back. After another quick peek, he reached inside again. This time he pulled an old book from the space.

CJ sat in the rocking chair and blew dust off the book. The word *EKKO* had been burned into a stiff cover made of tree bark, or maybe a shaved piece of wood. The book was full of hand-drawn pictures, and written captions, all sketched in ash, but the words looked more like numbers, or unfamiliar fonts. Whatever language it was—it wasn't English. The pages also seemed to be made of thinly sliced wood; they crackled as he turned them.

"Just what the hell were you into, Grandpa?"

There was a sketched picture of his amulet on the first page—the amulet he'd had since he was a kid, the same amulet in the picture of his grandfather. The amulet that opened the silver case. He turned the page and saw an image of a group of musicians dressed in frilly clothing. On the next page he saw a man in a long cape pointing a thin tube toward a crowd. The drawing had zigzagged bolts of lightning coming from the tube. A few people seemed to be running from the streaks of light. Others appeared mesmerized. Page by page, he saw different drawings: one of a graveyard, another of people lying in coffins, their eyes wide open. Then there was a rough sketch of a violin, and he could have sworn it had a blue tint to it. Another page showed several tunnel-like passageways inside a stone cavern. On the very last page, he saw people rising toward some clouds in the sky. It was the only picture without a dark presence or gloomy shadows. He looked at the silver case sitting across the room.

'*Hayson*,' the ghost had called the case—or the cylinders inside the case, which seemed to make more sense.

"What the hell are you?" CJ whispered.

Dead Bear

It was a ten-hour trip back to New York City, and during the drive the series of discoveries in New Hampshire kept running through CJ's head, consuming his thoughts … tormenting his curiosity. The Hayson was one toy he wouldn't set on a shelf and forget about. The brief encounter in the forest had topped his list of adventures, no doubt, but it also left him clueless, and that meant one thing; he had to figure out what these Hayson things were all about. What they did. Why they did it. Where they came from.

He made a few calls from the road and told a handful of club managers an inspection was due, that it was time to tighten bolts in the ceiling and install updates on the gear. Since he'd worked at most of these places for many years, he had enough authority to make that call, mostly for having firsthand knowledge of their equipment. But if that wasn't enough credibility, he'd been given keys to their buildings long ago. Pulling an all-nighter was nothing new for CJ, and no manager ever questioned his late-night routine, nor did they stick around and watch him work. But this inspection couldn't happen in a week, or a month, or next fall; it had to happen right away.

By the time he'd crossed the George Washington Bridge, three managers had returned his call.

He ended up taking the Haysons to a club called Sublines, a larger-than-normal venue in the heart of Times Square. More of an entertainment factory than a nightclub, Sublines was busy every night of the week, and even though the owner of Sublines was a terrific person, the appearance of the club lacked ambition.

On top of that, no money had ever been spent to improve the sound gear, and no one seemed to care about the thirty-year-old lighting system. He'd spent many nights in Sublines rebuilding decrepit gear, swapping out parts from broken-down equipment lying around in storage. Sublines was concerned about one thing—being sued, and that was that. If one light didn't work, then use another; that was their motto when it came to stage gear, which simplified his decision as to what club to call on. If any technical gear were damaged while experimenting with the Hayson, no one at Sublines would have a clue.

Built as a large, open-aired club, Sublines offered a great view of the stage from any one of the sixteen hundred seats in the arena. And even better, it was below street level, tucked away under a forty-story skyscraper. There was no way a passerby could see inside, making it the perfect place to experiment with the unknown.

Being one of the oldest venues in Manhattan, Sublines had also been built on top of an ancient Indian burial ground, and the spirits often came alive at night—to say the least. In addition to the semblance activity, the venue rumbled during the wee hours from the different subway lines surrounding the club. Behind the massive north wall of the venue, the 2 and 3 trains never seemed to stop. The N and R trains had tracks running along the southern structure of the club. Two floors lower, under the east section of the showroom, the D train shuffled New Yorkers to and fro all night long.

CJ entered Sublines well after the nightly show had ended; homemade supplies in hand, silver case in tote, ready to take on a paranormal curveball. After the staff had left the club, he locked the doors and turned on every last light, making the showroom as bright as possible.

In anticipation of facing the bear, he pulled a heavy-duty, orange extension cord from his bag. He snipped the female plug from the end of the cord, then removed about eight feet of outer wrapping, to separate the wires inside. He cut the ground wire off completely, then removed about eight inches of insulation from the other two wires, leaving the ends of both wires bare and exposed.

The wires weaved nicely through the tines on a dinner fork, tight enough to lace up two pieces of flatware. CJ wrapped the excess wire around the handle, creating a set of weapons that could transport a massive amount of voltage. Then he put a layer of foam over the super-

45

charged forks and wrapped each handle with a few feet of duct tape.

He singled out a wall socket and isolated it from the main circuit breaker—in case of a power surge. Then the showroom lights would stay lit, and he wouldn't be alone in the dark with a wild animal.

This seemed to be the best way to defend himself against the bear; he could test the cylinder a few times while keeping the animal under control. After learning how the device worked, he would get the bear back in the Hayson and take it to Jersey. If he released it in the Palisades, Fish and Game could pick up the ball from there.

The perfect plan.

He moved some tables and chairs around in front of the stage, building a confined, but open space to release the bear. Then he placed the hard-wired forks on a table and plugged the orange cord in the wall. His hands shook a bit, and his heart started racing as he aimed the cylinder at the floor and pressed down on the side-switch.

A fury of blue lights flew out from the Hayson, and the faintest hint of a tone, or a slight pitch, rang through the air, but no bear.

CJ set the cylinder on the table and grabbed a different Hayson, then slammed down on the side-switch. The second Hayson made a loud crackling sound, as though he'd opened twenty bags of freeze-dried coffee, then the cobalt-colored lights streamed through the air. As the blue web settled on the floor, churning and stirring from within, he grabbed the forks and stepped behind a row of tables.

Then it happened—the lights began to take shape and the massive bear began to materialize, looking just as it did when he last saw it in the riverbed: unconscious and lying on its side. As the lights began to fade, the bear began to come around.

It shook its head a few times and let out an angry growl, then it got to its feet, first the front legs, then the back ones. It turned its head and saw CJ, and that triggered a rapid rise, a beanstalk type of rise that seemed to never end. The tables and chairs looked like toys next to the bear, now standing nine feet tall.

CJ became paralyzed, or maybe it was the table behind his butt, holding him there. He broke out in a sweat and the taped-up forks started slipping from his hands.

With its nose curled back and its mouth wide open, the bear swung at CJ with its massive paw. CJ ducked and the paw connected with a table instead. The table flew through the air and crash-landed by the stage.

CJ kept the forks aimed at the bear.

The bear exposed its fangs and made another lunge, but this time CJ managed to shove one fork in the side of its furry neck, grazing the creature—giving it a good shock. The animal went into a brief spasm and fell on its chin. It rose fast, though, then shook its head, trying to gain some balance on its spread out paws. CJ ran behind the next row of tables.

That's when he realized he'd bitten off more than he

could chew. He needed to get the animal back inside the Hayson—and fast. He tossed the forks and reached for the Hayson, but his fumbling hands knocked the cylinder off the table.

As if in slow motion, the giant bear lowered its legs and sprung into one big leap. One paw snagged a cocktail table and sent it flying through the air—right into CJ. The little table slammed into CJ and knocked him down. The bear became tangled in some chairs, briefly, just long enough for CJ to grab the forks. It didn't take long before the bear was crushing the chairs and clawing tabletops, clambering over the furniture. In two seconds flat, the beast was on top of CJ, lowering its head to take a bite.

CJ thrust the forks into the bear. One fork fell to the side. The other went straight into the bear's ear, piercing the soft gristle and giving CJ a solid hit.

The creature flew backward as though someone had yanked it away. Lights flickered as the huge beast rolled around on the floor, smashing even more tables and chairs into pieces. CJ stepped back and watched what resembled a small tornado in action, dodging furniture as it flew through the air.

He ran to the wall and yanked the cord from the socket, but the bear had already stopped flopping around. Now motionless on the floor, the animal lay tangled in orange cord and broken furniture.

CJ started pacing the floor in hyper-speed, trying to grasp his emotions. He was sad, scared, and out of breath. The nerves in his neck were twitching in a steady rhythm. He held the Hayson to his face and stared at it. The fascinating new toy didn't hold the same appeal as before. In a rage of anger, he flung it across the room.

This wasn't tough; this was wrong. Tears swelled in his eyes and he felt like a lowlife, or a scumbag. Could he even say the word—poacher—the lowest form of mankind?

CJ sat on the edge of the stage with a bottle of bourbon, taking swig after swig. Regretting. Waiting. Wishing all of this would go away.

Would the bear have killed him back in New Hampshire? Should he have not hiked through the forest? Should he have waited to witness the interaction between the bear and the ghost? Should he have left the silver case behind? How could one simple hike in the forest leave him in a situation like this?

There had never been a time when CJ didn't know the difference between a reason, and an excuse. Right now he wanted an excuse so bad he thought about making one up, and if he dug deep enough, he could find a reason to lie to himself—just to get rid of his guilt—but nothing could take away the sudden shame he felt inside.

This time he'd screwed up like never before.

He kneeled next to the bear and took one paw in his hand. "I'm sorry you won't be going home," he said.

"You must take his hide," said a voice from behind him.

CJ twitched and tried to spin around. That spastic

move landed him on his butt.

An Indian woman was standing only ten feet away, sort of. She was semi-transparent, wearing an animal-skin sheath, with bones and claws hanging from her neck.

CJ stood and stepped away from the bear.

The squaw crept past CJ and approached the bear, stooping low and tiptoeing toward its head. She reached for a strap on her thigh and withdrew a knife.

"No, wait!" CJ said. "Don't do that. He's ... already dead."

Her arm froze with the knife in midair. She seemed confused, then searched the bear's hide and combed through its fur. "You did not hunt him?" she asked. "Why did you slay him?"

CJ froze. Embarrassed, he looked away.

"Chakawain is sad," she said, then lowered the knife. "If you did not kill for his hide, you have brought great sorrow to Mother Earth." She lost her ghostly haze and began to cross over, piercing his soul with her black eyes.

"No, I didn't hunt Chakawain. It was an accident. I made a big mistake."

"I am Chakawain!" she corrected him, then turned to the bear. "He is Nah-hak. He is not your enemy." She rubbed her hand along the bear's back and started dancing circles around the fallen beast, all the while wailing an Indian mantra.

"I swear," CJ attempted to say. "I didn't—listen, I

didn't plan on this. I wish I could take it back."

She stopped singing and faced CJ. "You cannot." Chakawain placed one knee on the bear's shoulder and grabbed a handful of its thick fur, then she gripped the knife. "I will take his hide. Then you must answer for your mistake."

"Whoa!" CJ reached for the silver case and took out another Hayson. "Wait! Use one of these."

Chakawain lowered the knife, as though she'd been scolded, and all of a sudden she seemed fearful. With her eyes focused on the Hayson, she said, "Chakawain is sorry. She did not know." She turned to the bear. "It is your mission, not mine."

"My mission? I don't …"

She got down on one knee and placed the knife in her open palms, then bowed her head and raised her hands, presenting the knife to CJ. "You may take his hide."

"That's not … that wasn't my plan." He waved the Hayson. "I wanted to get him back in here."

She cocked her head, suspicious. "Will you not take him and make stew?"

"*Stew*? No, no. He's—"

Chakawain sprung forward and put the knife to CJ's throat. "Do you bring harm, or good?"

"Easy now! Eassssy …" He watched her wrist. "Good … I guess, but I don't, I didn't mean to kill … all of this is …"

Chakawain squeezed her eyes. "You are not the

Wanagi. Who has sent you?"

"No one sent me."

"Then it is true." She lowered the knife. "The time for Tatetob has come."

"Ta what?"

"You carry the four winds," she said and suspiciously glanced around. "You must hide and you must be swift. They will soon arrive, in search of you."

"In search of me? Holy shit! Who? Who's coming for me?"

Out of nowhere, a faint, blue tint covered the chairs and tables, and Chakawain's dark eyes suddenly held the reflection a of tiny blue spark. CJ spun around and saw an orb in the ceiling. It was bright, yet hazy at the same time, as though a magnificent star was shrouded in fog. Slower than a snowflake, the sphere drifted to the ground.

As the orb reached the floor, it faded, leaving a man in dark clothing standing by the broken tables. He wore a fedora but kept it low, concealing his eyes. He looked like an FBI agent from the forties, and no sooner than he appeared, did he take gentle steps toward the silver case.

CJ reached across the table and slammed the case shut.

The Agent stood lifeless.

CJ took a step back.

The man saw the amulet dangling on a string from CJ's pocket. He raised his head only enough to flash a probing smile. "You have the key," he said. "Give it to me."

Chakawain faced CJ. "Do not give this man what he wants," she said.

The Agent extended the palm of his hand, concealed in a black glove. "I'll take it now."

CJ shoved the amulet deeper in his pocket. "I don't have a key."

The man tilted his head, slightly, just enough to zero in on CJ's pocket. With his eyes still hidden, he took a step forward and said, "Give it to me."

CJ backed away. "Not without some answers, creepy dude. I recognize you. Why have you been crawling through my head? I've seen you in my dreams. Why?"

"Stop wasting time."

Chakawain stepped in between them. "There is a dark cloud above this man. Do not trust him."

"Really, Pocahontas?" CJ said, "… cause a minute ago you wanted to stab me. And you," he faced the Agent, "back the … just back off. You don't scare me."

The man went to the silver case and rubbed his hands along the edges. "We have followed you for thirty years, waiting to get what belongs to us."

"Sounds like you've been searching the wrong place."

"You've done a remarkable job … avoiding us, that is," said the Agent, staring at the silver case. "You have my compliments. But you can't hide anymore. The Haysons belong to us."

"Do not listen to him," Chakawain said. "He brings

evil to Mother Earth."

The man sneered at Chakawain, then turned to CJ. "Give it here!"

"Hey! Both of you!" CJ shouted. "*You* have to participate with *me*. I'm the only one around here with a heartbeat. What I say goes—*got that*?" He shook the Hayson in the air. "If you don't believe me, then bring it on."

The Agent took slow steps toward CJ. "You accepted the legacy and disappeared, believing you could do as you please."

CJ stepped back. "No, I didn't."

"You broke your promise ... your word."

"Nope." CJ circled around a table. "Didn't do that, either."

"You won't be trusted again," the man said. "The ties between us are no longer honored—no longer wanted. I am stronger. I will sustain long after you die."

"Then you'll have to wait till I kick the bucket, 'cause I'm not giving you anything. I want some answers."

The man slammed his fist on the table. "There can only be one keeper! *One*!"

"You must not listen!" Chakawain said. "You must have courage!"

"I'll give you one last chance," he told CJ.

"Do not listen!" Chakawain shouted. "He is evil!"

CJ covered his ears. "*Dammit*! Someone make sense!"

The Agent seemed to ease up on the tension, even snorted a slight chuckle as he stepped closer to CJ. "Hand it over while you still can. I won't let you disappear again."

Chakawain tried to pull CJ away, but her hand sunk to the middle of his arm, clutching only CJ's spirit.

Then the agent-looking man grew larger and taller, and with a head now the size of three men, he leaned forward and screamed, "*Give it to me!*"

CJ's hair flew back and a strong wind pushed him into a table.

Chakawain split into long streaks of light and whisked away backward.

CJ screamed back, "*Nooo!*" Then he pushed the side-switch on the Hayson. The blue lights streamed across the showroom, but the man was gone.

CJ spun in circles, searching the showroom. "Katcha …" he called out. "You still here?"

The he saw it—the empty tabletop. He ran to the table and looked underneath and all around. The silver case was gone—along with the fourth Hayson.

Chakawain materialized a few feet away.

"Listen." CJ went to her. "I didn't mean to hurt the bear—I didn't, but I gotta get that case back. I don't want to search the universe and I do *not* want the Suits crawling through my head. How do I bring him back, right now?"

"It is too late. You have walked through the clouds; now you must travel the sky. You must stop this evil man. It is your mission."

He pulled the amulet from his pocket. "This is what they want. This thing! Not me. Why?"

"You must be careful. His kind will now hunt you, as you do them."

"Okay, this is just *waaay* too fucking weird." He ran his fingers through his hair, contemplating. "Okay, you know what?" He faced her. "No. I don't have to do any of this. I was fine before all of this. I'll be fine when I take this back where I found it. I'm not—"

"Do you wish to find your parents?"

CJ froze.

She cupped her cold hands around his fist, tightening his grip on the amulet. "You must find the answers you seek."

Chakawain went to the bear and placed her hands on its massive back. After a quick beat, a cloudy image of the bear rose from the carcass, then rolled to its feet. She turned her back to CJ and started walking away, the ghost bear moseying beside her until they had both vanished into the north wall of the club.

CJ stood motionless, staring at the bear carcass, and the damage he'd done to the showroom.

After a few more shots of bourbon, he contemplated calling for help, but there was no way to explain what had happened. And even if he told the truth, no one would believe him. He sat thinking … wondering what to do with a dead bear in the middle of New York City.

Within a few minutes, he had a plan.

Sublines produced a variety of different shows and occasionally the stage had to be reconfigured to accommodate whatever act might be rolling in. There were platforms and stage wedges piled high in the storage room, along with the equipment needed to haul the heavy sections around. After studying his options, CJ rolled the piano dolly in the showroom, then he secured a hoist to a ceiling beam.

He tied the orange cord around the bear's legs and body, doubling and tripling the cord in some areas so it could sustain the giant mammal. The rank stench of the bear's fur triggered a cough, as mud, and dung, and different odors of the forest seeped into his lungs.

One crank after the other and soon the heavy creature was suspended high enough to slide the dolly underneath. He cleared a path through the club, then rolled the beast out of the showroom. When he saw the back door he remembered something; there were cameras in the hallways.

"Dammit."

CJ knew the security guard that worked the graveyard shift. His name was Anderson. CJ had run across him many times while working late-nights at Sublines. He had to somehow divert Anderson from watching the video monitors in the security office, and he had to disguise himself for the camera in the loading dock.

CJ went to the green room, where artists either left clothes behind, or stored the garb to wear for the recurring shows. In searching through the lockers, he found T-shirts, pants, and a couple of jackets, along with a few dresses, robes, and an assortment of wigs. Then he found some waist-high, black dominatrix boots hanging next to a leather whip.

"Radine would pay double for that show," he said, closing the locker.

He gathered some clothes and tossed them in a box, along with some empty beer bottles he'd pulled from the trash. He placed everything next to the dead bear at the back door of the showroom. After he'd mapped out his plan, he called the security office.

"Hey, Anderson, it's CJ … down in Sublines."

"Hey, CJ. Who was down there tonight … anyone good?"

"Eh, same ol', same ol' … hey, listen—people are beating on the front doors. You know … the glass ones … upstairs? I can hear it all the way down in the showroom, but every time I go up there, no one is around. It seems to be happening every ten minutes or so, and I'm trying to finish some repairs, and … well, do you think you could check it out?"

"Probably some drunk tourists, CJ. But I ain't doin' nuttin'. Yeah, I'll check it out."

He knew Anderson would take at least ten minutes to get downstairs before taking a haphazard walk around the building, which would take another ten to fifteen minutes—even longer if there happened to be some women tourists roaming around. After that, Anderson would stop by an office somewhere in the skyscraper and grab a treat from one of those honor-system snack boxes, taking another few minutes before he would make it back to the security office. If all went as planned, CJ would have half an hour to complete his task.

Sublines had another exit downstairs—catty-corner to the back door. That side exit led to a hallway that zig-zagged through the basement and then ran behind the stage wall of the club, with Sublines' main office being halfway down the same hall. After passing the executive office, the corridor continued around a few more curves and eventually led to the back door of Sublines, where the dead bear lay on a dolly just inside the club, only five feet from the freight elevator.

He stuck a black T-shirt in the back rim of his pants before he went through the side door. If and when seen, that camera would show the front side of CJ coming out of Sublines, heading toward the executive office with zilch in his hands—nothing unusual at all.

He went down the hallway and into Sublines' main office. There he grabbed a broom and headed for the camera farther down the hall, a camera that captured a panoramic view of the freight elevator, and the back doors to several businesses—one of them being Sublines. He approached the wide-shot camera from behind and underneath, using the broom handle to place the black T-shirt over the camera lens, leaning the broom against the wall afterward. Now he could open the back door to Sublines without the camera capturing his image, but he had to move fast.

He threw on a pair of baggy pants and a thick down jacket, followed by a tangled wig, which he placed on his head backward to cover his face. Then he placed another wig on top of the first one, as a wig should be worn. The winning touch was the oversized robe he slipped on over the clothing. Now the camera at the loading dock would capture an image of a sloppy, heavy woman, with disheveled hair.

It took almost ten minutes to roll the heavy animal into the elevator—much tougher than he anticipated, but Sublines was only two stories underneath ground level. It would only take about half a second to go up two floors.

When the elevator doors opened at the loading dock, he stepped out and started flinging the beer bottles at the lights in the ceiling, shattering the bulbs—except the upper-right corner, leaving enough light to see the edge of the dock. If the loading dock camera recorded anything, it would be a heavy woman tossing beer bottles at the lights.

He rolled the bear out of the elevator and untied its legs, then he pushed and pried with everything he had until the bear rolled over the edge of the dock. He got back in the silver elevator with the extension cord, the empty box, and the piano dolly.

As the elevator doors closed on the shadowed view of a dead bear's paw, he knew this night—and that image—would haunt him forever.

CJ stripped out of the clothing and placed everything in the box with the extension cord, then he rolled the dolly and the box of clothes back inside Sublines. He knew the freight elevator, like many elevators, had a built-in memory that would trace the last ten stops, so he pressed several buttons when he got out, sending the elevator on a sporadic journey. By the time the elevator stopped on the thirty-ninth floor, Sublines would be erased from its memory.

If his time guestimations were correct, he'd have only three minutes to get back inside the club.

He removed the T-shirt from the camera lens and returned the broom to the executive office. CJ then stuffed the T-shirt in the front of his pants, and went back to the side exit. The side-door camera would now capture him going back into Sublines like any other day and, once again, with nothing in his hands.

The costume and the extension cord went in a large trash bag, along with strands of fur and chunks of mud he'd swept from the showroom floor. Then he went high in the ceiling and hid the trash bag on top of a gigantic air duct.

Given the cleaning habits of Sublines, the bag wouldn't be seen for twenty years.

He went to the broken tables and saw one Hayson lying on the ground. Then he remembered tossing a different Hayson across the room. He got on the floor and started searching under tables and chairs. While he was down there, he heard the sound of a closing door.

"Hey, CJ," someone hollered.

CJ peeked over a table and saw Anderson walking

into the showroom. He forgot Anderson had keys to every door in the building.

"Fuck me," CJ muttered, then bolted across the showroom. "Did you run 'em off?" he asked as he approached Anderson.

"Din't see nobody, CJ. I bet they came late for a show, got pissed, and banged on the door." Anderson took a bite from a candy bar. "Smells like shit in here. Pipes backed up?"

"I think so. Been this way all night. Listen ..." CJ said, inching toward the lobby. "I appreciate you looking into the banging. You never know when somebody might break a door down, ya know?"

"Oh, I've seen it all working late-night in this nut house, CJ. Nuttin' ... and I mean *nuttin'* ... could shock me at this point."

CJ had a visual of the dead bear's paw. "Yeah. Well ... thanks again," CJ said as he opened the door, hinting Anderson should walk through it.

Anderson followed the lead, but then he stopped and turned around. He held the door open. "Hey, I ain't busy if you'z wants me to look at dat plumbin."

"No, no, that's okay. I think someone's taking care of it tomorrow; besides, you don't want to get all nasty."

"I said I'd look—not *do*." Anderson let go of the door and walked away.

CJ stood still, waiting for the clicking sound of the door latch before he moved a muscle.

Then he bolted.

He found the Hayson he'd pitched across the room and placed it in his tool bag with the others. Then he took another glance where the creepy agent in the suit had materialized. The only things noticeable were the broken tables and damaged chairs in front of the stage.

"Shit."

But then he noticed a dim glow of lights in the ceiling, coming from a smaller lighting grid in a different section of the showroom.

It didn't take any coaching to see an opportunity there. He went to the smaller grid and cleared the area underneath, stacking the tables and chairs in the aisle. Then he put the furniture the bear had destroyed in the space he'd just cleared out. CJ brought the ladder over. He climbed to the ceiling and loosened the hardware, and just like that, the heavy truss came crashing down. Now it would appear as though the grid had come loose and smashed the furniture below.

To finish the swap, he hauled the undamaged tables to the open space in front of the stage, replacing the seating the bear had smashed.

He'd get a call about the grid on the floor, no doubt, but that would be the lesser of all evils here because he could come back anytime to do, what Sublines would consider, some repairs.

Finally, he grabbed a can of spray paint and coated a section of other grids above the stage. After tagging a few wires, it looked as though he'd done some repairs. He painted the trash bag full of dung and fur, and just as a safety measure; he sprayed even more paint in other places to rid the club of the bear's pungent smell.

He called Anderson again.

"Hey … it's CJ. I looked into the bad smell. It was a backed-up toilet. Just wanted to let you know I plunged it and flushed it down. It's all taken care of, but thanks for offering some help."

"*Dat* … was a toilet? Are you kiddin' me? I hope it wadn't nuttin they serve down there … you know what I'm sayin'?"

"Hey, it is Times Square."

"How late you gonna work, CJ? It's 5:00 A.M."

"Holy shit! Time really flies when you're in the ceiling all night." Anderson didn't reply, but CJ knew he'd planted the seed. "Come down and see a show, all right?"

"If these bastards ever give me a night off."

"G'night, Anderson."

Done. Everything was back to normal except for some broken tables, and the slight issue of a dead bear on the loading dock. All he could do was pray no one would connect him to the animal. Surely no one would finger-print the broken bottles—and he'd reported strange activity to Anderson. Still, only time would tell.

Hopefully the dead bear would be such a mind-fuck for the building crew they'd remove it without asking questions. There could be fines, and reports, and loads of paperwork involved. News would spread and inspections would follow. Yep, most likely the workers would sweep this incident right under the rug, and Anderson would never say he'd seen it all—ever again.

Sliced

"CJ, pick up the phone!" said Radine, her voice shrieking through the tiny speaker in the answering machine.

CJ lay on his bed, exhausted.

"CJ, you always do this. You ask me to call, then you turn off your cell phone and ignore your answering machine because you're lying around on your lazy ass. Get—"

"*What?*"

"See … I knew you'd pick up. You're so cute. You're so talented. You're so *fired* if you don't get here on time!"

"You lost me at hello. Goodbye, Radine."

CJ rose onto one elbow and grabbed a stack of mail from the worktable, then sorted through the pile until he found his schedule. After pitching the unwanted letters aside, he leaned back and studied the itinerary. He lowered the papers to see the clock on the wall.

"Shit!"

In less than an hour he was standing by the X-ray

machines at LaGuardia. He flagged down a security guard and explained he had a metal tube in his bag, along with some tools and items that might trigger the alarms.

The guard looked at a monitor and speed-tapped the keyboard, then told CJ he had nothing to worry about; he hadn't been selected for a random search.

As he was boarding the airplane—doing the snail-crawl down the skinny aisle—he noticed a man in a dark suit and hat, glaring at him with a pair of squinted eyes. CJ froze for a beat, thinking of the agent in the black suit at Sublines. A few steps closer and CJ realized the man was sitting in the seat behind his. The man's cobalt-blue eyes were glued to CJ, even as CJ reached for the over-head bin. CJ shot a look back, a quick glance, but the man looked away.

"Excuse me." CJ waved a stewardess over. "Can I sit behind this man?" He pointed to the aisle number above the seat. "That's my lucky number."

CJ peeked at the man as he passed by, and once again, the Suit looked the other way. As he put his tool bag in the overhead bin, he noticed a slight blue sheen on the rim of the man's hat.

"What the …"

The flight was the hourly shuttle from New York to Boston—one hour tops, but always felt more like twenty minutes. CJ had his eyes closed and his head leaned back when he felt the plane begin to make its descent. The in-side of the airplane seemed too quiet. He opened his eyes and looked to the right. The seat by the window was empty, and even though he'd been napping, sort of, he wondered how the woman sitting there could have slid by without waking him. He leaned over the armrest and looked toward the bathrooms, to see if the woman might be returning to her seat.

The aisle was clear.

When he turned to look forward, he tried to sneak a peek at the man sitting in front of him.

The Suit was gone.

CJ stretched his neck above the headrest and looked around.

Every seat was empty.

"Dammit!"

He stood and reached for the overhead bin, but the thin door swung open on its own and knocked his hand away. Wrenches and cords started flying from the compartment, slamming CJ in the face and chest. It was an unearthly attack, and it came out of left field. He dropped down low and covered his head. Suddenly there were screeching sounds and fluctuating, high-pitched tones piercing the air.

Just as sudden as the commotion started, though, it stopped with vacuum force.

CJ stood slowly, his eyes locked on the opening. He inched closer, bit-by-bit—until he was eye level with the compartment. Just as he peeked inside, an arm sprung from the overhead bin and grabbed him by the shoulder. The arm lifted CJ as though he weighed nothing, then it tried to pull him through the thin gap, slamming his body against the compartment with a series of tugs and yanks. CJ beat on the arm until it dropped him on the empty seats.

He stumbled into the aisle and leaned back while the mysterious limb flailed around, grasping this way and that, as if it were blindly reaching through a hole in a fence. All of a sudden the arm extended even farther— enough to snatch him by the hair and yank him into an empty seat.

CJ knocked the hand away and got back in the aisle, the skinny aisle, the aisle too thin to move around in. He tripped on his own tools and plunged backward, crashing into the seats behind.

Even during the excitement, he wondered why he hadn't plummeted onto empty cushions. Instead of landing on metal armrests, CJ fell on legs, and breasts, on Air Mall magazines and bags of peanuts. Before he knew it, he was stretched out on the laps of people, all of whom were not around just a few seconds ago.

CJ crawled off of the passengers and apologized. He looked to the left and right. The plane was full of passengers again—people that had been shaken up thanks to him. One woman had her child's face smooshed to her breasts, cuddling her kid in fear.

None of the passengers seemed to know anything about the strange arm; they were only aware of CJ falling, of the commotion he'd caused, of the clusterfuck of wires surrounding his seat.

CJ sat down and started stuffing wires in his tool

bag. As he reached for a wrench in the aisle, he looked once more at the seat in front of him. The man was gone. CJ glanced at the overhead compartment and said, "Just like that?"

The seat to his right was still empty, but since he'd just fallen on top of people, it only made sense the woman chose to finish the flight somewhere else.

The airplane landed and had begun to slow down for the final taxi-in. CJ heard the pilot welcome the passengers to Boston.

The frightened mother smothered her child's face to her thigh and bolted up the skinny aisle, and that's when CJ noticed two flight attendants were reviewing a clipboard, pointing his way with their ink pens.

He pulled out his phone and hit a digit. "Radine? It's CJ. I'm here."

"No, you're not here. That's the problem."

"No, really, I'm on the way."

"You're an hour late, CJ."

"No, no, I'm ..." He glanced around. The faces on the plane were different—not the people he'd boarded with. "I'm ... uhh, I'm on the way."

"How much longer, CJ? You know I don't give a shit, but your boss, who's also *my* boss, wants to know when you'll be here."

"Tell him I'm spending his profits on some new gear. He'll care more about the money than me being late." CJ hung up and rushed through Logan.

As the cab barreled through the Ted Williams tunnel,

he had a chance to concentrate, to stop and think about what had just happened. He started replaying the actions in his mind, thinking about the other people on the airplane. Step by step, he tried to connect the dots.

Was the Suit on the plane the one he'd encountered at Sublines? It dressed the same, except, there was a bluish tint to the one on the plane—an energy of some kind. Was it a ghost? If so, how could he sit on an airplane—in the middle of the day? Were there others like him? Were these confrontations going to happen more often now? Is this what Chakawain had warned him about?

He recognized the screeching noise coming from the overhead bin, easily confused with the high-pitched shrill of feedback—except, there were ghostly shrieks fluctuating in the background, voices resonating through the sound. Other phantoms in the past had manipulated the sound in one way or another; some had even played with the knobs on the soundboard. Come to think of it, most of the spirits he'd run across had something to do with sound. Was music the driving force behind everything? Even the Robin Hood dude had a flute in his hand.

But then, there had never been problems with any spirits before—they were always fun. Well, adventurous at least, like Chakawain. But this was different. An angry, mean spirit had paid him a visit in a public place, and he couldn't get away by leaping from a catwalk, or sliding through a trapdoor. Once again, and very soon after the last encounter, he'd visited some unfamiliar territory.

Then he realized he'd just seen something new, a behind-the-scenes view of the space between time; the place where ghosts lingered, and he'd been taken there— without requesting it.

It seemed pretty obvious, *now*, since ghosts could travel anywhere they wanted. The spirits had to go somewhere, but why hadn't he comprehended that before, especially when he was young? And what happened to the hour he'd lost?

This episode triggered some old memories, events from the past that he'd shrugged off as a simple game. Even though the Hayson was new territory, having skirmishes with the spirit world wasn't new by any means. He'd seen how ghosts used tricks and schemes to get their way, but no ghost had ever attacked him like the one on the airplane. That downright hurt.

Of all the years he'd been a sound technician, the last few days had changed everything—forced him to open his eyes. There had to be something in his past he'd missed, a detail he'd simply overlooked. He closed his eyes and thought hard, trying to remember.

Daylight filled the cab as the car came out of the tunnel. He covered his eyes and slumped down in the backseat, trying to recall some ghostly encounters from his youth.

CJ dropped his hands and yelled out loud: "Seattle!"

The cab driver yanked the wheel to the right and pulled over on Summer St. He turned down his radio and eyeballed CJ in the rearview mirror. "You changing mind?"

CJ sat quiet.

Cars whooshed by.

"Please to telling me sir."

"No, no ..." CJ said, finally looking up. "Go to the piers. Same place. No changes."

There wasn't much to remember about Seattle, except he was super young, and those were his first recollections in a night club, and the spirits he'd seen there came around on the same night his parents had died, and that's when he came across the amulet again, and that's what opened the silver case, and ...

"Holy shit."

The Hayson was drawing him in, pulling him toward ... what? How did the Hayson tie in with music?

Wait a minute. Was he supposed to find the old book? Had the bear been planted? Why did he get up out of the blue and go to New Hampshire? How would Chakawain know about his desire to find his parents in the afterlife? What the hell was going on here?

Okay, too many unanswered questions. Chakawain was right. It was time to accept his theosophical journey—so to speak. That would be the only way to keep these agent-looking men at bay. Clearly they were hunting him down, so he had to find them first. He had no choice. This whole Hayson thing was luring him into a world he wasn't too familiar with—but needed to be.

One thing was certain; if the game was about to change, he had to stay a step ahead of it, and if music was the medium, it was time to test the Hayson in a musical setting. And it was definitely time to take charge.

Then the light came on.

If he could force the ghosts to slice through time, the paranormal events would open up a whole new world of sound, a playground where he would have some leverage. Yeah ... this Hayson thing could work well for him. And heck, why stop with the sound? Some far-fetched visuals would definitely blow the ticket-holders away.

The Settlement

The cab drove across Four Point Channel and barreled up Atlantic Avenue until it pulled over to the right, stopping at an old seafood warehouse turned music arena. A place called The Settlement. A place where CJ had grown, technically. A place he called home.

Somewhere around twelve years earlier, he was called in to oversee the first TV pilot The Settlement ever produced. From that day on, CJ and The Settlement had tackled the computer evolution side by side.

There was chitchat of paranormal activity at The Settlement, but none CJ could ever validate. Most of the rumors had been generated long ago during the fishing boom, when the pier held one of Mr. Hibbons' warehouses. Supposedly Ann Hibbons was never hung for being a witch, but instead lived out her days in seclusion after the warehouse had been abandoned. It was said she died and rotted away in the back section of the wooden pier—just crumbled into the bay with every old splinter and bolt until someone in the sixties decided to rebuild.

When the fish factory re-opened, and the newspapers printed pictures of the remodeled warehouse, her image was seen peering out from a window up high. At least that's what some claimed, and that was enough to create a good ghost story.

CJ had already learned that having a haunted reputation was terrific advertising for a rock-n-roll mega bar. Many clubs had planted such rumors on purpose, but luckily for The Settlement, the tales had been told long before the club had occupied the pier.

But if The Settlement had any reputation at all, it was one of well-produced shows, excellent sound, and top-grade talent, making this showroom one of CJ's favorite places to work.

CJ ran into The Settlement and gave Radine a drive-by kiss on the cheek.

"Wait a minute, CJ!" Radine stuck her arm through the booth window, flapping papers in the air. "People are looking for youuu," she sang.

CJ halfheartedly turned around. "I'm late, Radine."

"I lied for you. So you owe me. Now, first … come closer."

"Really? Are you gonna do this every time?"

"Closerrr."

She leaned over the booth and put her weight on one elbow, and with her free hand she brushed and teased his hair. "You're lucky to have me as a friend, you know that?"

"My hair is fine. Who's looking for me?"

"No, it's not," she said, then sat. "But now it's bearable. And the question from upstairs is ... what are you spending money on, and why?" Radine flung the message in the air and rolled her eyes. "Also ... a guy named Larry called. He said you have his number and he needs you to call the Dark Star yesterday. ASAP. It's an emergency." Radine placed that message on the counter slow and easy, protecting her designer fingernails. "Now the best part ... you're not gonna like this, but the opening band is already downstairs." Radine turned on the faucet. "I told them what you said, CJ, but they kinda snuck in one at a time. I wasn't able to stop them."

"How many are—"

"I can't do everything, CJ. I just can't! I'm stuck in this booth, and people are calling, and asking questions, and calling, and walking in—" The phone rang and Radine glared at it. She lifted the receiver and slammed it back down. "I'm trying to stop the walk-ins but I can't do it, CJ, I just—"

"Whoa, whoa, whoa ... take it light. Take a breath."

"But, CJ you know I—"

He seized her face and planted some kisses on her forehead. "Don't," *Kiss.* "Hang up," *Kiss.* "On people."

Radine laughed and tried to hit him. "You're right, CJ. I love youuu." She straightened her breasts and said, "Now go away."

He snatched the messages from Radine's hand and headed down a long stairway that led to the lobby of the club, stopping on a midway platform to make a call.

"Larry? CJ. What's up?"

"CJ! What the hell happened in here the other night? Can you tell me, please? My phone is ringing off the hook with complaints. Customers got so drunk they don't remember going home … telling me they're sick as a snake, threatening to sue! You left a broken speaker on the showroom floor! What the hell happened in my club?"

"I don't—"

"My bartender also called in, says he's *dead*. And that was a few days ago. How much can you guys drink in one night? Were those your friends that invaded my club?"

CJ had a flashback of the semblance by the ladder. "I … I'm not sure, Larry. Chris told me he'd put the speaker away. I showed him how to adjust the levels on the other speakers. A new speaker is on the way."

"I haven't heard from Chris, and there's a band in my lobby waiting for a sound check. I got no soundman. No one! I'm screwed!"

A brief and awkward silence followed Larry's tantrum.

"Do you know what that means, CJ? It means I got no show! You can't pay bills with no shows! You made this mess, now you need to clean it up."

"Larry, I can't. I'm in Boston with two bands tonight. No way at all, man. Let me get on the horn. I'll call you in a minute. I'll find someone for you."

CJ ran down the remaining stairs and headed for the

office.

CJ had begun rummaging through paperwork when he heard the office door open and creak inward. He didn't turn around, but still said, "Talk to me."

"I'm looking for CJ."

CJ kept rifling through papers. "Who needs CJ?"

"Tina."

"Tina who?"

"*Duh* … Tina with Sweet Hipsters … the band?"

"Hi, Tina with Sweet Hipsters … *the band*. What do you need CJ for?"

"We're playing here tonight."

"What time?"

"Umm … 7:30 or 8:00."

He punched a stapler and asked, "What time is it now?"

"Umm … it's like 3:30, but we scheduled a four o'clock sound check, with CJ."

CJ spun around and faced her, and then he stood. "I scheduled that with you?"

Her expression said it all, which was, so busted. She clinched her hands together and said, "I'm not sure who scheduled it. Look—call our manager. He can give you the details. Can I use your computer? I have a list of names for you … or you can print them out."

CJ stood silent.

Tina cocked her head, surprised CJ wasn't responding. "For my guest list, *silly*."

"Is that all?"

"No, actually." Tina got excited. "I have more." She pulled some notes from her back pocket and shimmied her shoulders. "I need to explain how I want my CDs sold. My method is a little unusual—very original and, well … *definitely* needs a meeting."

"Right, 'cause … you're the first one to sell CDs at a bar."

"I told you we're different," Tina agreed, then shook her papers at silly CJ. "I need my own dressing room, and I need someone to hang our posters. When you call my manager, will you—"

"*Easssy*, Tina … back to the basics. Here's how it works. We start sound checks around 5:00, but you never sent me a tech list—did you? So I don't know what kind of gear you need—do I? Number two: I'm callin' nobody. You sign my checks?"

As soon as he snapped, he recognized her, this, the situation—the I me I me, entertainer, the kind that never knew they'd killed their career by living on a private planet, where the atmosphere was rich with vanity, where the only goal was to narcissistically desire the neon lights, which would obviously make them a star, until they woke up twenty years later and realized—it hadn't. He'd seen hundreds of them come and go over the years. Not a pretty sight. Tina was a full-fledged member of that coalition, and it seemed she'd been orbiting that planet for some time.

That only made it harder not to feel some compassion. He wasn't here to judge; he was here to help. He could see she wasn't a bad person, and God help this poor girl if she ever had to change a flat tire on the shoulder of a dark highway.

"Okay, look here … gimme your tech list. If I get ahead of things I'll come in the showroom and get you guys rolling. Okay?"

"Perfect. We have two guitars, one bass player, I sing, and the drummer—"

CJ imitated a buzzer sound, as if she'd lost the prize. "Make me a list," he said.

"But I can just tell you! We have—"

"Whoa," he laughed. "Read my eyes. On … a piece … of paper." He held his stare. "Who am I—your secretary?"

"I *just* don't have time to deal with all of that."

"So you're gonna tell me you spent time making that bullshit list, but you don't have a tech list for your band?"

Tina winked at CJ and kicked in to the next phase of her plot. She twirled her hair and bent one knee in, then she lowered one shoulder and smiled real big. "Most men are happy to do this for me."

"Yeah? Well, this is not some East Village beer joint, Tina. Be a pro, or hit the road. I'll see you at five, for sound check."

Definitely appalled but at the same time humbled, she wiped a non-existent tear from her eye and said,

"Well, if you could just make *one* phone call, we could find out how this got so crazy."

"That might be a good idea, Tina, but it's not happening."

CJ grabbed the edge of the door.

Tina jumped back as it closed.

CJ walked in to the showroom around 5:00 P.M. to find the showroom looking like a bomb had gone off. There was a surplus of gear onstage, enough for an entire day of Bonnaroo, with trunks and coffins stacked high as the drums. A rat's nest of cords had been tossed on the floor in front of the stage, waiting to trip any person who might walk by. Instrument cases and backpacks had been scattered across the cocktail tables in front of the stage, somehow leaving room for half-eaten sandwiches and soda bottles.

A few band members were hanging out onstage when CJ approached them.

"Before we do anything ..." CJ nodded at the cables on the floor, "... those have to go away. And you ..." He singled out the drummer, who was smoking. "Where's your ashtray?"

The drummer threw a puzzled look at CJ.

"If you're gonna smoke, you're gonna use an ashtray. Capisce?"

The drummer flicked the ash in his pocket and snubbed the cigarette on the sole of his shoe.

"Who has a tech list for me?" CJ asked, then headed for the sound booth.

This booth in particular, sunken in the center of the showroom and squared off by a half wall, gave him clear and open access to every speck of audio and video in the arena. He'd installed every piece of equipment in this club and knew this system like the back of his hand. In addition to the stage gear, he'd installed the video and computer configurations in order to keep up with the webcasting, video matrix, and dozens of flat-screen monitors throughout the club. Every road leads home, as does every cable in The Settlement, allowing CJ to control the entire club from this booth.

Even though CJ wasn't a pilot, he'd always compared working a sound booth to flying an airplane, and that meant both hands should be on the steering wheel at all times. The booth at The Settlement was his chance to try out his version of a cockpit, so he placed the power amps in a rack to the far right. The rack beside it held the system EQs, designated reverb, wireless transmitters, and sound compressors—all being gear he could operate with his right hand.

To keep his left hand busy, he'd positioned a couple of lightboards in the center of the booth, shelved a few feet above the soundboard, level with the dual CD and DVD players.

By his feet were four video monitors, mostly used for managing Pro Tools and overseeing live webcasts.

Over the years, running shows from this booth had

become every soundman's dream, because everything worked, and every piece of equipment was reachable from one spot.

As CJ powered up the racks of equipment, a constellation of green and red lights filled the booth, then a low-growling hum began to resonate from all the tiny fans in the machines.

Then he turned on the microphone labeled VOG: for, VOICE OF GOD, a must have tool for every club that produces live entertainment—not only used to speak to musicians onstage, but the same microphone the unseen announcers use when speaking to the audience, or better yet; the voice that comes from the sky when a show is about to begin.

"Okay, drums, you there?" CJ asked over the VOG, just as someone leaned over the half wall and handed him a tech list.

"Holy shit!" said CJ, eying the list. "Who are you, Steely Dan? Let's trim things down a little."

The Sweet Hipsters seemed to contain not one, but five lead players, each being more crucial than the other. CJ focused on setting the guitar player's levels, but the bass player insisted on thumping out a comical amount of steady notes, as though he were in a race with his own fingers. His volume was too loud to hear CJ, begging him to stop.

The musicians continued to amuse themselves with ego-driven riffs and musical trills—all at the same time.

As the battle for supremacy escalated, the volume

levels grew to decibels intended to wake sleeping dogs in China, and it seemed each musician had assumed the job title of Musical Director—without informing the rest of the band. The rhythm guitar-player lit a cigarette. The drummer slammed in to a 1970s version of 'Wipeout.'

CJ placed the tech list on his nose and blew a puff of air, sending the paper gliding.

Once again he'd been handed a group of unprofessional musicians, behaving more like a bunch of children onstage. After a few more attempts at organizing the madness, he went to the main breakers and shut down the power to the stage.

"Okay," said CJ, approaching the stage. "If you want me to set some levels, you'll have to work with me. As much as I'd love to see the reaction from the audience tonight, you know, when you sound like a blundering mess, I can't, because I have to think about the club. So … we either start … and finish … a sound check—or you leave right now."

The musicians hugged their instruments and stared into space, insulted by the ultimatum.

"You don't know who we are, do you?" The bass player snorted. "We have a song playing on the radio."

"Really?" CJ raised his eyebrows. "Then maybe you can teach me a few things. How do they treat you at Madison Square Garden?"

The guitar player shoved the neck of his axe at CJ and said, "Just do the fucking sound, you grunt! We've played bigger places than this dump, and had *way* better sound men than you."

"Then let me be the moron you remember on your road to success, but right now, I'm trying to help you. We can do this in one hour or not at all, but I'm not spending three hours watching you beat off onstage. What's it gonna be, guys? Are we doing a show to-night?"

The Sweet Hipsters kicked off their set at 8:00 P.M. with only a few customers in attendance. No surprise there, though. Opening bands hardly ever drew a decent crowd. While many backup bands could easily fill a club; that happened at home, on their own turf. Most bands hit the road for two reasons: to increase their exposure, and to build a following, and that took many years of enduring a grueling road life, traveling as a backup band, schlepping crates in the wee hours of dawn. Tonight the club wouldn't fill up with patrons until half an hour before Nathan Juju hit the stage.

The Sweet Hipsters were good, though. The employees watched them perform their music with pride, unconcerned that very few people were in the showroom.

During the bridge of one tune, the Sweet Hipsters vamped in to a repeated pattern of diminished, chord progressions, which placed a musically altered presence in the showroom. As with any augmented note, or peculiar rhythm, a touch of mystery often accompanies the eccentric tones, ultimately affecting a customer's liking, or loathing, of a song. But CJ knew mystifying chord progressions could also open enigmatic doorways to the unknown, and that's when the hairs on the back of his neck began to rise. With that, he knew a semblance was about to come around.

From the center of the sound booth, he stood and scoped out the club, searching for a semblance. Maybe it was Ann Higgins, or possibly the spirit from the airplane, or who knows, perhaps Genghis Khan. He noticed a shadowed figure just then—back in a dark corner of the showroom, but he couldn't make out whom, or what it was. He flagged a server to the sound booth.

"Go see if that person needs anything, all right?" CJ said.

"What person? Where?"

"In the corner." CJ pointed to the dark figure. "Right there."

"What are you talking about? There's no one over there, CJ."

"That's him."

"Who?" The server asked, then walked away, saying, "It's true. You are crazy."

Not two measures later, a tiny speck of light zipped through the air and zigzagged over the empty seats in the showroom. As it came to rest high above CJ's head, the spark of light grew into a vaporous—yet lucid figure. The phantom hovered above the sound booth, and it seemed to be fixated on Tina.

CJ heard the unmistakable thud of a microphone hitting the floor. He turned and saw Tina sitting on her butt, looking dizzy and flushed. She seemed disorientated, shaking her head to get her bearings. CJ watched her for a few beats until she composed herself and got back on her feet—albeit still confused.

The ghostly image flew to the back of the show-room, where it was dark, where it gathered momentum, where it geared up to go into a full-fledged haunt.

CJ took the Hayson from his bag and suddenly, his heart skipped a beat. He gazed at the Hayson, spellbound and anxious—frightened and excited. After a few head spins to confirm the coast was clear, he pushed down on the side-switch. A streak of shimmering blue lights soared from the Hayson and headed for the dark corner of the showroom. A brilliant light flashed through the arena, illuminating the rows of empty seats.

The ghost bolted to the left.

The lights from the Hayson stayed on the spirit's tail, though, until the blue madness caught up with the semblance and tackled it to the ground. CJ held the Hayson low and ran to the dark area, hoping to see a face, or maybe identify the ghost. The only thing he saw was a spirit kicking and fighting to break free. Then the blue netting and the captured spirit vanished with a blinding flash—back into the Hayson. CJ tucked the Hayson under his shirt and ran down the empty aisle, back to the sound booth.

The server approached the sound booth at the same time. "What the hell was that, CJ?"

"Make sure the green room is locked!"

The server bolted.

CJ pulled an XLR cable from a bin and plugged one end into the soundboard. After a few more head spins, he placed the Hayson at the other end of the cable.

Unaware of the consequences, of God knows what might happen, he placed his finger on the volume slider and slowly pushed it forward to increase the output. Then he slammed down on the side-switch.

The ghost wiggled through the cord like a fluttering garden hose, juddering wires and shaking connections as it raced into the power coils of the amplifiers. From there the supernatural life force surged through the equipment like an electrical storm, seizing and dominating the racks of gear—adjusting frequencies and rearranging decibels as it traveled through every sound-based device in the booth.

Held by the magnetic lure of the machines, the in-carnation then swept across the face of the soundboard like a nuclear wave, sheathing the knobs and sliders in a light-blue, florescent haze. CJ stepped back, preparing for a massive surge of energy, but all of a sudden the commotion stopped.

A sporadic light started flickering on his jeans, coming from the video monitors down below. He squat down and saw the semblance inside the screens, leaping from one screen to another ... running its hands along the inside rim of each monitor, looking for a way out. CJ reached under the video screens and turned them off, one by one.

With no other diversions available, the ethereal force raced up a pillar of cables that led to the ceiling. Then a speeding cobalt-colored light traveled through a network of wires above the empty seats—heading toward the stage.

Within a quarter beat the semblance had reached the SNAKE behind the stage, where it conquered, occupied, and altered every element of sound.

A loud snap suddenly penetrated the airwaves, clearing the air of all preexisting noise, and for a full measure, the showroom resonated with an eerie, silent cadence until the enhanced clarity had settled in.

Tina stood frozen onstage, staring at the ceiling with a baffled look on her face, which only added more confusion to her already hazy state of mind. But all her uncertainty flew out the window when she placed her hand on the microphone. Tina had no choice but to submit to the supernatural influence, and without missing a beat, she began to sing.

The new sound had a mysterious authority, and the various tones produced from the instruments and vocals went from a blundering mass of noise, to delicate layers of chromatic ingredients. The abrasive decibels suddenly had a smooth and tender approach, as each note now crooned through the air—resembling the way a ghost would make an appearance: by rolling into a space with ease, no longer fragmented in the conflict between speed of light, and speed of sound. The timbres and pitches had become authoritative and mature—raw and genuine, without restrictions.

Tina became irate onstage, performing as if she'd discovered a new mission. She tossed menacing looks across the empty showroom. She sang with a devilish conviction. Her newly found, crisp vocals had transformed her into a confident and focused singer, and she began to dominate the stage with a flare of hostility, pacing in a feverish rage, stomping from side to side with a masculine passion.

She stormed to the guitar player and punched him in the chest, and even as she walked away, she turned her head back and snarled. Her fearless stride became dissident and rebellious, cunning and calculating, crafty and seasoned. Tina reached for the crowd the same way the arm had searched for CJ on the airplane, grasping at thin air, clinching her fist in desperation. Tina had become a rock bitch, and she won the small crowd over with her new presence.

During certain light transitions, a smeared image of someone, or something, streaked across the stage, arriving in parallel intervals—fading in and out of sight.

The sound in the club became enticing, and Tina's new persona had not only captivated the few people in the showroom, but had drawn them closer to the stage. Appearing both fascinated, and curious, the musicians perked up and looked across the stage, as if this new vitality could be seen. Strangely enough the new energy helped them focus, and within a few measures the band was performing with the same unrelenting spark of enthusiasm as their lead singer.

Toward the end of the set, Tina purred the last few words of a song and lowered her chin. She didn't raise her head after the passage, though, nor did she smile at the small crowd. She seemed hesitant to continue.

The rhythm guitar player picked up on the temporary halt. He stepped up to his own microphone—eager to cover for Tina, smiling as he opened his mouth to speak. When he wrapped his hand around the microphone, his words became locked on the tip of his tongue, and his body froze, and he stood mesmerized—bound by the energy from beyond. With a stiff back and a gaping mouth, he peered over the showroom, paralyzed.

The ghost had taken a journey through the veins of the musician—and then it was gone.

The guitar player swallowed and took a wheezing breath of air, then his eyes darted back and forth as he woke from the stunning trance. Still somewhat distant, he softened his face and fingered a chord on the neck of his guitar, and with a subtle, poetic demeanor, he went in to song.

"*Does a sleeping dog dream at night?*
Is Rosebud really alive?
Is there really treasure, there,
where the rainbow touches down?
Gimme yours. Give you mine."

On the tail end of his last word, the band vamped in to a heavy rock groove and continued with the set.

Before the Sweet Hipsters had finished their last song, CJ reversed the switch on the Hayson and retracted the ghostly energy, forcing the blue lights to stream back across the ceiling, back to the sound booth. The semblance then receded through the amplifiers and zipped back into the Hayson. CJ grabbed a sharpie and wrote *Settlement* on the Hayson, but the ink evaporated, even after three attempts. He placed a red rubber band around the cylinder and tossed it in his bag.

The rest of the night flowed with ease and the headliners, Nathan Juju, broke a new record at The Settlement, reaching a customer attendance of twenty-two hundred. Despite the earlier activity, Nathan Juju sounded great without any unearthly aid. Their only distraction was Tina, who strolled across the stage at random times, clinging to the magic of the night, trying her best to dance with the lead singer, E.

While the crowd was shuffling out the doors, CJ gathered a few cords and a 3-PIN lighting cable from the sound booth. He took them to his office, and there he started snipping and splicing, screwing and connecting, weaving and tightening parts until he'd assembled an adapter to use in the future. Tina entered the office as CJ was tightening the last few fittings.

"CJ?" She called out softly. "I ... I wanted to thank

you. Everyone's told me what an amazing job you do, but I've never felt magic like that. The way the sound made me feel, CJ … like, like something just crept into my soul and pushed every emotion I have *straight* to the surface." Tina put her hands to her hips and bent her head sideways. "You're gonna do okay in this business."

"Gosh, I hope so, Tina."

Not long after the showroom had emptied out, CJ started wrapping up the night, inspecting the stage and making sure the equipment in the sound booth had been powered down. He saw a cord on the floor of the sound booth, and then he noticed a CD sitting on a rack of gear. The table next to the booth was empty so he set his tool bag on it, then swung the half-door open and stepped inside the booth. When he reached for the CD, he accidentally nudged it. The CD fell behind the rack of gear.

He dropped to the floor and lay on his side to reach under the rack. While down on the ground, he heard footsteps coming toward the sound booth, getting louder as they got closer, finally coming to a halt when the person arrived.

CJ stayed low, groping for the CD. "Talk to me," he said from the floor.

After a minute of silence he ditched the CD and stood.

No one was there.

A sharp needle suddenly pierced the side of his neck.

The needle then withdrew, stretching his skin as it pulled out. CJ stumbled. Before he could get his bearings, it happened again—another stab—right after the first puncture. He covered his neck with both hands, but another needle went in between his fingers.

"Dammit!"

The cord on the floor came alive and coiled around his body, strapping his arms to his torso with lightning speed. A force from beyond then shoved CJ in the corner and held him there, forcing him to stand immobile inside the booth. CJ squirmed until he heard more footsteps run by the sound booth. Then he froze. More footsteps came and went, this way and that.

A cloudy figure emerged right beside his tool bag. An image of his mother then materialized within the murky cloud, fading and reappearing in the center of the haze.

CJ lowered his head. "That's a trick … and it's pretty low. What do you want?"

"Give her back," said a voice, slicing through the air as though each word had come from a different place.

"Give who back?" CJ asked.

"Release her," the strange voice growled.

"Fuck you. Release *me*!"

One end of the cord magically rose and hovered in the air at his chest. The metal tip suddenly snapped from the cable and fell to the floor, then the outer sleeving started peeling away one layer at a time, exposing one thin wire. The cord curled and aimed for his chest, as though it were about to stab him.

The amplifiers suddenly had power again, and the colored lights appeared. The fans on the machines began to hum. The other end of the cord moved on its own to the soundboard, and with a slight click, it slipped into an open socket. The volume slider then slithered upward, going from no power, to full tilt, sending a massive amount of wattage into the cord. The floating wire at his chest rose even higher and stopped, suspending the needle-like wire only a few inches from his neck.

"You cannot have her," the ghostly voice told CJ. "Give her back."

Still unable to move, CJ eyeballed the wire at his neck. "Who, damn it. *Who*?"

The cloudy figure hovered above his tool bag, then a ghostly arm sprung from the haze and pointed straight down, straight at his tool bag.

A blue orb appeared on the other side of the sound booth, high in the ceiling at first, but then it slowly descended to the middle of an empty aisle only twenty feet away. As the orb faded, a man in a black suit and hat materialized. He started walking toward the sound booth.

The wire at CJ's neck spun around like the head of a snake, as if it were watching the man come closer.

"No," CJ hollered, bouncing his weight against the half wall, fighting to break free.

Spirits appeared from nowhere just then, several of them. The floating phantoms surrounded the man in the suit, as though they were trying to confine him.

The cord unraveled from CJ's torso and flew toward the Suit, then wildly coiled around the man's body like it had done to CJ, circling the Suit with fifty feet of wire.

The cloudy figure at CJ's tool bag suddenly reached for CJ. It grabbed him by the neck and yanked him through the half door, then released CJ at the table. "You've taken the wrong one," the voice said, once again pointing to his bag.

CJ's tool bag started bouncing on the table.

It was then that CJ got the message. His eyes wandered the showroom. He looked at the semblance hovering in the air. He glanced at his tool bag. An image of an old woman caught his eye; she was thirty feet away, dressed in Pilgrim clothing, hiding behind a pillar. His eyes darted to the man wrapped in wire, who, even though encircled by spirits, was coming closer.

CJ pulled the Hayson from his bag and held it above his head. He pressed down on the side-switch and the blue lights shot toward the ceiling. In less than a beat, a glimmer of a semblance emerged from the blue netting. The other spirits joined their previously captured companion, then soared away in all directions, leaving CJ alone with the Suit.

The cord binding the Suit dropped to the floor and circled his feet.

CJ aimed the Hayson at him and said, "Where's the silver case? Give me the Hayson. You took them from me. They're mine."

The Suit stepped over the mound of wire, his chin

lowered, hiding his face under the fedora.

CJ fired the Hayson and the blue web seized the man. As the lights retracted, CJ stared at the Hayson, a little shocked, and a lot stunned. "Holy shit," he said. "I got you." He sat in a chair and held the Hayson to his face. "I really got you."

A server station down the aisle was filled with napkins. CJ grabbed a stack and placed them to his neck to stop the bleeding. When he lowered the tissues to gauge the wound, there was no blood.

He flung the cord in the trash and walked away cursing.

Overcast with thoughts, yet finished with his duties, CJ walked upstairs and past the ticket booth.

"Umm, good night, CJ," Radine called out.

CJ kept moving, hugging his bag.

"CJ!"

CJ didn't stop for Radine, though. He didn't stop for anything. He walked outside and ended his night with a solemn walk through the North End of Boston.

In a perfect world he would have popped in to Legal Seafood and gorged on the legendary lobster bisque, but what he really needed was a stiff drink. There was a watering hole just a few blocks away, a place he knew well. He walked down the brick streets and made a left on Snow Hill, entering a small bar with a handmade sign on the window that read DASH.

At first glance, DASH seemed the same as any other late-night scene, but this place was a techie's bar. Most of the soundmen and stage crews in Boston made their way to DASH after work because drinks were served until 4:00 A.M., and depending on the bartenders mood, sometimes even later. The fact that cocktails were served in coffee mugs after 2:00 A.M. didn't seem to keep any techies away.

Behind the bar was a good-looking, blond-haired man about twenty-five years old. As an aspiring actor, he specialized in comedy improvisation.

Most evenings, he and CJ would talk as if they had met each other for the first time. It was a stress breaker, because the conversations they concocted would become so farfetched, one of them would start to laugh. The one who laughed first was the loser in the game, but the real mission was to get strange looks from other patrons at the bar.

The bartender bumped fists with CJ when he walked in. CJ went to the far end of the bar and pulled out a barstool. The bartender walked over with CJ's drink: Wild Turkey on the rocks. CJ ordered one drink and DASH bought the second; CJ would drop a twenty-dollar bill and all ended up well. Same routine, every visit.

The bartender set CJ's drink on the bar and said, "A guy named Larry called here looking for you. I didn't know you were in town."

"Shit!"

The DJ came over next. He shook CJ's hand. "Got anything on you?" he asked.

CJ pulled a CD from his bag. "Yeah, try track number seven; tell me what you think."

CJ began to relax and get lost in the music. He heard the bar stool next to him slide backward. He paid no attention to the person sitting down; he glanced at his tool bag, instead. Since it had a Hayson inside, he lifted the bag from the floor and placed it in his lap.

Little by little, CJ began to unwind.

He started thinking about the strange men coming around lately. He'd seen them before, he knew he had, but it didn't click during the encounter at Sublines. It was the confrontation at The Settlement that really triggered his memory.

As though another door to the past had just opened up, he remembered a recurring dream just then—one that started long ago, when he was a kid ... about being in a club after hours, a dark and smoky club playing slow and haunting music, similar to Bessie Smith. The music is echoed and distorted in the dream, as though the same record were playing on two different turntables—one spinning a bit slower than the other.

Four or five men have gathered around a table, their backs to CJ. They're dressed in black suits and hats. The men are a good twenty feet away, but he can still see a violin on the table—a blue violin with some kind of sheen, or hazy glow around it. He knows not to look for a light, not to search for a Profile or Lico projecting a blue silhouette. He'd already looked for the light source in previous dreams and never seen one; it just wasn't there. Even so, the violin bore a cobalt sheen around the edges.

Instrument cases are stacked on the table next to the men, who never seem to be talking, just staring, each of them gazing at the blue violin.

Compelled to approach them, CJ moves closer. After a few steps, he sees the shoulders and body of another man sitting at the table, facing the men in dark suits. As CJ walks even closer, one man grabs the violin and walks away. The other men leave right after, exposing the man sitting down. Even though the group of men walk away, every time, and even though CJ moves closer to the man seated at the table, in every dream … that's when he wakes.

"Hey man," said the bartender, waving his hand in front of CJ's face. "Hey!" He snapped his fingers. "Tough night?"

CJ looked to his left. The bar stool was empty. He gripped his bag and said, "Do I know you?"

The bartender broke out laughing. "So who played over there tonight? Anyone good?"

CJ looked down at his tool bag. He wanted to talk about the unusual night, about the otherworldly music and the ghostly battles, about cuckoo Sweet Hipsters and awesome Nathan Juju. And he wanted to cheer about his new toy, sort of. But instead he faced the empty barstool next to him, then said, "Eh … same ol', same ol'."

CJ downed his drink and caught the last shuttle home.

Deals

CJ arrived ten minutes early at the location Dean Autry had requested, a sterile-looking, glass monster of a structure resting in the shadow of the Chrysler Building. He entered the lobby and scoped out the directory. Intertwine Music wasn't listed. The suite number Dean gave him was listed, though, so he went to the seventeenth floor and entered Suite 1753.

The reception area was cold and stale, and the girl behind the desk seemed lifeless on the phone. She cupped the receiver with one hand and waved him inside with the other, greeting CJ and sending him down the hall to the first door on the left. CJ went in the room and found it to be the same as the reception area: dull and boring.

Two black leather chairs faced each other in the middle of the room, a small table to the right of each chair. Another table in between the two chairs held a phone, several notepads, and some ink pens.

CJ sat facing the door.

As he sat there waiting, he wondered why there were no pictures on the walls. He went to the door and glanced down the hall. There were no records on the walls, no music was playing, no Punk Rocker was racing down the hall with a mail cart—nothing.

"This is definitely not a music office," said CJ, closing the door.

On the way back to his chair, the door clicked open and a young man walked in with some paperwork.

"Hi, CJ. Dean will be right in. He wanted me to thank you for coming in. Can I get you something to drink?"

"No, no. I'm good. Thanks."

"I brought a contract to look at while you're waiting. Dean's excited about having you on board." He handed CJ the paperwork and left the room.

CJ sat, but he soon felt uncomfortable. Something seemed wrong. The room had the same vibe as one of those fly-by-night operations—the kind that set up office in a hotel room, but a few days later … they're gone.

Soon enough, though, Dean Autry blasted through the door with a surge of authority, hosting a gruff and rugged demeanor—like someone who'd be branding cattle instead of sporting a thousand dollar suit.

CJ stood to greet him.

"CJ? Dean Autry." He shook CJ's hand and they sat. "Thanks for coming in. Here's the deal, mate. Nathan Juju is flat out cooking with a new album right now; however, this will be their first major tour in several years. We'll not be labeling this project as a comeback tour, but reviving their live-performance status should, by and large, boost their overall record sales."

His enthusiasm took a sharp turn for the serious, and CJ suddenly felt the intensity of Dean's beady eyes peering out from under his wrinkled eyelids.

"I'll need you to oversee the tour, CJ. Audio and lighting, of course ... but—" Dean crossed his legs, finger in the air. "You'll not be required to oversee each performance. We've commissioned another audio mate to travel with the crew and run the live shows. You'll remain a day or two ahead of the tour, CJ, as we primarily want you to prep the rooms."

"Prep in advance?"

"Precisely. You'll travel ahead of the tour," Dean went on, pulling paperwork from an envelope. "We haven't the resources for the rather large stadiums, but we'll not play the small clubs, either. I've found that most mid-sized arenas are bloody miffed when it comes to sound. I suppose it's because they pay their technicians mere pennies. After discussing the subject thoroughly, we've decided to pull out the big guns for this tour; we're holding back on nothing."

Dean reached in his jacket for a pen. "We want you to tweak the sound systems in these venues prior to the concert date. We've gone to great measures to assure each arena is dark the night before Nathan Juju performs. This has taken some precise and careful planning, but it will allow you the time needed to attend to any technical difficulties. When the crew arrives as scheduled, you'll have made the necessary adjustments, to our specifications, of course, and the show will be nothing short of the mutt's nuts."

"Now," Dean continued. "One slight stipulation. We'll oversee the live sound for backup bands, as well. We'll not be putting so much effort into a blinding success, merely to have some air-locked wanker alter the preparations; therefore our crew will operate sound for each opening act as well. It's in the contract and there's no getting around it."

"So … you want to occupy the sound system in these arenas. Have you worked that in advance?" CJ asked him. "Soundmen don't give up their booth so easily. Neither would I."

"You've worked in most of these arenas, CJ, if not designed their entire sound system. Quite frankly, by knowing key players in these venues, you can pull strings—move things along much quicker than normal… if by mere association alone." Dean stared CJ in the eyes. "And before you say it … let me. *Yes* … we're exploiting your working relationships, and we're exploiting you. We want these venues to be ours when we arrive. We'll need you to make that happen."

"Okay, but shouldn't I rehearse with Nathan Juju for a while to get their feel?"

"You copped a feel last night and it was excellent. I haven't a shred of doubt regarding your technical skills."

"Wait a minute," CJ said. "I think I caught wind of

this at DASH last night; that there was a falling out with the soundman. So it's true that—"

"Yes," Dean confirmed, a little loud. "We've had issues with that lairy sod for quite some time, and I've no more patience for issues. This tour was put together for one purpose—to make money."

"What about consulting with him? Shouldn't—"

"Would you care to talk about the past, or the future?"

"No, no … the future, Dean," said CJ, somewhat distracted by Dean's bushy eyebrows. "But if the tour launches next Tuesday, that's only—"

"*You* will leave on Tuesday. The crew will depart on Wednesday. As I stated, you'll travel ahead of the tour."

"That's three days away. Holy mama, Dean. I hate to pass this up, but I—"

"I simply won't take no for an answer, CJ. You'll have an exhaustive itinerary—it won't match the rest of the crew. You'll be on your own. But from what I've witnessed so far, you can bloody well do anything." Dean grinned and tilted his head. "You've been in the front line with a few of our artists in the past, and I hope this leads to a brilliant working relationship in the future." Dean raised his eyebrows, smiling as if the cat had just eaten the mouse. "We'll provide you with an assistant for the next few days—to help with any conflicting schedules."

Dean thumbed through the contract to find a specific page, then he folded the papers back and started reading.

"Eighteen-fifty per week base pay, with a weekly per diem of three hundred. Of course, there will be a proper bonus at the end of the tour, to the tune of fifty-five hundred. All travel and hotels will be taken care of, naturally. Mail service once a month." Dean looked CJ in the eyes. "We need you CJ. You're the only one who can tag this tour with such short notice."

"And you've talked this over with E and the band? I mean ... we've worked together a few times, but it's never been very magical. Even last night was just okay."

"Last night was spectacular. And the sound ... well, the sound was absolutely brilliant. And speaking of magical, you made that poor bird onstage sound like bloody Ann Wilson."

"Thanks, but that place has top-of-the-line gear."

"Yes, and you control it."

CJ rubbed his amulet, thinking.

"A woman named Sara is going to—"

"Look, Dean. I'm honored, but I need a few days to—"

"*Give* Sara names and numbers." Dean clicked his pen and slipped it in his jacket. "She'll ring anyone you wish, and say anything you ask her to say."

And just like that Dean had blown him off, ignored his opinions, tossed his concerns out the window.

"I don't really work like that, Dean. Who's gonna work for me at The Settlement for three months? They rely on me up there, and they've been real good to me over the years, and ... that's just them. What about the other clubs? These aren't chump-change gigs. I can't have some woman just *call* these places and tell them I won't be there." CJ tossed his contract on the table. "I wouldn't leave those guys hanging, just like I wouldn't leave you hanging. I'd like to think I'm a little more reliable than—"

"Sixty-five," Dean offered. "Four thousand before you leave, with the balance at the end of the third leg." Dean took CJ's contract from the table and flipped it open, first scratching and then scribbling on one page. He initialed his writing and handed the contract back to CJ.

CJ raised his eyebrows, realizing his salary had just about doubled.

Then he started weighing the pros and cons. This much traveling had been a blast when he was younger, but he wasn't twenty years old anymore. On the other hand, this was a major touring company, putting him at the top of the game with a dream gig. If he accepted, there would be no turning back.

This deal was moving way too fast.

"Listen, Dean. I need a few hours to make some calls. I've got to make sure no one gets screwed here."

"I don't have a few hours, CJ. I'll need your answer now."

"Then I'll think about it while you look for someone else. If you don't find anyone, call me and I'll have an answer for you."

Dean smirked. "You don't allow any codswallop, do you? Which is precisely why we want you, CJ. You walk in to a showroom and make it yours."

Dean slid the contract in an envelope and smiled as he handed it to CJ.

"Three hours from now, I'll have Sara, your new assistant, deliver information to your home. Give her whatever she needs to get the ball rolling. We'll schedule a production meeting on Monday, at which time you'll receive the technical specifications and meet the entire crew. Meanwhile, Sara will be at your disposal to wrap up any loose ends." Dean stood and shook CJ's hand. He went to the door and stopped. Dean turned and said, "With you on board, this tour will be the dog's bollocks. I'm bloody sure of it!"

CJ took a walk through midtown, preoccupied with the deal he'd apparently accepted. He noticed a window display at Colony Record Store in Times Square. The theme was: GONE BUT NOT FORGOTTEN, a presentation of famous musical heroes from the past who still held value in today's market.

Spinning in the center of the exhibit was an old 78-RPM record of Duke Ellington's: "Black, Brown and Beige."

CJ took a closer look at one of the old band pictures. Something seemed familiar. There was a man in a dark overcoat that caught his eye. The man was standing to the side of the band with the rim of his hat covering his face, his image half-smeared, as if he'd turned away right when the old photograph had been snapped.

CJ stared at a band member in the snapshot, and he could have sworn the musician's eyes moved.

All of a sudden CJ realized this tour with Nathan Juju was an opportunity in disguise. He could search for the silver case and the missing Hayson, he could embrace this new upsurge of semblance enlightenment, but most of all, he could design some remarkable stage shows. And since the amulet had led him to the Haysons, maybe the Haysons would lead him to the afterlife—to his parents, where he could finally apologize. And since ghosts were already a part of his diet, well, the pieces seemed to be falling into place.

CJ's home was only fifteen blocks away. He decided to walk.

"Just a few more calls and I guess I'm gone, DeBussey. You're taking care of Dog and working the brunt of the gigs, so … I guess that's my life in a nutshell. I'm laying a lot in your lap. Are you sure you're cool with all these jobs?"

"Yeah, yeah, CJ … I'm cool. Piece of cake. You'll hear only good news. Sounds like you'll be climbing through rafters with a hundred pounds of cable around your neck."

"This tour shouldn't be all that. Hey, if you hear from a woman named Sara, get back to her. Let the details fly, all right? I mean it, you can tell her anything.

She works with a bunch of musicians, so she's heard it all. You might even like her; I hear she's kinda sexy."

DeBussey laughed. "If you're passing her off on me, she must be a barker. Thanks, but no thanks, CJ; besides, you don't want to burn any bridges here. You know what happens when that stuff goes sour. She'll blame you."

"Good point. I need to work again when this tour is over."

While CJ gave DeBussey information about the gigs he was handing over, he sorted through his key cabinet, placing the keys DeBussey would need inside a purple Crown Royal tie bag. "Oh, yeah," CJ said. "You're gonna have Mark Barrett and Lillias White at the Limelight this month. Give these guys all you got. They're some of the coolest people on Earth. If you have to buy any gear to make them shine, then call me for a Fed-Ex number. I'll pick up the tab."

"Okay, but I get all screwed up with the overseas time changes."

"No need. This is a US tour."

"But Dean lives overseas, doesn't he? He's mentioned in *Billboard* all the time, and everything happens in London."

"I think he flies across the pond every couple of days. Probably has a home in both countries."

"Dude, what's he like?"

"He seems all right. He's definitely been around since the Earth cooled; that's for sure. He's a no-nonsense guy. I guess that's why he deals with the A-list of talent."

CJ grabbed the Hayson he'd used to capture the Suit in Boston. He wrapped a T-shirt around it and hid the bundle inside a 1958 Traynor speaker, an heirloom of sorts, sitting on the bottom shelf. He piled some heavy gear on top of the speaker as a safety measure. Even if DeBussey needed equipment for a job, he'd never use the antique speaker and the Hayson would remain tucked away.

DeBussey started laughing. "CJ, dude ... this is a great thing, man! It's a long way from playing the subway twenty years ago! Remember that? Huh? Do you remember playing under the Delacorte Clock in Central Park?"

"Yeah ... Remember your guitar strap ripping from the weight of all those coins?" CJ placed the other two Haysons in his tool bag.

A buzz from CJ's doorman interrupted their conversation.

"I gotta go," CJ said. "I'll call you tomorrow and ... thanks, DeBussey. I really mean it."

CJ tossed the purple bag of keys on the table and opened the door.

A lady with blonde hair just past her shoulders was standing in the hallway.

"You must be—"

"Sara," she said. "It's a real pleasure. I've looked forward to meeting you for quite some time, CJ."

"For a few hours, anyway."

"Oh, no. This goes way back. The tour, I mean." Sara handed CJ an envelope. "Here's your itinerary and a list of personal phone numbers. My number's in there, too."

"Thanks. I guess I'll be seeing you around."

"Not quite. I'll be here in New York, but trust me, I'll be with you every step of the way. Let's have a great tour."

"Yeah. Let's."

CJ closed the door and sorted through the paperwork. There were contact numbers for hotels and arenas, as well as car service information. The airline tickets were in his name, paper clipped to a check for four thousand dollars. A Post-it on top read: *CJ Singleton. April 22, 2008, through June 22, 2008. Next delivery: The Foley Hotel, Salt Lake City, UT; June 16, 2008.*

He studied the itinerary, quickly realizing Dean was right: he had worked at most of these venues. He opened the key cabinet and started grabbing keys, tossing each set in a black microphone pouch.

CJ put the keys on the table and reached under his bed for the book he'd found in New Hampshire. It took a minute to scope out his apartment, to find the ideal hiding place, but after pondering the dozens of bins to choose from, he stashed the ancient object under a pile of *Rolling Stone* magazines in his closet. The book made a small lump in the stack, but not enough to draw attention. CJ patted the heap of journals and said, "No one will ever find you here."

New Orleans

The first stop on CJ's new tour was the awesome city of New Orleans. Sara had booked the band at a large rock club on the corner of St. Louis and Chartres, across the street from the Napoleon House. It seemed only fitting Nathan Juju would kick off their touring hiatus at a venue called The Resurrection.

CJ's travel arrangements were effortless, and a car was waiting for him when he arrived at Louis Armstrong International. The driver's instructions were simple: give CJ a ride to The Resurrection, but take CJ's luggage to the hotel. The driver would then return to the club six hours later—unless otherwise instructed.

Nathan Juju, however, would remain in Hudson, New York, for another night, following suit of many well-known groups that would prepare for a tour by re-hearsing away from their fan base. By playing the first few shows at a college gymnasium, the band could work out the kinks in the music while still performing for a small crowd. But the main reason Nathan Juju stayed under the radar was to sneak in a couple of concerts without the press catching wind of the show. After the run-throughs in Hudson, the band and road crew would travel to New Orleans to begin the tour.

It came as no surprise the door to The Resurrection was cracked open when CJ arrived. He was on time. He entered the lobby and took about ten steps, then he stopped. The ghostly presence was overwhelming, and the old brick building reeked of history. His inner senses went haywire, and that's all it took to know there would be no shortage of semblance activity inside.

As he left the lobby and went in the dark showroom, he heard someone say, "Are you, CJ?"

CJ spun around to see a twenty-something kid with a bleached-blond buzz cut.

"I'm Steve. I'm the Assistant Operations Manager. I'm here to show you around and tell you about our amazing club."

Steve kicked into his spiel as if someone had dropped a quarter in the slot, listing the club's features in a rapid-tongued tempo. CJ had to turn away, though. Steve was too much—too fast. Instead of listening to Steve, he took a Maglite from his bag and started searching for sound gear and speakers. He inspected the catwalks and ran the beam of light along the massive walls.

There was a cloudy figure sitting on a catwalk only fifty feet above them. CJ fixated on the image. It was a woman, her white chin resting on the lower bar of the railing. Her legs were swaying in a steady rhythm, as a child would do on a bench. She appeared bored and lonely, focused on the empty stage.

She noticed the beam of light and turned her head toward CJ, now interested in the stranger down below. CJ kept his light planted on her face, and even though the distance was too far to see each other's pupils, he knew they had locked stares.

"We hold twenty-eight hundred in the seats," Steve said. "And two hundred standing. Frank Sinatra sang here many years ago. How 'bout that?"

Steve continued to rant, but CJ kept his eyes on the woman. She grabbed the top of the railing and stood, then eased her way toward the back of the club. After twenty feet, or so, she disappeared. CJ's first instinct was to run after her, to find her, to start the game, but he knew he'd have to wait. Right now, he needed to focus on the job. And it wouldn't be a bad idea to pay attention to Steve, who was still chatting in double time, explaining every last feature of the club.

"All of our gear is state of the art," Steve said. "And we just installed fourteen new Profiles in the lighting grid. We have—"

"Can I see the sound booth?" CJ asked him, cutting to the quick.

"What? We haven't done the official walk-through yet. Are you sure you want to move on?"

CJ grinned. "Maybe later, Steve. I need to get in the

booth. Cool by you?"

Steve took CJ back through the lobby and up a set of stairs that was closed off to the public. At the top of the stairway, Steve opened a door to a giant maze of catwalks, all of which were either suspended from the ceiling, or mounted high along the inside walls of the club. The catwalk at their feet led straight to a garage-sized cage, dead-center of the ceiling, attached to the massive beams that crisscrossed the inner shell of the roof.

With CJ's spotlight as their guide, they walked across the metal grid to The Resurrection's sound booth.

The workspace had been built high in the air and boxed in with dark-metal, chain-link fencing—except for the face of the structure, left open for an unobstructed view of the stage. Steve unlocked the cage and they stepped inside.

"I need the logs, Steve. And I need to know where the main cutoff switches are, too."

"The breakers are over there," said Steve, pointing to the back of the sound booth. "And the logs..." Steve paused.

"The specs, Steve ... system configurations? I also need a map for the SNAKE, from backstage to the soundboard."

Steve bit his lower lip and walked away.

CJ went to the soundboard and leaned forward for a better view.

The club underneath was pitch black. He could feel a shadowy presence as he studied the lighting grid above the stage, jam-packed with Fresnels, and Pars, and Pro-file spotlights.

Behind him was a catwalk leading away from the sound booth. CJ ran a beam of light along the walkway until it merged with the catwalk running along the back wall. He shined his flashlight to the left, and to the right, and then farther each way, discovering the metal walk-ways ran the four corners of the club. Midway along the right side, he saw another chain-link cage mounted high against the brick wall. He scoped out the other catwalks, but something kept pulling him back to the dark cage. He held his light on it, captured by its ancient magnetism.

"There you are," CJ said.

"Yes, I'm back."

CJ spun around and planted the light in Steve's face.

Steve chuckled. "Kinda spooky in here with the lights off, isn't it?" Steve had a cup of coffee in one hand, notebooks in the other. He offered both to CJ. "Which one first?"

CJ grabbed the coffee. "You rock, Steve. Hey, I'll tell you what. Leave the logs with me, and I'll leave you alone for good. I won't bother you for anything. How's that for a deal?"

"Well, actually ... if you really don't ..." Steve seemed thrilled by the offer. "Are you sure?" he asked, shoving the notebooks in CJ's chest. "Just in case, though," Steve pointed behind CJ. "There's a phone be-side the soundboard. Dial eleven-o-one and you'll reach my desk. I'll be there. Just call. I'll be at my desk. I'm always there."

As much as CJ wanted to toss the notebooks aside, he couldn't. He was here to work and that was that. The ghost activity would happen at the right time. He knew it.

Thirty-minutes later CJ took his eyes off the logs, like he'd already done a few times. From his seat at the console, he scanned the dark club, wondering where the woman he'd seen earlier was hiding.

There were conduit pipes at the back of the sound booth, extending down from the ceiling and feeding wires to an assortment of breaker boxes. He went to them and started flipping switches. The Resurrection became visible one section at a time, revealing a sea of empty seats below. The vacant chairs sat like brokenhearted ghost ships—waiting for their passengers to return.

He stared at the chain-link cage across the showroom. It was still dark up there, but now he could see a tarnished stairway running up the side of the wall, leading right to the cage.

"Yep, that's you."

After studying the soundboard, a beautiful, thirty-two channel Neve, he grabbed a CD he had burned for himself and used at every club. The disc played rap, country, classical, and rock music, mixed in with some spoken word, live comedy, and even a few old radio commercials from the '40s. Since it was made to limit each style of music to one minute, he hit PLAY on the CD player and made his way downstairs.

Turning on the lights made it easy to walk the showroom, but CJ needed to analyze the sound. It was time to gauge the highs and lows of the frequencies, to monitor the clarity, to pinpoint unnecessary vibrations. He listened for hot spots—where the sound could be overpowering, and he searched for flat areas—where the sound could be dull. He went from corner to corner, up and down each aisle, paying serious attention to every nuance that might deny a listener from hearing great sound.

As he approached the mid section, he came upon one area that was lifeless—almost muted of sound. He shined his light high in the ceiling. It appeared one speaker had shifted in its mount and was now facing the wall. Since the problem was so simple, he decided to go ahead and fix it. Normally he wouldn't make any adjustments without contacting the owner of the club, but he wanted to avoid the phone-tag downtime and red-tape explanations. Screw the insurance; it needed to be done.

He found a tall ladder and gathered the tools he needed. Then he made a harness, so he could suspend from a ceiling beam and work hands free. Last, but not least, he stashed a Hayson in his tool bag.

Halfway through the repair, he saw movement from the corner of his eye. He stopped turning the wrench mid twist. It was the woman he'd seen earlier. She was standing on the catwalk to his left … watching him. Being much closer now, he could see she was younger than he first thought, and even more intriguing: she was beautiful. He felt compelled to stop and stare.

He'd run across plenty of ghosts while working in

dark clubs. It came with the territory. It was the spirits he couldn't see that scared him, but he had a clear view of this one, and even felt a lustful attraction to her. Something inside him was stirring around big time.

Her good looks were obvious, but she possessed a mysterious attraction as well, much more alluring than any woman he'd ever laid eyes on—ghost or living. Maybe it was her simplicity that captured him, as if she had no motive or ulterior thoughts behind her pleasant stare. Her modest look of truthfulness seemed to match her simple sundress, and there was an unusual curve to her smile, complemented by her long white hair that covered one of her eyes and bundled at her shoulder before flowing down her back. Her beauty seemed effortless. Then her lips opened just slightly, but no words came out.

He swung to the ladder and unhooked his harness. "I've got time for this," he said, scaling down the steps.

As CJ descended from the ladder, he saw her walking high along a catwalk, approaching the top of a stairway against the wall. He threw his tool bag over his shoulder and headed up the stairs, but after seven or eight steps, he came upon an old gate. He climbed over the handrail and scaled along the outside edge of the stairway until he'd passed the gate. When he jumped back onto the stairs, she was only ten steps higher, staring into his eyes, encouraging him to follow. He could vaguely see her breasts through her old white dress, and the slim outline of her body had his groin throbbing.

"This is crazy," CJ said. "*She's a ghost.*"

As though a switch had been turned on, she became playful, possibly from being recognized, maybe from leaving her drabby world behind. For whatever reason, she was suddenly lively and vigorous, skimming her hand along the brick wall as she ran down the metal grid.

CJ took a few steps and heard creaking noises, though, giving him a subtle warning. The catwalk could easily be too old and unstable for a human.

Fifteen careful steps later he was stopped by another chain-link barrier, but this wasn't just a gate; it was one of two gates, both accessing a cage mounted to the wall. Being twice the width of the catwalk, it protruded in the air, making it impossible to climb around. Then it hit him; this was the same dark cage he had seen from the sound booth.

She had already passed through both cage doors and continued to run along the catwalk on the other side, but when she realized CJ wasn't behind her, she came back to the gate on her side. With CJ in front of one gate, and her standing in front of the other, the eight feet of space between them seemed like miles, but when she smiled and placed her small white hands against the wire, CJ knew he had to get to the other side.

He inspected the old cage and studied the struts and brackets. It appeared the top and bottom braces hadn't been maintained in ages; they'd rusted over the years. The weight of the structure had caused the cage to slope downward. What must have once been a sturdy storage area, was now a decrepit box of wire mesh, deteriorating with time.

He fumbled with the lock on the gate and found that it, too, was old and rusted, but one solid blow from Dr. Hammer would cure that condition. When he applied the treatment, the shackle hurtled to the left and the gate dropped a few inches.

CJ pushed and pulled, and the gate creaked and groaned, until it opened inward, barely, just enough to squeeze through. The mesh floor also looked deteriorated, and he wasn't sure it would support his weight. He reached inside and grabbed the wire-mesh wall, then gripped the rickety cage door with his other hand.

He was thin enough to squeeze through and step on the mesh, and so he did, but the chain-link floor creaked with hardly any pressure.

As he was sliding back out, his tool bag snagged an old piece of wire. He shouldered the cage door—a bit too forcefully. The top hinge snapped from the wall and the gate dropped another eight inches, pinning him in the doorframe.

The female spirit stood patient on the other side. Waiting. Wondering why he'd been held up.

CJ didn't know the wire had ripped his bag, and with each struggling movement he only opened the slit wider. Then a few tools spilled out, and a couple more wrenches after that, and those caught his eye. He watched the tools bounce on the chain-link, then slip through the open gaps and fall to the floor of the club.

Realizing the Hayson could also fall from his bag, he stopped squirming. He needed to grab the cylinder, but that meant he'd have to let go of the gate, and if he let go of the gate he'd fall into the old cage.

CJ was stuck.

Her expression was now that of an innocent child. She stood on the tips of her toes, trying to peek over his shoulder, still curious as to why he'd been delayed. A few more wrenches fell from his bag. She tilted her head sideways and watched the tools fall to the ground.

The tools didn't matter much, and the bag had even less value, but the Hayson had to be protected at all costs. He peeked down and saw one shiny edge of the cylinder. Judging by the size of the tear, it would take one more shuffle for everything to come pouring out.

'*Dammit.*'

He let go of the gate and grabbed his bag, but that spun him into the cage and tangled his other hand in the wire lattice above his head. The weight was too much, though, and the mesh wall ripped along the top. CJ dropped a good ten inches. With one hand tangled above his head, and his back against the chain-link siding, he hugged the tool bag to his chest, trying to free his twisted feet without falling on the mesh floor.

She seemed all too confused at this point. She walked through the gate and across the cage floor with ease, approaching CJ with a look of compassion on her face. She made a few attempts to help him, but her hand passed through his arm each time she tried to grab him.

His tangled fingers started turning blue, and with his feet still stuck in the gate, his back had bent the wrong way. His spine was beginning to hurt from the awkward bend. Just a few minutes ago everything was peachy. Now he was trapped.

She tried pulling his fingers from the wire, but she was useless when it came to helping him. To make matters worse, he felt a sharp pain every time her cold hand touched his skin. Then she tried pushing on the chain-link cage, only to have her chalky white hands sweep through the wire mesh.

Then she saw the Hayson through the tear in his bag.

"You?" She backed away and put her hands to her face. "You are the one?"

She rushed her hands to her lips, realizing she'd spoken, knowing she would cross over and enter his world.

That gave CJ a ray of hope, though; that she might be able to help him.

But she became furious, instead, and her frown molded a tortuous V in the middle of her forehead—not the kind of vibe he was hoping for. She seemed attracted to him earlier. Now she appeared to loathe him.

She kneeled down and inched her face close to his, and with an evil snarl she began growling. She opened her mouth as though she were about to bite him. But locking her eyes with his was just a ploy, a distraction, a way to creep her hand closer to the Hayson.

CJ noticed her hand crawling closer to the Hayson.

He pulled his bag closer to his chest.

Either she realized her intimidation tactic had failed, or she recognized the terror in CJ's eyes, but for some reason her anger transformed into a look of kindness.

She placed her palm on CJ's face and rubbed her cold soft hand against his cheek. With a tender smile, she tilted her head sideways and said, "You are safe now."

He started seeing color in her face, and then her beautiful, light-brown eyes and shiny black hair began to emerge. As she crossed over into his world, he could almost smell her breath. Powdery. Enticing. Woman. She became more beautiful and gentle with each soft touch, and for a fleeting moment, he forgot how bad the situation was.

There was something mysterious in her eyes, a touch of passion in her trance that gave him hope, but suddenly, without any warning, she raised her hand and slapped his face. Then she slapped him again ... hard enough to shake the cage. Then one more time, with even more force ... and then again—another violent, angry slap. The cage slumped down a few more inches. She raised her hand for another smack when CJ slipped his arm through the strap and caught her wrist in midair.

It was a sensible action on CJ's part, but it threw her off balance. She reached for the cage wall and clutched the wire, then yanked herself closer to CJ. His tool bag swayed back and forth, dangling from his arm. With the two of them planted in one area, and her wrestling to get away, the additional weight started pulling the old cage from the wall.

"Let go!" she hollered, struggling to break free. All of a sudden the Hayson fell from his bag and rolled across the chain-link floor. The struggling came to a screeching halt and they each held their breath until the Hayson came to rest in a crease only a few feet away. Her eyes became fixated on the Hayson. He tightened his grip on her wrist.

"That's right," CJ said. "It's mine. Do you want it? Tell me why."

She went into a raging madness just then, pulling and twisting and fighting as hard as she could. Her tugs only shook the cage, though, with the Hayson rolling a few inches every time another hinge snapped. The weight of two people soon became too stressful for the old bolts. Braces and beams started grinding as they inched from the brick wall. The cage suddenly plunged a good two feet, and it appeared to be on the verge of collapsing when she screamed with a ferocious, deafening assault. As though fifty metal wheels of a subway car were screeching to a halt, her shriek seemed to go on forever, taking him in and out of dimensions, driving a skewer through his head.

Now that she had stunned CJ, she gave a tug with the strength of fifteen men, yanking his feet through the gate and heaving his body to the middle of the cage.

The wire mesh ripped like cloth and the chain-link folded over him, but that sent the Hayson rolling his way. He grabbed it and held it to his chest. For every action there's a reaction, and when the entire frame twisted, the chain-link floor started ripping at his feet. CJ's legs began to dip, and with each snapping of the wire his lower body dropped ... link by link, until his legs were dangling thirty feet above the seats below.

She stood with her back to the brick wall, glaring at CJ. It was a hateful look, a stare that seared his dignity. Then she began to lose her humanly color, and her beautiful eyes became milky white again. She extended one hand to offer help, but pointed to the Hayson with her other hand—suggesting a trade.

"No," he said, afraid to make the slightest move.

She pointed at the Hayson again, forceful and demanding.

He closed his eyes and lowered his head. Feeling the pain, he said, "No."

Furious now, she left the cage and went back to the catwalk. She took a step back and raised her hands in the air, then she let out another haunting, demonic scream. The brick walls began to rumble and her hair flew forward, then her dress pressed against her back as a forceful breeze stirred up from behind.

The power of the wind attacked CJ like a hurricane. Even the old cage began to sway.

Then he heard it; the unmistakable sound of water, swishing and flowing. Then he felt cold liquid seep into his boots and soak his feet. Within a few seconds the rising water had reached his knees. The ice-cold sensation traveled up his body and soon reached the bare skin on his stomach. As the water rose even higher, the chain-link started to loosen and his fingers slid free from the twisted bind, but he was still sandwiched in between the two layers of wire caging.

While he was becoming submersed in water, the showroom began to darken, and within a few heartbeats the club had become jet-black. He saw her standing on the edge of the catwalk, only five feet away, glowing with a radiant, brilliant sheen, as if she were an angel.

Before he could grasp what was happening, water began splashing at his shoulders, and then his tool bag became weightless and started to sway. Still trapped in the wire cocoon, the water level reached his neck.

When the water touched his chin, he turned his head sideways, muting the sound in one ear. As the water crept even higher, he filled his lungs with air and closed his mouth. The white woman became squiggly and warped when the water covered his eyes.

CJ wiggled and jerked his body, trying to break free.

With one loud snap, the cage finally dropped and pulled him underwater. He flopped like a fish, but the cradling wire held him prisoner as it sank in a downward spin. After a few twisting rolls, the wire mesh slipped over his head with a scratching, relentless force, propelling CJ into a gravity free spin.

He started paddling and kicking his feet, but his equilibrium had gone haywire. The pitch-black water left him without a shred of light. He swam this way and that way, and up seemed down, and he went in circles aiming for nothing. CJ ran out of air and his chest became gripped in a tight vise. He swam faster in every direction, but he was fully dressed and wearing heavy work boots.

Worn out from the ordeal, CJ's exhaustion got the best of him and he stopped kicking his feet.

'*So this is how I die?*'

A high-pitched ringing invaded his ears, and the sensation of water against his skin began to fade as he sank more and struggled less, hearing only the fading pulse of his heart, beating at half speed.

CJ closed his eyes.

He felt someone pulling on his fingertips, prying the Hayson from his hand.

He opened his eyes.

The female spirit was only a few inches away.

CJ grabbed her and yanked her close, and her once lovely hair began to swish against his face as she kicked to swim away. Each of her tugs pulled CJ closer to the surface.

He'd held his breath so long his eyes had begun to pop, but suddenly his head emerged from the water.

As he gasped for air, he saw a drifting log. He grabbed it and held on tight, coughing, vomiting, watching as she swam away and climbed onto something.

He couldn't trust her enough to look away, but he knew better than to get too close. He clung to the floating log and looked around. He wasn't in the club any longer, but that was meaningless right now. At least he was alive.

She had perched herself on an old dock made of tree logs and branches, held together with fat mounds of coiled ivy. CJ paddled to the same wooden platform and pulled himself up, then scooted backward over the bumpy logs until he was ten feet away from her.

Exhausted from the encounter, he sat and caught his breath.

Clarise

"Resurrection. Steve, here."

"Steve, it's Dean Autry in New York. Has CJ arrived?"

"Yes, sir! He's in the showroom right now. But the wall in my office isn't rumbling, and that means the stage is quiet. Is this guy any good?"

"He's the best, Steve, and I must speak with him right away. Have him ring me, will you?"

"I don't know if I—"

"I'm in the office," Dean said and hung up.

Steve huffed out of his office and opened the door to the suspended catwalks. Apparently it had become tiresome to reach around the doorframe and pull a megaphone from the inside wall, to lift the oversized funnel to his face and talk into it as he'd painfully done at least a hundred times. The cone went to his lips and Steve said, "Hey CJ. Calling CJ. Please call extension 1101. CJ please call 1101."

He lowered the cone and listened, then put the cone

to his mouth again.

"Just bang on a pipe, okay? So I know you heard me. Okay?"

Steve listened for a reply.

The only sound he heard was his own finger, scratching the megaphone.

He tossed the bullhorn in his office and headed downstairs to the lobby, where he opened the showroom door and saw the bright stage far away, with rows of colored lights beaming down at full capacity.

Steve got to the stage and climbed up from the front, then tiptoed across the black floor as if it might cave in. He shaded his eyes from the intrusive lights and peered across the empty club. "*Where the fuck is he*? Call Dean, CJ!" Steve hollered and stood quiet. "I don't have time for this shit." He jumped off the stage and went toward the lobby. Steve couldn't see the puddle on the dark floor, until he slipped and fell in it. "What the hell is this guy doing in here?"

Before Steve could get bent out of shape, he saw the ladder in a back section of the showroom. He got off the floor and went there. Wires were dangling from the ceiling.

"Cee Jay ... every light in the house is onnn ..."

CJ sat on the dock, his eyes glued to the semblance. He knew not to use the Hayson. Doing so would trap him here alone, but he could threaten to use it—if only to get some information. Still out of breath, he aimed the Hayson at her and spoke.

"Who are you?" CJ asked her. "What do you want from me?"

"It is you who wants," she said. "Why do you torture us? Why must you take us from our homes?"

"What homes? Where are we?"

"Why have you chosen me? I have done no harm."

"I didn't choose you. I don't even know you. Who are you?"

"I am Clarise. Why have you come to take me away?"

"Clarise, I need you to help me."

"*Help you*? You want to hurt me … and yet … I should help you? You are evil. That is what you are!"

"*Me*? Hurt *you*? You just tried to kill me. *Why*?"

"It is what we do when one from the living tries to harm us." She leaned forward and snarled. "Now you are trapped! You will not survive here, and others will never know what you have seen. Your death will be cruel and painful!"

"Hey! I didn't search you out. I thought you wanted me to follow you. Was I wrong?"

She glanced at CJ for a brief second, like she couldn't deny what he'd said, but she turned her back to him anyway.

"You're right," CJ said. "I don't belong here, but I have to protect myself from things like this."

She spun around. "What things?"

"Things like this. Places like this. Being taken away from where I belong."

"And what of where I belong? You want to take me away. You have tricked me into finding …"

"Finding what, Clarise? Where are we? What is this place?"

She scanned the pond below with sadness in her eyes. "This is Artha. My home."

"Okay, good. See … that didn't hurt. Now, if you show me how to get out of here, Artha, I'll leave now and I'll never come back. I promise."

"You are not able to come and go as you please," she said softly.

For a split second he wasn't sure if he was dead or alive, but he had to be alive; his heart was beating way too fast.

"Tell me about your home, Clarise. Tell me why I can't leave. You can come and go. Why can't I?"

"Because you are of the living."

"Last I checked."

"When one leaves the living, they are brought here, to Artha. When they awaken, they are shown the way back to the living. It is the only way to learn the path. You may see us in your world at times, but we are the only ones who may come and go as we please." She pinched her lips and said, "When you take us away with your evil Hayson, we cannot find our way back. Why have you taken so many of us?"

Oh yeah. The Hayson. He realized he still had it

aimed at her. God she was beautiful.

But then he remembered: cut the nice crap. This was a battle to get home. "Clarise ... people in my world don't know where I am. They're looking for me right now. They know a lot about ghosts, too. They're better than me at this stuff. You don't want them showing up, do you? So ... tell me how to get back and I'll let you go."

"No! You are a liar! You trick and deceive. I know of you! We all know of you!"

'*Dammit.*'

He had to turn away, unable to look her in the eyes, and no way in hell could he admit all of this confused him. He wasn't sure how she knew about the Hayson, but she did. And since her English was from a different era, he couldn't help but wonder how long she'd been here, too. Unless he wanted to join her in this place, for God knows how long, it was best to shut up and listen.

"How did you find the Hayson?" she asked him. "It was hidden hundreds of years ago. It should have never been found. The one before you was much too evil—so cruel to many of us." She dropped her shoulders and protruded her lower lip, tugging at CJ's heartstrings. "Artha is my home. Now you will behave as the one before you. You have come to take me away."

After a few beats of no response from CJ, the pity party came to a screeching halt. She took a deep breath and re-claimed her confidence, out-and-out losing her sense of helplessness. Clarise flung her hair back and placed her hands on her hips. "I will not let you take me away! *I. Will. Not. Go!*"

"If you don't take me back home, Clarise ..." he shook the Hayson. "... I'll use this. I really don't want to. But I will if I have to."

Clarise threw him a wicked look, and her hands began to twitch. She took a few steps toward CJ, trembling, submitting against her will. Then she spun around and dove in the water.

CJ rushed to the edge of the dock and aimed the Hayson at the pond. The water was black. He couldn't see her, but he pressed the switch anyway, only to watch the blue lights dance across the surface of the pond. He sat on his knees at the edge of the dock.

She had disappeared.

"Shit! Shit! Shit!"

Frustrated, he sat on his butt and looked around at this place called Artha.

The dock extended ten or twelve feet from the shore, barely resting above the surface of a round pond, a precise, sphere-shaped pond—as though a perfect circle had been cut into the land. A ring of short grass grew along the shore, with a wall of strange-looking brush growing behind it. The foliage had foot-long pine needles sprouting from corkscrew-looking trunks that rose fifteen feet high. They were cactus, they were dogwood, they were unearthly, and they grew in unison with the ring-shaped pond.

He noticed the water was motionless, as smooth as a

sheet of glass. Then he realized the air was inert, null and void of crickets and bugs. There were no stars in the sky, either—just an oval-shaped moon, but as he stared at the moon-like figure, he discovered it was actually two moons … one resting slightly behind the other, both shining a small amount of light on the pond.

He stood and went toward the brush. At the foot of the dock was a thin path leading in to the spiny bushes.

From the first step in he couldn't see his hand in front of his face, but he could tell the ground was muddy, or swamp-like, because his feet slid sideways with every step. The furry stems weren't very soft, either. Hayson in hand, he entered the darkness.

After only a few steps he heard some splashing in the pond behind him. He kneeled down and peeked through the edge of the brush. Bubbles were surfacing on the far side of the pond.

Hoping Clarise might be returning, he crouched low and waited.

Instead of Clarise, he saw an oversized frog rise from the pond and hobble onto the shore. It looked to be at least three feet high, with eyes the size of coffee cups bulging from its head. Then it sprawled out, as frogs do, the lower half of its legs resting in the water, stretching eight feet from head to toe.

He figured it was a phantom spirit that had taken another form so it could travel safely. And that made him think he should stay put, wait in the dark brush until morning, if there was a morning here, then figure out how to get home.

After a short time he heard some faint, mumbling sounds, like voices nearby, possibly a conversation. He leaned his head and listened, trying to pinpoint the source of the voices. Maybe it was best to get off his butt and start searching.

He slid through the dark path, using the twisted trunks for support. Eventually the trail led to an open field, and across the meadow he saw a fire burning. He crept along the outside edge of the brush until he came to the fire. The flames were larger now that he was closer.

A few horses appeared from behind CJ just then, walking at a slow pace, dragging a wheel-less wagon toward the fire. He hit the ground, realizing he wasn't alone. The horses had no driver, but they pulled up to the fire and came to a halt, as if they knew just where to stop.

On the far side of the horses, a man came out from the same dark brush CJ had stumbled through. The man tiptoed by the horses and crept up to the cart, and there he bent down and started picking through the shipment. After watching for a minute, CJ could see limbs and legs hanging over the side of the cart. The horses had delivered a wagon full of dead bodies, and it looked like the man who'd come from the brush was robbing the corpses of any valuables he could find.

CJ crawled closer, scraping his belly along the edge of the brush until he was ten feet from the cart.

The thief rolled a body from the top of the pile and it hit the ground, but that heartless action uncovered another man on the wagon, lying on his back with a dagger buried deep in his chest.

The thief took a step back, then dropped to his knees and cupped his hands to his face. "Sweet mother of Mary. Could it be?" he whispered.

The horses grew restless so the thief jumped up and unhooked the cart, allowing the horses to turn around and stroll back in the direction from which they came.

The thief approached the corpse again. He knelt down and gripped the dagger with both hands. The knife wiggled and that frightened him. He backed away, just a foot or so, then waved a cross symbol in the air and kneeled down once again. A little less hesitant this time, he grabbed the dagger and pulled. The knife slid from the corpse's chest as though it had been lodged in a pile of sand.

Some shouting blared out from across the field.

The thief scurried away from the corpse and headed straight for the brush, straight for CJ, too. When he saw CJ, he stopped and stared with a terrified look on his face—until he realized CJ wasn't the one looking for him. Then he sprinted off with the dagger, down the same path as the horses.

CJ backed into the dark brush.

The yelling got louder as two men in gladiator-style outfits came toward the fire, dragging the thief by his arms, forcing him back to the cart.

"Put it back!" one guard yelled. "Put it back or we're all doomed!"

The thief tossed the dagger on the ground and started weeping. "I cannot!"

"You must!" the other guard shouted. "You removed it. Now you must put it back." He snatched the dagger from the ground and placed it in the thief's hand. "Hurry! You haven't much time. Hurry!"

The corpse on the wagon moved his arm, then balled his fist.

"Quickly!" The guard shook the thief's wrist. "Place it back into his chest! Quickly!"

The thief hesitated at first, but then he went to the corpse, weeping and trembling. He gripped the dagger with both hands and raised it above his head, ready to pierce the corpse's chest when the fire beside them erupted with a blaze of yellow flames. The guards hollered and jumped away from the fire.

As the flames subsided, the guards lowered their arms. The corpse was standing upright, one hand clinching the thief by the neck. The corpse jabbed his thumb in the thief's jaw and forced his head sideways, then pulled him closer. With his mouth an inch from the thief's ear, the corpse started whispering a chant.

The thief started punching and screaming, but the corpse lifted him by the neck and held his struggling body high above the ground. With one quick twist, he snapped the thief's neck and tossed his lifeless body on the fire.

One guard bolted. The other guard grabbed the dagger from the ground before he, too, ran away from the corpse.

CJ stayed low to the ground, watching from the brush.

The corpse spun his head and zeroed-in on the brush, though. He sniffed the air, sensing someone close by. His eyes were black and empty, and his long ratted hair made his face seem small. He wasn't very tall for someone with such strength, and the tattered robe draping over his body looked as though it could fall off at any time. He started taking gentle steps toward the brush.

CJ jumped from his hiding place with the Hayson aimed and ready, and without missing a beat, he slammed the side-switch and sent the blue streaks jetting toward the corpse.

"No!" Clarise cried, leaping from the brush. "Father!" she said to the corpse.

Clarise ran to CJ with her fists in the air. "You cannot do this!" She pounded on CJ's chest, then dropped to her knees and wept.

CJ pressed the switch and the blue web withdrew, releasing the corpse. He took a few steps back and aimed the Hayson at both of them.

"Clarise! Take me back!" CJ told her. "Now!"

Sitting on her knees, she looked up at CJ. "I cannot lose my father, not again."

"Then take him with us—but now! Now! NOW!"

She seemed torn between fear and trust, yet she stood and grabbed her father's hand.

The fire had spread across the cart and was raging

out of control, burning the hair and clothes of the other dead bodies.

The guards came running back to the scene, this time bringing reinforcements. A few ran to the fire, trying to contain it. Two other guards approached Clarise, her father, and CJ.

One guard lunged for Clarise. CJ slammed him in the face with the Hayson, knocking the guard to the ground and the dagger from his hand. The corpse saw the dagger and he started hissing and backing away, until a guard reached for the dagger. Then the corpse stomped the ground, challenging the guard with another menacing hiss.

That muscled warrior bolted.

CJ snatched the dagger with one quick swoop and slid it between his waist and pants.

The guard on the ground started coming to, but he seemed weak and dizzy. Other guards were trying to put out the fire by beating it with their capes, but that only sent hundreds of red ashes soaring high in the air. The cinders then drifted down with the ease of heavy snowflakes, showering everyone with tiny red coals. Small yellow flames erupted in the field as the floating ashes began to land and ignite.

"Listen to me!" CJ turned to Clarise. "We have to go!"

"Yes. Yes!"

Clarise grabbed CJ's hand and bolted, pulling both CJ and her father into the dark brush. As they barreled through the muddy thicket, the long needles started poking CJ in the face. He covered his eyes and held on tight as the three of them slipped and stumbled to the pond.

Clarise pulled them onto the dock with such force that it collapsed and crumbled to pieces, plunging them in the water alongside the scattered branches and twine.

CJ took a deep breath just as Clarise yanked him underwater.

"I don't know where he is, Dean. That's what I'm trying to tell you," said Steve, pacing the floor by CJ's ladder. "There's water on the floor. Maybe he got scared and pissed his pants. Maybe he had a heart attack in the ceiling. Maybe … he got scared, had a heart attack in the ceiling, and *then* pissed his pants! I … don't … know! We've had some bad luck with this kinda stuff in the past."

"Phooey! That showroom belongs to us tomorrow night … and that means … you must locate CJ!"

Steve pinched the bridge of his nose. "Well, I don't do spells, Dean, so I can't really conjure him up."

"I'm not concerned with your superstitions and séances, Steve. *Find* CJ!" Dean said and hung up.

Before Steve could put his phone away, a section of the ceiling started swirling and spinning in circles just above the recently damaged, old cage.

"What the…?" Steve said.

Clarise, her father, and CJ suddenly fell from the inverted whirlpool, blasting into The Resurrection with a gush of water and broken branches.

The catwalk against the wall caught Clarise and her father, and it held them there until the water had rushed down to the floor. CJ landed on the rail, bounced into the wall, then fell on the same grid. The dagger flew from his pants and spiraled down to the showroom, landing in a section of empty seats.

Before a moan could be wailed, the braces on the catwalk gave way and the metal grid came swinging down, slamming them against the wall of the club. The three of them then rolled off the catwalk and plunged to the showroom floor.

As if he were frozen in time, Steve stood motionless, his jaw hanging down. Water gushed under the seats. Branches bounced across the floor.

Flat on his back, CJ spoke first, saying, "God, that hurt."

"Let go!" said Clarise. She pulled away from CJ and rushed to her father.

CJ sat up and shook his wet hands. He looked around. He was back inside The Resurrection.

That was good news.

Then he saw Steve standing close by.

That was bad news.

Steve's face was white, and his hands were frozen in

midair. He'd seen everything.

CJ got up and stumbled over to Steve.

"You have maintenance here, right?" said CJ, wiping water from his eyes. "That was some mess up there, Steve." He waved his hand in front of Steve's face. "Hey! Steve!"

It took a minute, but Steve faced CJ and said, "There were … that was …" Steve flung his arms down. "What … in the *fuck* was that?"

"It was a leak, Steve. A pretty big one." A cagey grin spread across CJ's face. "I, uhh, I fixed it, but you need to get that cleaned up. Someone could slip and fall." He grabbed Steve by the shoulder and spun him away from the mess. "Why don't you call someone to clean this up?" CJ told him, walking toward the stage, dragging Steve along. "We'll get a bite to eat and you can tell me about the lighting system."

Steve stopped and turned around. He opened his mouth. He pointed. He couldn't seem to speak.

CJ spun Steve around and slapped him on the butt, then pushed him up the aisle. "Go call a cleanup crew, all right?"

Steve staggered out of the showroom.

CJ didn't think Clarise and her father would stick around, but he went back anyway. Sure enough, they'd vanished. He gazed up at the ceiling and spoke out loud: "I still need your help, Clarise. I could've captured both of you but I didn't. Don't forget that." He stood silent, waiting. "Clarise? Can you hear me?"

"Hi-ya, Dean. How's—"

"What the hell is going on in New Orleans, John? You're the bloody road manager, and your arse is in one hell of a sling if CJ doesn't produce. Furthermore, if your arse gets in a sling, then *my* arse gets in a sling, and you know what … John? My arse does *not* get in a sling! Hold on!" Dean lowered his phone and punched a digit.

"Hello!"

"Dean? I found CJ," said Steve, a bit rattled. "He was fixing … a leak?"

"A *leak*?" Dean put the phone to his face and hollered, "Why would you have this man fix a bloody leak? He's not there to fix your pipes, you bloody numpty! Do you know what this man gets paid? Bloody hell, man!" Dean lowered the phone to his side and gazed in the air.

"I was tied up on the phone, Dean, because some guy named … E, called? Is that a name, or a code? Whatever … the guy said he'd be here in a few hours. He didn't want me to tell you, but CJ seems kinda busy … so I am telling you, okay?"

It was one of those days for Dean. He rubbed his forehead and stuck his hand in his pocket, shaking whatever coins he had. Dean brought the phone back to his ear, ready to get to the bottom of this, ready to be rational.

"There was an accident, Dean, and it looks like he cut his face … I think, or maybe he has acne. Does CJ have acne? I don't remember. I just met him this after-noon and it was dark. I had a friend once with really bad acne. It took years to clear up."

Okay, screw rational. Dean clinched his jaws and said, "I need … to speak … with CJ!"

"We're going to lunch in a minute. He wants to talk about the lighting system."

"Have CJ ring me and keep him away from your *bloody pipes*!"

"But … I didn't ask him to fix—"

Click

"… anything." Steve sat calm for a beat; then he pounded the receiver on the desk. "I don't like you!" He reached for his Rolodex and grabbed the number of a contractor.

CJ spent the next hour searching the walls of the club, looking for doorways that had been sealed off, or hall-ways that had been bricked up. These could be passage-ways to Artha and Clarise had to have used one of them, and she had to be close by—just on the other side.

In a back section of the club he found a ladder mounted to the brick wall, running floor to ceiling. He started climbing, searching for unusual patterns in the bricks.

While high on the ladder, CJ saw a row of old post-ers that had been glued to the wall long ago; prints of women holding parasols and small children wearing suspenders. The fonts and artwork had to have been over a hundred years old. The posters were a real find and he wanted them. He grabbed the bottom edge, but the antique paper crumbled to pieces. Then he tried peeling one poster from the top corner, and again, it cracked and broke off into tiny flakes.

As he watched the specks of poster drift to the floor, he saw Clarise standing below. She was looking up at him.

CJ started climbing down.

"Father is not well," she said. "We have to go back."

CJ became cold and hard as he jumped off the ladder, bypassing the last few steps. "You don't have a choice."

"He is not well. You must let me take him back. If you let him go … I promise to return."

"Of course he's not well; he just came back from the dead! Ten minutes ago he was stiff as a—" CJ stopped talking and turned to the left.

The contractor Steve had called in was standing six feet away.

E

Celebrating the launch of the tour, the road crew and band members of Nathan Juju had invaded Tanzy's restaurant for a bodacious lunch. The band had one more dry run scheduled that night in Hudson, NY, the last dress rehearsal before the troupe would finally hit the open road.

John, the road manager, and Alan, the stage manager, sat at a private booth, far from the ruckus.

"I haven't seen E all day. Have you, John?" Alan said.

"He's probably hanging out at some newsstand, rearranging the magazines."

Alan laughed. "Why in the hell would he do that?"

"He opens the rags and places his picture at eye level. He's been shooed out of Penn Station more than once for doing that. Doesn't seem to stop him, though."

"Doesn't the clipper service do that?"

"They only collect the ads, and trust me, E has every one of 'em. No, this is different. E likes to wear a disguise and rummage through the slicks. Says it helps his media-magnet image. Gives him an air of mystique. With a name like Eddie Bessinger, I guess he's always trying to fill the *rock legend* shoes."

"Eddie Bessinger?"

"Shh! Keep it down!" John looked over his shoulder. "No one knows that. E would rip my titties off if he knew I told you. I only know because I handle the books."

"He's one strange bird, I have to admit. But he's committed to his music. I'll give him that. He can definitely leave an audience in awe."

"Right?" John slid a menu his way. "What a mix. Gifted voice meets self-imposed rock god. I guess he is a rock god, in a way, but he also thinks, I mean really *believes* he should be curt and flamboyant. I've seen him be downright mean at times. It's pretty unattractive. But like you say," John opened the menu, "he's talented." John ran his finger down the menu and paused at the Reuben Sandwich. "I don't envy the road crew at all, having to listen to his bitching. Vocals are hard enough, but he's hammering the techies with his guitar, bass, and piano, too."

Alan leaned forward. "Good thing he doesn't talk onstage like he does in person. Have you noticed how people leave his meetings with migraines? What a tongue, man."

John laughed. "Sometimes I'd like to tie his hands down and say, *stop petting your hair*! Man, that gets on my nerves."

"Now that we've trashed him, do you know where he is?"

"Ask Reynolds," said John, waving the server over. "He's the gossip monger in the road crew. He'll know."

Alan went to Reynolds' table and came back.

"You ready for this?" Alan slid in the booth. "E caught a car to Albany this morning."

"Why? What's in Albany?" John asked Alan, then raised his head. "The airport, Alan. Shit! That's what's in Albany!"

"So what's your point, caller?"

"Fuck!" John slammed his hand on the table. "He's headed to New Orleans. I told him not to do this!"

"Dude, what are you talking about? We have one more dry run. *Tonight*. He can't *leave*."

"E's pissed off, Alan. His last soundman jumped through hoops every time E snapped his fingers. CJ doesn't do that. E wants to shake CJ—send him a message. He told me so last night."

"What message? That Dean's gonna kill him? Cause Dean's tea is gonna *boil* when he hears about this."

"The message that he's in charge. E doesn't like it when someone stands up to him. He's got an ego as wide as the Mississippi." John put his hands to his face. "I have to call him. I have to stop him." John slid from the booth and ran outside.

E stared out the tiny window, brushing his eyebrows. He ignored the vibration from his phone, as if he could make it go away, as if it hadn't been buzzing non-stop for thirty minutes. He knew it was John. He saw the list of messages. The buzzing finally stopped and E tucked his phone away.

Then the buzzing returned.

"Okay—alright," said E, punching a digit. "*What*?"

"E, where are you? Why did you leave Hudson?"

"Should be over Pittsburgh. I see a city down there. Maybe it's Philly."

"E, I know what you're up to, and I really don't want you to go through with it. Just go to the hotel when you land. I'll cover from this end. If Dean finds out, he'll—"

"Chill out, John, I've got everything under control."

"Dammit, E. You have a show tonight!"

"We have a dry run—a rehearsal. The band will do fine without me. We've practiced till we're blue in the face. Besides, you heard the show in Boston the other night. We kicked ass."

"You're putting me in a bad place, E. I don't appreciate you dumping this in my lap."

"Fine, John … I'll call Dean and tell him it was my idea. That'll get you off the hook."

"There is no off the hook! The tour hasn't even started yet and you're breaking the contract, man. Dontcha get it? Dean could pull the plug in a heartbeat. If you don't care about yourself, then think about the guys who need the paycheck. Everyone has committed to a three-month tour. They've rearranged their lives, E!"

"It's one night, John … one night; besides, Dean's not gonna can me … *I'm the star*!"

John put his foot down. "No, E! The lead singer doesn't just disappear!"

A flight attendant tapped E on the shoulder and asked him to end the call.

E buried his face in the window. "Why can't I disappear?" he said. "Who would we play for … the stupid janitors at the college? The same fifty kids who came to last night's show? Do ya think they gathered up a few hundred of their closest friends? C'mon, man … get real. That's no concert! Where's the inspiration? Where's the screaming babes? I say let the band jam for a night— without me."

"Okay," John continued. "Fuck the moral obligations … let's talk legal. You're putting the entire tour on the line; you know that, right? You realize that people have contracts … and they can sue … right?"

"Sir!" the stewardess insisted.

E shooed her away with the back of his hand.

"Nobody's gonna sue, John. They're lucky to be on this tour."

The flight attendant leaned over the seats and closed the shade.

E browsed the stewardess up and down, then looked away. "Look, John … this has to be done. CJ needs to learn a few things about me. If he thinks this tour's gonna be easy … or that I'm gonna cut him any slack, then he's got another think coming. CJ needs to know who the *real* boss is, and I'm going down there to set him straight." He winked at the flight attendant. "I'll call Dean when this hunk of tin lands."

Dean stood beside an open suitcase holding two white shirts in the air, both on a hanger, both neatly pressed. He lifted one, then the other, as if there was a variance in the whiteness, as if one were more attractive, as if either were any different than the other fifty in his closet. Sue Champion was relaying her spoon-fed saga on the four o'clock news, disaster and doom, death and mayhem, smiling as though someone were tickling her pussy from under the desk.

His phone rang. Dean glanced at the caller ID and answered compassionately, sporting a big smile. "Eee … cat-daddy … how are the rehearsals? The numbers are coming in. Tell me you're ready for a splendid tour."

"Dean, I'm in New Orleans, and I'm here to talk to CJ."

"Come again?"

"I just got off the plane and I'm heading to the club. You can't stop me and you can't keep me away from CJ. I understand how you want to try this new concept, Dean, I really do, but what you're doing is wrong. I have to oversee the audio, Dean … *me*! It's *my* music!"

"You left the group?" Dean paused. "New concept? E … I can't … I can't believe … *keep you away from CJ*? What the…?" Dean put his hand to his forehead. "We've gone through all the necessary steps with tech—including your demands! Have you lost your bloody mind?"

"If I need to fix anything—like CJ's attitude, this is when it happens. It's better I do this now, than halfway into the tour. Don't worry, I just need to make sure CJ understands my vision, my art … my world. Everything happened so fast in New York. I'm still a little skeptical."

Dean remained quiet.

"Why don't you meet me at the club, Dean. Once you see how I do things, you'll understand."

"Dammit, E! You gave me your word you'd follow the bloody itinerary. What if you'd been scheduled for press? No, E, I don't approve! What's next, you've flown to Moscow for lunch?"

After a tense moment of silence, Dean let out a sigh. "Give me a few hours, E … but listen! If you arrive and find the place in shambles, don't blow a bloody gasket on me. I'm hearing about some building issues and I'm not quite sure about the condition of the club. Whatever we decide, we will decide together. If we don't get this tour off the ground on a peaceful note, it's all to pot—do you hear me? We'll not begin this jaunt with a kick in the teeth. I'll not have it … and I'll not spend the next three months babysitting egos. No more than usual, that is."

"Don't worry, Dean. I won't hurt the kid."

Dean lowered his phone. "It's not the kid I'm worried about."

CJ kept the construction worker in the corner of his eye as he approached Clarise. "God, that's really good!" CJ applauded. "The show is only one week away and you already have the lines down pat. Kudos, baby. And the costume ... wow! It's great. Just great!"

The worker squinted his eyes and glared back and forth. "Do you know where Steve is?" he asked.

"I'll be seeing Steve in a few minutes," CJ told him.

"Do you know anything about a leak?"

"A leak? Does anyone know about a leak? Hmm, look around, man. There are no pipes back here."

The worker nodded his head at the broken catwalk sitting in a puddle of water, tangled in branches and twine. "Then what's all of this?" he asked CJ.

"Oh that? Yeah. It was a stage prop. But it fell apart. It's pretty damaged now. In fact ... that thing is toast. We'll have to build a new one."

The worker crossed his arms and frowned at CJ, seeming to reject the charade.

"Listen," CJ said. "Steve probably saw the water and thought there was a leak. How's this? Let's just *tell* Steve you fixed it and everyone walks away happy. Cool?"

The worker squinted his eyes again, this time looking Clarise up and down. "You show people are freaks, ya know that?" He turned and left the showroom, getting a good ten feet away before CJ faced Clarise.

"Where's your father?" CJ's voice was tense. "I can't have him running loose in here."

Clarise crossed her arms and turned her back to CJ. "He is safe for now. I will not let you harm him."

"I told you I wouldn't hurt him—and I won't hurt you. I just need your help tomorrow night. Can I trust you to come back?"

Clarise spun around. "It seems I have no choice. How soon can we take Father back to Artha?"

"We can go now, but we need to hurry." CJ lifted her chin with his thumb. "Get your father and we'll go, okay?"

For a fleeting moment he stared at Clarise, thinking how beautiful she was, how he felt a strange attraction to her. Even as she turned and went to the back of the club, he kept his gaze.

But the minute she was out of sight, he started pacing the floor, wondering if he could trust her to come back.

He'd used the Hayson in Boston without anyone knowing a thing—except for a few ghosts and the man he'd captured, and the Suit certainly wasn't saying a word—to anyone.

If he captured Clarise in the Hayson, then held her there until the show, her father might run around snapping necks trying to find her. Not only would that scare the hell out of everyone, but it would bury CJ in chaos. It was best to trust her, for the time being anyway. Obviously the spirit world knew what a Hayson was, but this had to stay under lock and key with the humans.

All of a sudden he remembered the dagger. It was able to contain her father once. If he threatened to use it again—send her father back to that cart, he could keep a tight rein on Clarise. Shady ... but perfect.

But he hadn't seen the dagger since he'd landed on the catwalk. He grabbed his flashlight and started looking around. While he was searching underneath the seats, he heard footsteps coming closer. CJ covered his neck and stood.

E was standing in the aisle, the dagger in his hand.

"E ..." said CJ, more than surprised. "You're here a day early, aren't you?"

"I like this," said E, twirling the dagger close to his face, eyeballing every ancient battle mark. "I think I found me a souvenir. It's like something out of Battlestar Galactica, but it's old."

"That belongs to someone here, E. I dropped it from the booth. I was just looking for it."

"We must go now," said Clarise, returning with her father.

E lowered the dagger and gawked at Clarise. "*Da-yum* ... hey, baby ... what's your name?" His hands flew to his ponytail, tying it back real tight, nearly cutting it off with the dagger. "Ever been with a rock star?" he asked Clarise. "We know how to get *funk-ay* ... if ya know what I mean."

His unfamiliar babble didn't register with Clarise. She turned to CJ. "We must go now. Father is weak and you promised—"

"Hold on," E cut in. "Don't leave. We can get Pops anything he needs. Hey, CJ," said E, undressing Clarise with his eyes. "Take Pops and get him fixed up. Looks like he needs a good meal. I need to spend a few minutes with the dish."

"Gimme the knife, E. Pops isn't going anywhere and I still need to wrap up a few inspections before I leave."

"Look, man!" E got in CJ's face. "You do what I say you do, and you *only* do … what I say … when I say … what you do!" E looked to the side, trying to digest his own words, but he recovered fast and said, "You wouldn't even be on my tour if Sara didn't pull you in."

CJ clammed up and looked away.

"Just know your place, CJ! *I'm* the one who makes this train move. Don't forget it!" E chucked the dagger and it bounced on the floor.

Both CJ and Clarise dove for the dagger. CJ grabbed it first and brought it up aimed it at Clarise's father.

E threw CJ a look just a hair short of shock. "Are you nuts, man? What are ya … a burglar now?"

"Yes! He is!" said Clarise, rushing to E. She grabbed his wrists and said, "Please help me. He wants to hurt Father!"

"Maaan … you are one cold bird!" E pulled away from her icy grip and held his hands in the air. "I don't know what you guys are up to, but I stay away from domestic problems."

But in a sudden maneuver, E slipped his arm around Clarise and said, "But if it's a real man you want ..." E yanked her close and tried to fondle her breast.

Clarise spun away and rushed to CJ.

Clarise's father stepped forward and planted a cast-iron, evil glare on E; then he began to whisper a chant.

"Father! No!"

The shrewd display of arrogance E knew so well seemed to fizzle and die, along with his manhood. "Oh, I see," E said. "You guys got something freaky going on here, huh?" He faced CJ. "Well, it doesn't matter, cause right now I need your little *boyfriend* to finish what he started." E snapped his fingers and walked down the aisle. "Follow me, CJ."

E took about ten steps when he stopped, turned around, and barked once again. "You think I'm playing, man? Get your ass over here, CJ!"

"Can't," CJ said. "Let's meet in half an hour, okay?"

"Dean's gonna be here in a few hours, CJ," said E, crossing his arms, defending his last ounce of authority. "And if this shit's not ready, you're outta here! You have one thing to do in the next few months, and that is ..." E looked to his left, choosing his words carefully, "... do what I say!"

E spun around and bumped shoulders with a teenage boy who had arrived to clean up the mess. "Get the fuck outta my way!" E shouted, shoving the young man out of the aisle.

The kid climbed over the empty seats and said, "What the hell, man?" He went to the mess and started stacking pieces of catwalk in a pile, all the while tossing giddy smiles at Clarise.

CJ grabbed Clarise's arm and spun her away from the kid's sight. Her father stepped forward and hissed, but CJ aimed the dagger at his chest and said, "Easy, dead man. We have to get you back to Artha. I'll keep the dagger. And you …" he faced Clarise, "… will come back here with me. Let's go."

Clarise took her father's hand. "We will go now, Father."

She led them down an aisle to the back wall of the club, where an arched doorway had been sealed off with a different style of brick. She closed her eyes and lowered her chin, and with that the center stones began to fade, exposing a standing wall of shadowy water behind the archway. CJ felt a tight squeeze on his hand right before she stepped into the unearthly passage, pulling CJ and her father with her. Before he knew it, CJ found himself floating in the pond at Artha.

The three of them paddled to the shore.

"We must not be heard," Clarise whispered. "The guards are looking for Father." Clarise helped her father to the edge of the tall brush and they sat. "We must leave you here, Father." Clarise faced CJ. "I have been promised free return," she reminded him, then turned to her father. "We will soon be together." She held her father's neck with both hands and kissed him on the cheek.

Clarise's father grabbed her by the arm and pulled her close. "And what of you, dear Daughter? How are you able to find me after such time?" His voice was brittle and his dialect ancient.

Clarise held her father's face and looked him in the eyes. "I promise to tell you everything, but now we must hide you from the guards."

CJ went toward the path but Clarise stopped him. "We will stray from the path," she said, then shoved the brush to the side so her father could go first. CJ followed.

While they were trekking through the foliage, CJ noticed some of the plants seemed to be glowing at the base, softly illuminated with a lime-green haze. Clarise steered her father around the dimly lit areas. After dodging one himself, CJ looked closer. He saw a body lying in fetal position, eyes closed. He couldn't tell if it was a man, or a woman, but the arms and legs appeared to be intertwined with the twisted roots of the plant.

Clarise picked a spot and laid her father on the ground. She closed his eyelids and kissed him on the forehead, then she motioned CJ to follow her.

"Wait," CJ said. "Who are all these people?"

"Shh ..." Clarise looked over her shoulder. "They have left the living and now they sleep. When they awaken, they will be shown the passage to and from Artha. Then they may travel as they choose." Clarise scanned one of the lime-green dells. "Some will go where they feel they are needed." She turned slowly, gazing at the others in the ground. "Some will sleep here for hundreds of years. If I could help them wake, I would do so. But I am unable."

"But … how did your father get here? I mean … how did he get here if he's not a spirit?"

Clarise looked away, somewhat baffled. She hadn't thought of that. "I do not know. I was not with Father when he left the living. When I, too, met with death, I began to look for Father. I searched many places for hundreds of years, never knowing he would be here, until I saw you … trying to take him away."

Search for father. Those words hit home base. CJ thought of his own father. Was he in here, too, joined by his mother? Did he have time to search for them?

"How big is this place, Clarise? I mean, how do you find someone in here?"

"There are many paths. They lead to many people and many places. You must search every day if you wish to find someone."

"Can I find someone with a Hayson? Would it be faster?"

"No!" Clarise yelled and then flinched. She looked over her shoulder, then back at CJ. "The Hayson is evil!" she whispered.

"It doesn't have to be—does it? Why is it evil? Tell me."

"You cannot change the course of a Hayson. Just like you cannot change the dead to the living. A spirit must remain free. If it is forced away, there is great danger."

"Is that why there are guards everywhere? You said you wanted to free the sleeping people. Why can't a Hayson do that?"

"What you ask is not the purpose of a Hayson. It is used to conquer the spirit world, as those before you have done. But you must not do the same. The Hayson will only cause sorrow."

"I know there were others before me, "CJ said. "I mean, I've kinda heard that, in a roundabout way. Now those guys are looking for me." He touched the amulet at his neck. "I think they want this more than they want me."

She leaned in for a closer look. "I have seen this carved in stone. What is it?"

He thought for half a beat. Was he being sloppy? "Just tell me—did the ones before me wear dark hats?"

"I have not seen one in many years," Clarise confessed. "They are forbidden to enter Artha. The capes they wear are darker than night, and they hide their shameful eyes. The Hayson is seen only before they take, and …" Clarise paused, this time pleading with CJ. "You must hide the Haysons, take them far away. If you wish to remain living, you must stop using them."

"I won't. Not until I find some people. I have to know about how they died."

"Then it is your soul that lies in agony—not those you search for."

"Well, yeah. I may have killed them."

Her face became detached, without a speck of emotion in her eyes.

"Not on purpose," CJ said. "You don't understand. I loved them. If I hurt them, I need to apologize. They need to know how sorry I am."

"If they left the living because of you, it is they who will find you."

"Why the fire, Clarise? Why the guards? Can they help me?"

"We must go back, and we must do so now. If you are seen, you will be taken and—" She stopped mid sentence and looked down.

"What? What will happen?"

"We will go now." She grabbed CJ's hand and pulled him through the spiny brush.

Sound Check

"I should arrive in twenty minutes, E," said Dean, stepping off the plane. He glanced at his watch. "It's 7:00 P.M. Have you crossed paths with CJ?"

"Yeah, I saw that little piece of shit. What were you thinking—hiring CJ, Dean? He's into some pretty weird stuff. Did you know he brought his chick with him … *and* her father? What is this, the Salvation Army tour? Do I gotta feed every non-working deadbeat in the country?"

"I'm not certain what you're referring to, E, but I'll be there shortly and we will all sit and discuss this. Try not to blow a gasket, ol'right?"

"I care about this tour, Dean, that's all. My music has to be top priority. I already called another soundman for a backup. I won't have that little fucker talking to me like that. If CJ gives me any more lip, I'm cannin' his ass. I'm telling you, Dean. I—"

"You'll do no such thing! This tour will be great, E. You will be great. *CJ* … will be great! Now just relax and I'll see you in a moment."

Dean jumped in a cab.

E fondled his ponytail as he paced the bare stage at The Resurrection. His phone started vibrating.

"Bob Dustin! The man with two first names!"

"I just got your message, E. What's going on? Where are you?"

"I'm in New Orleans. I'm trying to get this tour off the ground and this asshole, CJ, isn't cutting it. What's on your plate, Bob?"

"CJ? Are you sure? Dude, he's one of the best. I have a hard time believing he's not cutting it." Then Bob paused, as though he'd just shot himself in the foot. "But I know you, E. You're one of the top pros in the business. Your standards are high. What is it you need, E?"

"He brought his girlfriend with him, *and* her father, and God knows who else. I mean … what the fuck is that about, Bob? I swear to shit—what kinda soundman brings his whole family on tour? He's way outta line, man."

"CJ doesn't have a girlfriend, E. In fact, I think he's gay. Are you sure it's his chick?"

"*Gay*? Well, his boyfriend's got tits! She's pretty fuckin' hot to be a he! I don't know about that, Bob."

"You want me to come down?" Bob asked him. "I'll show CJ a thing or two about sound."

"Yeah. I don't like the way this is panning out, Bob. I'm too professional for this bullshit. I need to know that everything is in order. I came down early to check on things, and I don't like what I'm finding. CJ doesn't respect me, *or* the project. I don't want you to show him anything, I want him *gone*."

"Where you at, The Resurrection?"

"Yeah, I'm here now. CJ is around somewhere, but he wouldn't give me the time of day. I don't know if he's even worked on the sound yet." E threw his head back and sighed. "The band arrives tomorrow, Bob. I can't have everything fall apart. Get on the next plane, will ya?"

"Sure, E, I'll be there in a few hours, but talk to CJ before I take over, okay? I shouldn't be the one that bumps him."

"Don't worry. Dean is coming down, too. Let him burn the guy. That's what he gets for hiring the little shit."

Dean saw the cleaning van in the parking lot when he arrived. He went to the side entrance, knowing it would be open and he wouldn't have to bang on doors to get inside. He stepped out of the cab just as the side door swung open. A teenage kid backed his way out of The Resurrection, dragging a cluster of chain-link mesh to the pavement. The kid dropped the junk next to a pile of metal railings.

Dean stormed in the club, calling out for CJ and E.

Steve waited for over an hour in Neutral Ground, the South's oldest coffee shop. He'd finished his double Red Ruby, even scraped the plate after devouring Pat's Peanut Butter Pie. He'd given up searching for crumbs, and he'd given up on CJ. Steve went back to the club.

As soon as he entered the lobby, he heard shouting through the showroom doors. Steve reached for the door handle just as Dean kicked the door from the showroom side. The door slammed Steve in the chest and knocked him down.

Dean stormed in the lobby, huffing, in a rage. "Where are they?" he asked.

Steve shook his head, then sat up, one hand to his shoulder. "I don't ... why did you—?"

Dean shook his finger at Steve. "I want CJ! I want E! I want bloody answers and I—"

"Dean, baby. You made it."

Dean spun around in slow motion. "Have you any idea how hacked off I am? What the bloody hell are you doing here, E? And for fuck's sake ... where's CJ?" Dean took slow steps toward E, his nostrils flaring.

"Dean, now ... hold on ..."

"Excuse me," Steve interrupted. "Can I help you guys?"

"Shut up!" Dean and E shouted in unison.

Steve flinched and wobbled up the back stairs ... to the safety of his office.

"Now listen, E! I've invested more money than you realize on this run. What the hell were you planning to do? Would you like me to shank this project right away? Are you bloody *trying* to piss me off?" Dean shoved his finger in the air. "It's not too late to bag the whole tour!"

"No, Dean ... I just wanted to make sure—"

"What's with all the yelling?" CJ asked, stepping into the lobby. "You guys could wake the dead."

E threw his hands in the air. "*Now* you show up? I've been looking for you for hours, CJ. I had to call Dean."

CJ ignored the lie and said, "I'm working on the room, E. I think that's why I'm here. Am I wrong?"

Dean glared at E, his beady eyes searing E's pupils.

"Go inside, guys," said CJ, eager to end the scuffling. "Will you get onstage, E? I want you to hear something. Dean ... will you sit somewhere around the sixtieth row? I'll get to the sound booth and we'll do a vocal check. I wanna make sure you're happy, E." CJ winked at Dean and headed up the back stairway.

E snatched the microphone from the stand. He held it behind his back as he leaned over the front of the stage, semi-shouting to Dean: "I want you to see for yourself ... he hasn't done a *thing*!"

Then E heard CJ's voice coming through the stage monitors. "You have a ballad on your first CD. I think it's called "Georgann." Will you sing a verse, acappella?" CJ

171

asked him.

Still angry, still bigheaded, and still hoping to can CJ, E began to sing.

"*When I come home, at the end of the day-ee.*"

E stopped singing after one line. The sound had taken him by surprise. He gripped the microphone with both hands and brought it to his mouth, putting more gusto into the next line.

"*First thing I seee ... is, your beautiful fay-eece!*"

The tone was perfect. E's voice sounded rich and strong, with the texture coming from deep inside his throat. The reverb was not too much, but enough to leave a small trail at the end of each note. E began to sing some vocal scales and convicted long notes.

"*I ... ee. I ... ee. I ... ee knooow!*"

E slung the microphone to his waist after the power note. It was a dramatic move, a gesture only a lead singer could pull off. His voice resonated throughout the arena with a deep, clear sound.

Dean stood from his seat and walked down the aisle.

"Nice, CJ," said E, somewhat sincere, because everything had become about him again. "Maybe I got used to that little gymnasium in Hudson, but it really sounds good in here." E shielded his eyes and peered over the empty seats. "Can you hear that, Dean? What's it sound like to you?"

"It's the best I've ever heard you sound," said Dean, standing in front of the stage. "I need to speak with you, E. Let us step outside for a moment ... shall we?"

Clarise sat in the mud amongst the twisted trunks in Artha, her father's head resting in her lap.

"Clarise, my daughter. You are as beautiful now as such day I left you. I did miss you so."

"Father, where have you been for so many years? How did you leave the living? Why was the dagger in your chest? It brought me tears to see you had met with such fate."

"We have not time for talk. Hear me, Daughter. You must kill him, the one with the Hayson." His face became vile. "He shan't leave you behind."

Clarise looked away. "I cannot. He has brought us together again, and I have given my promise."

"Clarise, you must kill him! We will again hide such Hayson; hence, never to be found. Then all may be free from such fear." He brushed her hair away from her eyes and said, "Tease him with thy beauty. Lure him with such charm. Upon his weakest moment, you must take the dagger and force it upon his chest." He put his thumb to Clarise's chin and slowly raised her head for a dead on stare. "It must be done, dear Daughter … it must be done."

Dean followed E out the side door. He slipped his hands in his pockets and said, "Will you bloody trust me now? Do you see why I've done this? The tour will be phenomenal, E! You will get your status back and record

173

sales will fly through the roof." He felt a hint of kindness sweep through his soul just then. He fought it. Compassionate but firm, he continued. "I need you to trust in CJ. The boy knows his wires."

"Well, yeah, okay … I do feel better now. But you left me in the dark, Dean. What was I supposed to do? I've never had you as a promoter, and CJ's never run my sound. This is all so new." E combed his eyebrows. "It's just got to be right, Dean. I won't have it any other way."

"If this were a dog-and-pony show, I'd not invested a single penny, E, but this is a bloody great team. I need—" A Caribbean jingle rang from inside Dean's jacket. He reached in his pocket and fumbled around until the ditty stopped.

"Just have CJ stick around for the first few shows, all right, Dean? Just do that for me? When I see that everything's cool, I'll loosen up. Oh … and … get him to wash his face and clean up some, okay? That acne is outta control."

"'Nuff said. But I need you to back off and allow this tour to take shape. I swear, E, if you break your contract once more, I'll walk." Dean paced back and forth. "Thirty years, E. *Thirty years* of promoting tours. One would presume I'd have a clue by now, wouldn't they? Is it possible this new concept might only be new … to *you*?" Dean stopped pacing and faced E. "I'll have CJ stay for the show tomorrow night, but the very second it's over, he's off to Savannah—understood? We discussed this thoroughly during negotiations. I'm the bloke bailing you out of bankruptcy; therefore this tour is in my hands ... and I'm pulling my bloody rank! You *will* make your radio spots! You *will* show up for press interviews! And you will follow your itinerary ... to the tee!"

"Now hold on, Dean. I—"

"This tour must proceed without any more fits! I'm trusting you once more and that's it!" Dean snapped his fingers. "Over!" He turned around and headed inside.

"Just one more thing," E said.

Dean stopped walking. Still facing the club, his hands went to his hips. "Yes, there is one more thing. You screw up this tour and you're bloody finished, E. I'll fucking bury you. I'll bury you so deep, your career will need a tombstone, *but* ..." Dean spun around, finger raised, "... you'll be too *poor* to be dead because I'll bury your bloody bank funds as well!" With piercing eyes, he leaned in and spoke gently through his clinched teeth. "Are? We? Clear?"

E shuddered. "Yeah, cool."

CJ's ride pulled into the parking lot. The driver crept up behind E and honked his horn. E yelled at first, then jumped in the backseat, claiming to be CJ.

Dean hopped in a cab and called CJ, informing CJ of the changes in his itinerary.

CJ confirmed, then agreed to meet Dean for dinner later that night.

Frederick

In less than twenty-four hours, Nathan Juju would be rocking the stage at The Resurrection. The lights would be flashing and thousands of people would be cheering, but tonight, the showroom was dark and empty.

CJ aimed a spotlight on his wet clothes, and that placed a tawny glow in the sound booth. It also projected some monster-sized shadows on the far wall. CJ sat at the console, wrapped in a towel, spinning the Hayson in his hands. There was more than enough time to get the sound up to speed by common standards, but not by his, not if he wanted to combine ghosts with a rock-n-roll show. The giant shadows on the showroom wall had his mind reeling.

He'd heard the clarity in Boston, the effect the Hayson had on the music. It was breathtaking; it woke him up and reminded him how much he loved the art of sound. Maybe it was time to test the visuals, though—time to raise the stakes. There was no telling what this Hayson thing could do with the lights.

He still wasn't convinced Clarise would come back, though. He felt a sudden impulse to go downstairs and find her, strictly for the show. Purely business. His strange attraction to her had nothing to do with wanting to see her, to look into her eyes, to gaze at her beautiful smile. Professional thoughts aside, there had to be a way for humans to get to Artha, and he had to find the passage.

With the shutter on the spotlight opened wide, it took less than twenty minutes for his clothes to become crispy dry. CJ got dressed and went downstairs with the Hayson.

He went to the bricked-up passageway where Clarise had taken him to Artha. He called out for her. She didn't respond. Maybe she just refused to answer.

One thing was certain: the Hayson was useless without a ghost.

He remembered sensing the ageless energy when he first entered the showroom. Other spirits had to be around; he knew it. As he searched different sections of the club, shooting the Hayson in random places, he ended up at the farthest reach of the back wall. Something was suspicious about the congested area where the catwalks converged high in the corner. He could see a shape up there, but the lights were too low to cast a shadow.

As he went closer, he saw a squared-out burrow in the wall. It was the size of a treasure chest, safely concealed under the catwalk.

The ladder came to rest a few feet shy of the hole,

even after extending it to the last rung. CJ started climbing anyway. The over-extended ladder weakened at the halfway mark. It bowed toward the wall. He kept climbing, though, carefully, until he ran out of ladder frame to cling to. That had never stopped CJ before, and it wouldn't stop him now. He went higher, pressing one hand to the brick wall for support. Just a few inches from the opening, the hairs on the back of his neck began to tingle.

He held the Hayson above his head and pressed the switch.

The lights bounced around in the hole, emitting a bright blue flash. Maybe it was the darkness of the burrow. Could have been glare from the catwalk. But the Hayson seemed blinding, so blue he had to shield his eyes. As the unearthly lights dimmed, CJ inched higher and peeked into the space, where only a few feet away, an old man lay contained in the cobalt-colored web. CJ got a brief glance at the man's wide-striped vest and fringed-tongue shoes, at the streamlined part running through his slick hair. He had one shoulder to his chin when he opened his eyes and looked at CJ. Then he vanished as the blue web retracted, pulling him into the Hayson.

CJ hesitated, remembering what Clarise had done to him. He needed to be diligent. Watch for tricks. He took a deep breath and prepared himself for a new encounter, then he held the Hayson above his head and sent the apparition back into the hole.

As the blue lights faded, the semblance reappeared,

curled in a ball at first, but within a few beats the ghostly man opened his eyes and stretched out his limbs.

"Can you hear me?" CJ asked him.

The old man had a weary look on his face.

"Can you see me?"

He seemed stunned, incoherent.

"Come closer," CJ told him. "What's your name?"

The ghost straightened his legs and looked his body up and down. His hands went to his face and he rubbed his eyes. He glanced at CJ. He scratched his scalp. He scooted to the opening, but he didn't seem to notice CJ was standing on a treacherous ladder. He flung his legs over the edge, forcing CJ to back down a few steps.

Fixated on his white body, he brushed his legs, trying to beat the white dust from his limbs. As he patted his body, little gusts of frosty air blew against CJ's face.

CJ waited patiently, hoping the man would soon realize … it wasn't dust.

"Who are you?" CJ asked him.

"I'm Frederick," he said, patting his arms. "Who are you?"

"I'm CJ. I wanna help you."

"Help me?" Frederick rubbed his biceps. "How can you help me?"

As Frederick began to cross over, CJ started seeing a hint of color in the man's skin, but not much. The man was pale skinned, even after he'd crossed over. "Do you like it here?" CJ asked him. "Wouldn't you like to live somewhere else?"

"I don't *live* here. Oh, my, no. Why, I'm from Detroit. I must have fallen asleep." He licked his palms and slicked down his hair. "I know better than to drink in the afternoon, but New Orleans is so much fun. Why, there's singing and dancing everywhere. All day and night!"

A terrified look came over Frederick's face. He raised his head and said, "What am I doing up here? What time is it? I can't be late!" He peered over CJ's shoulder, looking for a way down.

"I don't think you need to worry about that. How long have you been here?" CJ noticed something sticking out of Frederick's vest pocket, like a rolled-up brochure, or a pamphlet tied with string. "What is that? Can I see it?" CJ held out his hand.

Frederick loosened the decades-old knot and unrolled the piece of paper, which he then handed to CJ.

The leaflet was dated July 28, 1918. It was a list of names, with numbers scribbled beside each name. CJ examined the piece of paper. "Tell me, Frederick, what happened to you?"

"I'm the stage manager. I was drinking at the speakeasy, next door—but please don't tell anyone. I can't go to jail. I'll lose my job!" He rubbed his face, trying to remember. "We had our drinks, and then ... I don't know. I was bringing in the payroll for the cast when ... something hit me. I ... I can't remember anything else."

As soon as Frederick realized what he'd said, he started trembling. He raised his legs and patted the bricks underneath. He spun his torso left and right, searching the tiny space. He faced CJ and shouted, "The payroll … it's gone! I'll be fired! I'll go to jail! Somebody stole the payroll!"

"It's okay, Frederick. No one's gonna take you to jail. It sounds like you were robbed."

Frederick seemed baffled—until the reality of his predicament finally set in, then he lowered his elbows to his knees and plopped his frowning face in his hands. "This just can't be. So many people will be angry with me."

"Nobody's mad at you. Try and relax; tell me about the show, Frederick. Tell me why you're here."

"Our show is *Barbarossa of Barbary*," he mumbled through his fingers. "Sixty-two singers and dancers on-stage at the same time. That's sixty-two people that won't get paid." He raised his head. "That's sixty-two people who will be angry with me! Oh, my. This is all my fault … all my fault. We've been touring for a few months now, but this is the first problem we've had … and I'm the cause of it." Frederick searched his pockets and patted his body once more, as though he had one last ray of hope. "Oh my. Why did this have to happen in New Orleans? We've been to worse places than this. Why here? I love New Orleans."

"It's okay, Frederick. The show is gone. In fact, everyone's gone, moved on. Tell me more about the show."

"Gone? Oh, my. Did they leave … *without me*? I suppose I've really done it this time."

"They left because … well, try to relax, okay?" CJ knew theater people couldn't refuse talking about themselves, and that seemed like a good way to divert Frederick, take his mind off being robbed. "Tell me all about the tour, Frederick."

Sure enough, Frederick's eyes came alive as he told CJ about the stage design and the canvas props. He laughed when he explained how difficult it had been to get everyone into places, but once the actors and dancers paid attention, the show was nothing short of amazing.

While Frederick was telling his story, CJ began to wonder how the old guy would fit in with a rock-n-roll show.

"Are you in the show?" Frederick asked, sounding suspicious. "I don't recognize you. And your costume … I don't recognize it, either. It's rather odd."

Then Frederick began to mutter, as another memory flashed through his mind: "Maria needs her thread. I have to find her." He looked past CJ and shouted into the showroom, "Maria!"

"Maria's not here, Frederick. She's gone away, too. What year is it, Frederick? Do you know how long you were sleeping?"

"I … I don't know. A few hours, I guess. I had such a strange dream. A beautiful woman was talking to me." Frederick rubbed the back of his neck. "I thought I was careful with the spirits, but I drank too much again. I guess I'm in trouble … *again*. Curses and damn!"

"Frederick …" CJ took hold of the old man's hands.

"Get ready for this, okay?" CJ looked him in the eyes and said, "You were killed."

"*Killed*? Look at me. I'm not dead!" Frederick cocked his head and said, "Are you touched?"

CJ began to feel some compassion for Frederick, a sweet old man who'd been killed for some payroll money over eighty-five years ago.

Frederick studied CJ's clothes and took a curious gaze at the cylinder. He squinted his eyes and lowered his head, then he looked deep into CJ's eyes.

"No!" he said. "I'm alive! And I want you to leave me alone!"

Frederick panicked and leapt from the hole. That enthusiastic move forced CJ to roll around the backside of the ladder. CJ hung from a rung while Frederick climbed down the front—way too fast. The ladder wobbled, then shimmied along the wall until it leaned to the right. Frederick made it to the floor just as the ladder finished its fall, tossing CJ to the ground.

Frederick ran up an aisle, heading for the lobby door.

"God, that hurt," said CJ, lying on his back.

Thinking the nasty music people had left his club, Steve decided to leave for the night. He went downstairs to make sure the stage lights had been powered down. When he opened the showroom door, he saw a strange-looking, fuzzy old man running up the aisle, coming straight for him. Steve slammed the door and ran to the front doors across the lobby. He dug for his keys while the old man jostled the showroom door. Steve had seen a few spirits in his day, too, and it seemed obvious the old man was an evil spirit lurking in the club. And there was no doubt in Steve's mind the ghost was coming after him.

Steve couldn't slide the key in the lock, mostly because he was shaking like a stick. After only a few tries, he wigged out and threw his keys on the floor. Then he ran up the back stairs ... to the safety of his office.

CJ stood and shook off the fall. As he got his bearings, he saw Frederick tugging on a door, trying to leave the showroom. CJ bolted up the long aisle and approached him from behind.

"Frederick! Listen to me, okay? Just listen to me."

Frederick made a dash for the stage and leapt onto it when he arrived. He then bolted to center stage and skid to a halt. Frederick stood frozen in his tracks, stunned by the rows of soft glowing lights. He spun in slow circles, gazing at the monstrous speakers, at the unusual gear high above his head—curiosity pouring from his eyes.

"Frederick," CJ called out from the side of the stage. "Listen to me, just ... hear me out." CJ tossed his wallet across the stage. It landed at Frederick's feet. "Look at it!" CJ told him.

Frederick looked down at the wallet, and then back at CJ, not quite sure what CJ was trying to tell him.

CJ softened his tone. "Open it. Read some dates."

Frederick was hesitant, but he picked up the wallet. First he pulled out a few receipts. He took a quick glance and flung them in the air. He removed some business cards and tossed them aside. Finally, he slid some money from the divide. This time he let go of the wallet.

"Yes," CJ told him. "Read the dates on the money."

Frederick held the bills close to his face, then he turned to CJ, his jaw hanging down. Frederick hadn't spoken for a few minutes, long enough to cross back over to his world. His body began to turn white again. He noticed the milky haze and frantically patted his thighs, then brushed his chest. As if in slow motion, the green money slipped through Frederick's hands and spiraled down to his feet.

Frederick studied his cloudy white hands for a few more seconds, then tears swelled in his eyes. He dropped to his knees and said, "I can't be dead. I have a show to do. I have—" He stopped whining and pointed at CJ. "It was you! You robbed me! You stole the …" Frederick noticed his arm when he pointed at CJ; it had begun to show some color again. "What's happening to me? What in God's name is going on?"

CJ jumped onstage and put his arm around Frederick's shoulder. He walked Frederick to the edge of the stage and sat with him. CJ spent a little time explaining the present day to Frederick, even elaborating on some of the modern stage equipment. Soon enough, the two men started behaving like young boys, squabbling over a bunch of gadgets.

To convince Frederick he was dead, CJ walked him to a large mirror by the lobby door and asked him not to speak. Frederick stood quiet, just as CJ requested.

Frederick began to lose all color in his clothes and hair, and soon ... every part of Frederick had become ghostly white again. The truth seemed to sink in when Frederick got a sobering look at himself in the mirror.

Frederick stared at himself in the mirror and said, "But ... you're not finished. You want to dance and laugh ... and *drink*!" He faced CJ. "I don't want it to be over."

"You can still entertain and bring smiles to a lot of people." CJ held the Hayson in the air. "I'll show you how cool that is."

"Cool?"

CJ chuckled and looked Frederick up and down. "How would you like to be in a concert tomorrow night? It'll be strange, but everything will be okay if you just trust me. After the show, you can go wherever you want. But I promise you, tomorrow night ... will be magic."

Both statements were mostly true, except Frederick could go wherever he wanted without CJ's help. But CJ was on a mission to find a ghost, and now it appeared he might not need Clarise after all.

After circling his desk for half an hour, Steve had worn himself out. In another attempt to leave the club, he went down the stairway and crept up to the front door. His eyes probed every nook of the lobby as he bent down to grab his keys.

While his head was near the doorframe, someone outside started pounding on the front door. It was a loud and aggressive banging, driven by anger. Steve flinched and backed away, then he bolted across the lobby to the showroom door. He cracked the door open and peeked through a small slit—just enough to see the chalky old man standing with CJ, both in front of the large mirror. Steve's eyes rolled back in his head and he passed out, landing flat on the ground. The door closed with a slight click.

CJ heard the latch of the door and ran over to find Steve lying on the floor of the lobby. Then he heard someone banging on the front door. He grabbed Steve by the ankles and pulled his body in the showroom. CJ went in the lobby and quietly closed the showroom door.

He grabbed Steve's keys from the floor and hollered, "One minute!"

The banging continued until CJ opened the door.

Bob Dustin was standing outside. He seemed frustrated when he stepped inside and said, "Does it usually take thirty minutes to get in here?"

"What are you doing here, Bob?" CJ asked, locking the door behind him.

"I'm looking for E. Have you seen him?"

"He's probably at the hotel. We did a vocal check earlier; then they left."

"They?"

"Dean and E. Are you working in town?"

"E asked me to come down, CJ. Did he mention me to you?"

"No. Nothing."

"E wants me to take over this gig. He doesn't want any faggot running his sound."

"Really?" CJ raised his eyebrows and suddenly, all the commotion and stress took him over the top. His anxiety soared to the highest possible octave. It took a beat before he could reply.

"You need to respect E, CJ. He's a pro and he won't put up with your unprofessional bullshit. Like that thing in your hand. That's not audio gear, so whatever you're doing has nothing to do with sound. Which means you're in here *fuckin' off*."

"I didn't know you'd seen every tool in creation, Bob. I'm so impressed."

Bob took a good look at the Hayson. "What the hell is that, anyway?"

"Oh, this?" CJ shook the Hayson and said, "It's called a nunya."

Bob scratched his nose.

CJ grinned and opened the showroom door. "Come inside, Bob. But walk slow, okay? I wanna get a real good look at that ass."

Bob backed up to the door, as in flat as a board flat,

as in sphincter squeezed tight, flat. "Don't get funny on me, CJ. The rumors of you and your weird shit are getting out of hand. It's time you took a walk, man." Bob pulled out his cell phone.

"You calling E?" CJ asked.

"Yeah, let's get this straightened out." Bob scrolled through his phone.

CJ aimed the Hayson at Bob and said, "Let's not."

Before CJ realized what he was doing, he'd pressed down on the side-switch and the blue lights came flying from the Hayson. Bob dropped his phone as the web of lights surrounded him, then sucked him into the Hayson.

CJ stood quiet, somewhat stunned, not quite believing what he'd just done. Steve was lying on the showroom floor, Frederick was dancing in front of a large mirror, and Bob was inside one of the Haysons. He plopped down on the floor next to Steve.

"Dammit!"

CJ leaned against the doorframe, thinking about the three-ring circus he'd created. He called out for Clarise, but he knew better—like she was really going to come to his aid. Frederick was still dancing in front of the mirror. CJ got up and approached him.

Frederick noticed someone behind him. He stopped dancing and turned around. "You again?" Frederick said.

Clarise smiled and gave Frederick a warm hug. "You have woken. You were there for so long."

Frederick pointed to CJ and said, "He woke me. He's going to help me."

Clarise threw a scowl at CJ. "Now you want him as well? How many do you plan to take? How evil must you be?" She pursed her lips and gave CJ a wicked stare.

"Okay, see ... there goes that anger," CJ said. "Let's not go there."

Clarise raised her arms and took a stance and ...

"*Wait*! Clarise ... wait! Listen to me. I have something for you ... for your father, I mean. I know why he's sick."

"What would you have that Father should need? Why do you trick me? I have returned as I said." She bent her hands back, aiming her palms at CJ.

"No, Clarise! No tricks! I think your father is a vampire. He needs food ... and ..." CJ shook the Hayson. "I have food for him."

"Father is not of the walking dead!" She spread her fingers into claws.

"Whoa!" CJ aimed the Hayson at her. "Easy, now ... Think for a minute, Clarise. The fire. The dagger. He's weak ... why is he so weak? Look at you. You're fine and you're ... well ..."

Clarise withdrew her hands, but not all the way. "We will go," she said. "But if you trick me, I will leave you in Artha to die—this I promise you."

Having dodged another episode by the skin of his teeth, CJ turned to Frederick. "You can't let yourself be seen, Frederick. Stay close to the place where I found you. If anyone comes in here, do *not* let yourself be seen. Do you understand how important that is?"

"Why, no. I don't. Can't I have a drink? Do I have to stay in here ... alone?"

"Yes. Just for a little while."

"Yes, you must," Clarise added. "We will return very soon."

Clarise and CJ went to the bricked-up doorway in the back of the club. For a brief moment, and as screwed up as all this was, CJ felt as though he and Clarise were a team.

Milo

Clarise and CJ crept through the dark brush in Artha, making their way to her father, who was fast asleep, still lying where she had left him.

"Father," whispered Clarise, nudging his shoulder. "Please wake. I must speak with you."

When he opened his eyes and saw Clarise, his smile grew larger than life. His face turned foul when he saw CJ, though; still breathing, still alive. He raised himself in a huff and leaned his back against a twisted trunk.

"You have done not what I spoke of, Daughter. Why is this?"

Clarise lowered her chin.

CJ threw her a curious look.

Clarise jettisoned her father's question and dodged CJ's glare. "Father, I must ask you. How did you leave the living?"

"I might be able to help you," CJ said, then looked away, as though he'd stumbled into a mental cadence—a thought process with an irregular beat. He suddenly saw

Clarise and her father as who they were—people with lives, sort of. Something hit home and he had to make a pit stop, check in with reality.

He'd ended up back in Artha because he'd offered Bob Dustin as food for Clarise's father ... just to save his own ass. Something was wrong with this picture. The little voice in his head finally spoke up and said, *not cool*. This situation felt more uncontrollable than being run off the highway by a Semi. Even so, he couldn't bring himself to leave; he was too close to finding out about the Hayson. He knew it.

CJ asked her father straight out, "Why aren't you a spirit?"

He snarled his teeth and hissed at CJ, and there was no mistaking the hatred he felt inside. Centuries of containment were summarized with one evil stare, aimed right at CJ.

CJ felt the tension down to his bones. He had to dislodge it, though. He had to bite the bullet and dive into the vampire's world. He stood strong.

Being only one foot away from the testosterone fest, Clarise became restless, shifting positions and sitting more upright , preparing herself for the words to come.

"How did you end up on that cart?" CJ asked him, nudging Clarise for support. "Tell us what happened to you."

"Yes, Father ... please."

The three of them sat idle, even muted for a few minutes until Clarise's father took a deep breath and began to tell his story.

"I began my life as Milo. I am uncle to the great Hucbach."

"Hucbach, the composer?" CJ asked.

Milo sneered and said, "Nay composer was he! 'Twas I who taught Hucbach his musical knowledge and …" Milo shook his head. "… nay musical genius was he. Upon his arrival to the monastery of Odopheus, he did bear the company of Pantalli … a composer commissioned to protect the great Hucbach." Milo chuckled all of a sudden, even bounced his shoulders as he said, "I did question—would such a service be of need … for a monk?

Pantalli did claim in return … 'twere my musical teachings that not be of need. Claim he did …that *I*," Milo put his hand to his heart, "am of fraud. Yet namian of fraud should be placed upon Hucbach, as nay a worthy composer should—"

"*Okay*, okay … someone was a fraud," CJ said. "We need to know about you … your life, Milo. Why were you on that cart?"

"'Twas one eve in the garden of the monastery, when Pantalli spoke to me with the promise of death should I not praise Hucbach, for all the villagers in the land did possess a great love for Hucbach." Milo raised his head and took deep, slow breaths, turning to the bushes, sniffing his surroundings, recalling the joy of breathing.

"Hey, Milo." CJ snapped his fingers. "Over here."

Milo grunted and faced the muddy ground. "Many a yer'e of agony did pass under such dreadful rule … until one eve, I did witness Pantalli gathering many great treasures, riches which did belong to Hucbach." He scrunched his nose and said, "I did question such thief … am I to observe this robbery—yet keep my witness secret? For this I cannot do.

Pantalli spoke with quivered breath, and his words did frighten my soul. With eyes of a demon Pantalli drew his sword." Milo seemed appalled. "I had not time to prepare for battle when … he did force his weapon into my chest, with nay mercy."

Clarise began to weep.

"Lie in the garden of Odopheus, did I … my eyes upon heaven through the night. I live not—yet—nay I will die? By revelation, I was gathered by those who did possess a great loyalty to Odopheus. Such a death in the garden of the monastery would surely bring distrust upon the greatest monk of all time, and thus cause great harm to his monarchy. Nay such scandal be known; they did remove my corpse from the garden."

"Who is *they*, Milo … the guards? Other composers?"

"I did not know at such time, yet, one with the breath of winter did place his hands upon me. I did sense a great evil near me." Milo stood and curled his arms in front of his chest, reenacting his story. "Such foul man did lift my corpse and hold me high. I did feel my body move—yet—nay I do walk? Travel to a chamber he did, with walls of stone ... only to place me upon the cold grund floor." Milo put his palm to his heart. "I cried to the heavens. With my soul I did pray for any God to cease my fear."

"Milo, listen to me," CJ said. "Hucbach, Odopheus, Pantalli ... these guys are in the history books, but they're legends ... even heroes. Why would—"

"I was of the living at such time! I speak the truth!"

"Shh ... Father."

"While I lie in such chamber and await the hand of heaven, God did speak my name." Milo rubbed his eyes and looked straight up, speaking to the sky. "Yet—nay God was he who spoke my name ... nay God indeed."

"Then who, Milo?"

"'Twas one of whom we villagers had fought to defeat. 'Twas the walking dead."

Milo kneeled down and took Clarise's hand, pulling it close to his chest. "With tears you did search for me, Daughter, but nay did I leave a corpse to bury in the grund. For ..." Milo paused, bringing her hand to his cheek. "For I did begin a new life on such day."

"What new life, Father?" Clarise asked, gently pulling her hand away.

"While alone in such darkness, the walking dead did feast on my corpse. Such demons drank of my blood and drew of my spirit. I cried for the heavens to take me, but nay one angel did arrive. Alone was I on such grund floor, left not seen for days ... until ..." Milo hesitated. "... I did awake ... with shame ... and pity ... and ... thy first new breath of life."

Clarise became fidgety. She scooted closer to CJ, and, without thinking, placed her head on his shoulder. She'd been searching for centuries to find her father, only to hear this horrible story: that her father was a vampire. Ironically, CJ became her comfort zone.

Milo spoke with trembling lips: "I chose this not, dear Daughter. I chose this not."

CJ cut in. "Is that why the dagger was in your chest? Somebody stabbed you with it while you were already … dead? I mean … I saw you on the cart. You looked pretty damn dead."

"'Twas the yer'e of 927. The mission had lost much faith. For the walking dead had begun to ravage all the villages in the land. A great fear had overcome the Flemish."

"Fear of vampires?"

Milo closed his eyes and nodded his head, agreeing. "'Twas Odopheus who began to cleanse each village of the walking dead. As such dagger did possess a curse, 'twas thine only means in which to cease a demon, until such demon may be burned with fire, never to breathe life again.

Such conquests became magnificent and the walking dead did quickly vanish from the land. Hence, Odopheus did acquire 'Privilege of Exemption' by the Pope. 'Twas during this ceremony such dagger did vanish."

"I'm confused," CJ told him. "Who took the dagger?"

"'Twas Odopheus whom did take this weapon, but place it, he did, in the very hands of the walking dead, for Odopheus did arrange a secret trade. In exchange for such dagger, Odopheus would cease to destroy the walking dead. Thus, in return, all walking dead would nay be permitted to feast within the villages for ever more."

Clarise looked away and stared into the dark brush. "Were you there, Father? Did you witness such hunting?"

Milo seemed afraid of her question, no doubt troubled by his past, and difficult to admit he'd been a part of the massacres. But his expression also held a hint of speculation, as to how Clarise wouldn't know this.

But Clarise did know; she had merely gone into denial, and she seemed so alive by dodging everything painful.

Milo answered quietly, "Yes, Daughter, I did witness many deaths of such."

CJ sat on the ground, his hands clutched around his shins. The little voice inside his head was begging him to stop, just walk away. But he couldn't. He had accomplished finding out Milo was a vampire. Great, but worthless.

"Where did the Haysons come from, Milo? How do you know about them?" CJ asked.

"'Twas the yer'e of 1173. Upon one eve in our Black Forest, a magnificent light did appear. 'Twas a glow of which we had never seen before. Our forest did shine bright as day—yet—it is night? 'Twas beautiful, this new spectacle." Milo looked CJ in the eyes. "Yet nay this light be beautiful, as such light 'twas a demon instead ... sent here to beset us! Behind trees and stones we fled, but it sought us! When such light did cease, nay but few of us remain. Gather us often, they did, as we fled through the forest under each new moon. Hence ... we were slaves to this new light." Milo hung his head. "'Twas a demon more vile than I."

CJ noticed the scars and wounds on Milo's neck; this guy was older than dirt, and he seemed to have some pretty crazy stories about the past. CJ had a visual just then, of an ancient history book with crumbling edges and aged, brown paper—suddenly receiving an update, an insert, a new chapter of bright white paper, which would be Milo's version of what happened long ago. This story would blow the lid off any music historian's previous renderings.

"How did all of that get over here, Milo," CJ asked him. "To America?"

"Upon our discovery of such demon light, all walking dead did gather. We set forth to steal this evil light and place it with such sacred dagger in shipment to the New World. 'Twas I whom did travel to the New World with such demon weapons, devices surely not of this Earth. Upon my arrival, I did bury the evil Hayson below a church in the New World, deep within the grund. 'Twas believed to remain hence. Until *you* ... you have returned with such evil light. You have come to hunt us."

Milo hissed at CJ and said, "I will kill you before you will place harm on my daughter."

"I'm not here to hurt Clarise. I have the Hayson, yes … but …" CJ stopped. All of a sudden his excuses seemed petty. He'd begun to somewhat understand Milo, and strange as it seemed, he felt a spark of sympathy.

"Who was controlling all of this, Milo? And what about the dagger?" CJ asked him. "If it was buried, how did it end up, well …"

Milo shook his head no. "Truth be said, I did not do as told. I did not carry such dagger to the New World, but instead, I hid such dagger near my home … deep within our Black Forest, pray tell it never be found.

Many a yer'e did pass, with nay a worry such dagger would be seen, until one night of thunderous rain. The walking dead did discover a farmer who had traded one cow for such dagger. 'Twas in route to market, this farmer, to quickly auction the dagger. Sadly, though, his journey was ill met by the walking dead, whereas such dagger was taken upon his death.

Until this wretched day, 'twas believed that I be of true word. Yet, when the walking dead did once again lay eyes upon such dagger, 'twas proof my words nay be true."

"Father, why did you stay?"

"I am not able to travel, dear Daughter, as who would befriend such a demon as I?"

"What happened then, Milo? Where did you go?"

"The dagger of curse 'twas thrust into my chest, as

such demons knew this would grant me access to Artha."
Milo took a deep breath and spoke softly. "Upon my arrival in Artha, I was bequeathed with the essence, yet—
such foes of the walking dead did accompany my journey. With black hoods and stench of rotting flesh they
did steal my essence. As I lie in agony, they did place my
essence into a small vessel, and furthermore," Milo
balled his fists. "They did demand I steal more essence
for the Octogeni Astri." Milo glanced at Clarise, then at
CJ, then back at Clarise. "I did no such thing!" said Milo,
affirming his innocence. "For I know not where the
essence is kept, nor did I know of such Octogeni Astri
they spoke of. The walking dead did once again pierce
my chest with the dagger. My corpse then discarded in
Artha, never again to be seen."

Milo rolled over and laid his head in Clarise's lap.

The stillness of Artha crept into CJ and made him
shiver. He sat staring at Milo … at his clothes, at his skin
… at the gashes in his robe. 'Octo astri? What the *hell*
did that mean?'

And that was that. CJ hit a red line. He'd got what he
needed. He'd learned the Hayson had been involved with
music all the way back to composers of a thousand years
ago. Now it was time to get the hell out of here, time to
get back to his world. Ghosts were one thing, but a vampire was way out of his league.

"Clarise," CJ whispered. "We need to go."

"Yes, we must." She lifted her father's head and
placed it on the ground, then said, "I will soon return,

Father."

As they slid through Artha, CJ felt overwhelmed—scattered between Milo's story and Frederick's initiation to death. And what the hell was he going to do with Bob?

Before he knew it he was back in the pond and Clarise was pulling him underwater.

Once back at The Resurrection, CJ went to the lobby, wondering if Steve had come around yet. Steve was long gone, but a cell phone was lying by the lobby door. He grabbed the phone and called Dean's voice mail.

"Dean? CJ. Listen, I got tied up and missed dinner. Sorry about that. I'm still making adjustments. I probably won't be leaving tonight. Will you have the road crew bring my backpack tomorrow? It's at the hotel. There's some gear in it that I need. It's real important, Dean. We can't run the show without it. Please do that favor for me? I'll call you in the morning and give you an update. Everything is fine."

CJ knew he needed to get some sleep or everything would go haywire.

But the night wasn't over yet. He had to map out a floor plan with Frederick and Clarise so he could do what he did best; design a stage show.

Nathan Juju

The road trucks crossed the Lake Pontchartrain Bridge at 9:00 A.M. the following day. After crossing one of the longest bridges in the country, they'd arrived in the beautiful city of New Orleans. The road crew stopped by the hotel to gather a few band members, then they drove to The Resurrection for the load in at 10:00 A.M.. One of the roadies brought CJ's backpack to the club, as requested. Steve let everyone inside.

No one could find CJ, though, until Steve went to the green room. Sure enough, CJ was wrapped in towels and fast asleep on the couch, still spooning his tool bag, the leather strap coiled around his arm.

"Hey! CJ!" Steve hollered from the door, keeping his distance.

Mark, the drummer for Nathan Juju, peeked over Steve's shoulder. The wardrobe doors had been propped open with chairs, and CJ's jeans had been stretched out across the top. His socks and a T-shirt hung from the chairs like a backyard clothesline.

"Geez, what happened to him?" Mark asked as he stepped inside the green room. He put his hand to CJ's shoulder. "I'll wake him."

Steve bolted down the hall.

The sound check went without any glitches, and the showroom had cleared out by 5:00 P.M.—except for the staff at The Resurrection, who were busy prepping the club for business. CJ was in the sound booth by 6:00 P.M., well-prepared with his plan of attack. Not only was he ready with the basic, technical details for the show, but Frederick and Clarise had helped him cook up something special for the stage show, something sure to please everyone, something a bit over the top.

At 6:30 P.M., the doors of The Resurrection swung open with a series of loud clicks as fans of Nathan Juju began to enter the showroom and occupy their seats. CJ programmed a simple, yet creative, light show, to get some energy flowing through the veins of the ticket-holders. One of his favorite duties was playing music and flashing lights for the crowd, especially since they were already geared up to see a show. If the club had any sort of video system, CJ would project his collection of vintage black-and-white cartoons—a hit with any crowd.

CJ saw Dean crossing the catwalk, heading for the sound booth. He removed his headset as Dean came inside.

"It's a bloody good thing I'm not fearful of heights."

"Can't be in this business." CJ rolled a chair his way.

"Have you seen Brandon? I can't seem to locate the wanker."

"No. Not since sound check. I don't know him too well, but I can tell he's a ladies' man. He's probably snagging a date for after the show."

"You bloody soundmen ... in this business merely for the birds—aren't you?"

"Well, he's a good-looking kid. I can see him doing that, but no. Not all of us start out that way. When I was young ..." CJ paused and then chuckled. "Maybe you're right."

"Ahh ... yes. Youth," Dean said, then sat. "You may not realize this, but I, too, was once a dashing young lad. My hair was frightfully black, and I had creamy white skin, very similar to Brandon as a matter of fact." Dean rubbed his face and sighed, and thirty years flew by with one reminiscent gaze. "But I have the feeling Brandon has lived a pampered life, unlike most of us, and that's what I wish to discuss with you."

"Talk to me."

"He doesn't seem to push the envelope, CJ. Let some of your magic rub off, will you?"

"He seems pretty smart, even above average when it comes to sound gear. What's the issue?"

"He possesses somewhat of a ... shall we say, a slight attitude. Have you noticed?"

"Yeah, he's a little cocky. I figured he didn't like

me. I can live with that."

"I suppose that derives from being short and all."

"He lifts and totes just like everyone else, Dean. There's no room for a diva on a road tour. I think he knows that."

"'Nuff said there, but he simply lacks intuition, which, as you well know, is a key factor for engineering a smashing show. I'll need you to look past the pissing contest and get the monkey up to speed, CJ. Can you do that for me?"

"Sure. My only concern is his stutter. He gets a little excited and *bam* … 'It's a—it's a— it's a …' Not the best way to announce a show, but what the hey."

"Brandon is a West Hamptons mate. Grew up with certain amenities. I believe his father provided him with everything he ever wanted. It's because of that he carries about a sense of entitlement. I don't believe stress has ever been a part of his diet. I'm afraid he may be a bit spiteful of you, as well. You hold plenty of top-notch experience over his head."

"Well, why did you hire this guy? You must have thought he could do the job."

"I'm afraid I've misled you. He can certainly do the job, but I'm looking to get more out of him. Simply enlighten the lad, will you? Since his father and E were flat mates, he had an advantage in securing this position. I'm afraid he'll have a tendency to be rebellious with a supervisor, especially one he's envious of."

"Listen. Dad's not around. And as far as I'm

concerned, nobody rides for free."

Brandon came into the booth just then, stuffing a folded bev-nap in his wallet. "Hey, guys," he said. "What time do you think we'll be finished tonight?"

Dean glanced at CJ.

"We'll be done in about three months," CJ said.

Dean chuckled and stood facing Brandon. "So we're fully aware of the logistics tonight, CJ will run this show and I'll need you to listen and learn from the master. Are we clear on this, Brandon?"

"Yeah. I don't see why, but I'm here, aren't I?"

"Splendid. I must be heading backstage now." Dean gave Brandon a pat on the shoulder and left the sound booth.

CJ wheeled the empty chair to the soundboard. "Have a seat, Brandon. It's curtains in ten. You ready to sail?"

"All set."

"Okay … there are some basic rules for playing background and walk-on music, Brandon. Let's get started. Wait," CJ said. "Ever worked with a rock violin before?"

"A violin is a violin is a violin, and yes, I have."

"Somewhat true, but mostly false," CJ corrected him. "There's a difference in the frequencies—a big difference. Tougher to mix with a loud band. We'll go over those settings during the show."

Brandon lowered his eyelids and glared at CJ.

"Let's start from the top."

Brandon grabbed a pen and paper.

"If the talent hasn't given you any music to play, follow these guidelines. Always play great music, but never play current radio hits that could work against the talent about to go onstage. The music the artist delivers, *live*, from the stage, has to be the best thing the audience hears all night—no exceptions."

Brandon scribbled a few words on the pad.

"Before you cue the walk-on music, remember these rules: select music with no vocals at all, or play a familiar song with the vocals removed. It's the same as cleansing the palate for the audience. If that's not possible, go to step two. And that is ... if the performer is a male singer, play music with female vocals that, again, won't conflict with the performer's style. If it's a female artist, swap the music to male vocals; same guidelines."

Brandon stopped writing. "I just use one of the cable stations. They have a huge selection of tunes."

"Yep, most people do. But that's mundane and average; besides, cable music skips. If you depend on cable, you ... are fucked—especially Time Horror Cable. Burn your own stuff, man. Test it before you play it live and always ... *always* have a backup. Never play music because you personally think it's great; play music that fits the show."

"I'd have to come in way early, CJ. There's not enough time to set that up before a show."

"It's called homework, Brandon, but having your shit together frees you up to take care of the artist. Hunt down music when you're not working. Make notes and log everything—year-round. Know your library and time every song to the second. Master the art of scouting music and make it a part of your diet. Get music from the big guns, the little guns, independent labels ... even local bands from every city you visit. Basically, anywhere you can find music—ask for it, and get it."

"Now," CJ went on, making a side note. "Some music will land in your lap via major record companies. Always accept it with a smile, but be selective. Just because a song has been plastered all over the airwaves, doesn't mean the song is good or that people actually like the tune."

"See, bad music will bring down the overall experience of any show. Don't give anyone—any reason to complain. If you've done your job right, the customer won't remember anything but the music they came to hear. Seasoned artists will have all that worked out, or they'll leave it in the hands of their own soundman, which ... in this case, would be you. Capisce?"

Brandon looked confused.

CJ reached for a volume slider to adjust the music. "Let the artist onstage know nothing else matters, Brandon, regardless of whether you like the performer or not. No matter how successful the artist is," CJ added, "sit with them for a minute. Ask questions and find out what they like in their sound. First and foremost rule ... it's always about the performer. Hang your ego out to dry and learn anything you can. Most of them know sound pretty well themselves; in fact, they usually have a trick or two you've never even thought of. I got my best lessons on reverb from Liza Minnelli—go figure. So, trick is … pay attention, be concerned … and never settle for second rate."

Brandon's eyes began to glaze over.

"Okay, let's just do this." CJ slapped on some headphones.

The warm-up band turned out to be a professional piece of cake. The musicians were focused and performed a thirty-five-minute set of rock music with very few lighting cues and no sound problems. They finished on time and left the crowd roaring.

CJ had three channels of communication linked to the crew's headsets: one channel had been linked to Steve, who'd be helping out as a production assistant: another to the green room intercom: and the third channel had been designated to Dean. CJ also had a direct line to Alan, but since Alan was the stage manager, his voice came through a small monitor by the soundboard.

"Headset check," CJ called out, testing the lines. "Dean, you on?"

"By the green room, CJ."

"How about you, E? You with us?" CJ asked.

"Nah … I'm at the library. Whaddaya think, man?"

CJ muted his mouthpiece and said, "Really? Pick up a book on manners while you're there, will ya?" He turned his mic back on. "Steve? You there?"

"I'm right here, CJ. What am I supposed to do? Should I stay by the stairs? Should I stay backstage? When do you—"

"Stay backstage, Steve. Don't do anything unless we call it, capisce? Say as little as possible and keep the lines clear. *Only* speak up if you see a problem, okay? You're a hero tonight, and the entire show is resting on your shoulders." CJ covered his mouthpiece and chuckled.

"Alan, are we true?" CJ asked, confirming no gear had been redirected through the SNAKE, and no cords had been replaced—without being tested—since the initial sound check.

"All lines are true, CJ," Alan said over the monitor. "But keep an ear out for Jerry's guitar. He has the lead-guitar syndrome."

"What the hell is that," Brandon asked.

CJ muted his mouthpiece and said, "Some lead-guitar players have a tendency to turn up their volume during the show, not once, not twice, but all night." He tore a strip of neon-orange tape from a roll, then stuck it to a volume slider. "Which, as you know, throws the overall sound mix out of whack, not once, not twice, but all night."

CJ noticed something onstage. He punched a button and spoke into his headset. "Hey, Alan, I see an empty table at stage left. Is it prop?"

"Clearing it now," Alan said.

CJ saw Steve run across the stage and carry the small table away. As soon as Steve was out of sight, CJ lowered the lights.

"Hey, Dean."

"Right here, mate."

"Get me a CD from the band that just played, will ya?" CJ winked at Brandon.

"Ol'right."

"Thanks. We go in two."

CJ took the house lights down to 50 percent, darkening the ambiance in the showroom and directing the crowd's attention to the stage.

After a small outburst of applause, he lowered the house lights and killed the music, leaving the club dark and silent, knowing the crowd would soon cheer in anticipation.

And so they did, and when the applause reached a steady roar, CJ blasted the intro of the song, "The Game of Love", which had the vocals removed, and featured an undeniably great guitar solo by Carlos Santana. The iconic guitar riff brought the eager crowd to their feet.

CJ lit the drums with a bright red, overhead spotlight. The powerful light hit the hardware and reflected a plethora of shiny flashes across the darkened club. As he brought up the stage lights, he started alternating the overhead lights from left, to right, on the downbeat of each measure.

Brandon watched every move.

"It's amazing how many people only watch the lead

singer during a concert," said CJ, over his shoulder. "When you introduce the stage to the audience—before-hand—they'll look around more, soak in the performance from corner to corner."

Brandon seemed intrigued by the intro, an art form of its own, a steady buildup of lights and sound meant to stir up the crowd—all in about ninety seconds. Once the opening song had mellowed into a steady rhythm, CJ placed a circle of blue laser lights at center stage, high-lighting the lead singer's microphone.

CJ lowered the music and turned on the VOG mic for the opening announcement.

"People of New Orleans! Welcome … to The Resur-rection!"

The crowd roared in response.

"Tooo—night! All the way from New … York … City! The Resurrection is proud to bring you … NATHAN JUJU!"

The first guitar chord rumbled across the stage with a monstrous attack. When then the drums and bass kicked in, CJ bumped the stage lights up to 60 percent. The band played an instrumental loop of one of their most popular hits, while CJ spun bright blue lights above the stage.

"In the wax to the max, mate!" Dean shouted over the headset.

E ran onstage just then. CJ increased the stage lights to 100 percent, then he sent hundreds of frenzied laser lights dancing across the heads of the crowd. The audience cheered and the ladies rushed up front to gaze at E.

"Takeoff!" CJ announced, submersed in the excitement, watching E with an eagle eye. "Do not take your eyes off the lead singer, Brandon," said CJ, again, over his shoulder. "Watch his every move and move with him." E made subtle hand gestures as he jigged across the stage, nods and signals regarding monitor levels and other slight nuances. CJ adjusted a few knobs in response. "Read his body language and give him plenty of time to acclimate to the sound levels."

CJ and Brandon had spiked the stage during sound check, and E was professional enough to follow the bright-colored lines of tape, knowing the outlined areas would guide him to the best possible sound onstage, or, prevent him from getting buried in another musician's sound mix. E also knew crossing those marks could cause a deafening feedback.

The violin player went into some diatonic riffs, using his own stage gear to reproduce a timbre-tuned, rock quartet, filled with semi-tones and harmonic modulations.

During the chorus of Nathan Juju's biggest hit, CJ did a quick blackout on every other four count, killing the lights onstage, but leaving E in a bright white spotlight. It appeared as though massive snapshots were being taken of the show. E's band seemed skeptical at first; the musicians weren't familiar with this routine, but they liked it and soon began to smile. Now the band had become energized as well. CJ spun the overhead stage lights at the end of the song, highlighting the cheering audience.

Earlier in the evening, while the crew was running cables, CJ had configured a way to shoot the Hayson into the dimmer pack—the main source of stage lights. He used the 3-PIN cord; the same adapter he'd made after the show in Boston, plus or minus a few parts. It was a cable constructed of three large copper stems, thick enough to send twenty-two hundred watts through each line; the massive amount of electricity needed for the five-hundred-watt bulbs. On the female end of the 3-PIN cord, there were three industrial-sized cavities, and those cavities had enough magnetic pull to lure the lights of the Hayson through the thick-gauged wires. CJ placed the adapter under the soundboard by his feet, knowing he'd have only a split second opportunity to use the adapter when the time came. Until then, Frederick was on standby.

Nathan Juju performed with nonstop energy for a good eighty minutes, filling The Resurrection with some solid rock-n-roll music. The audience seemed content with the show, but CJ knew it was time to take things over the top. With the encore fast approaching, he activated the smoke machine for a quick four count, just long enough to shoot a miniscule puff of fog over the stage.

That was a cue for Clarise.

Nathan Juju ended the song and ran off stage to wait

for the roaring demand of an encore. When the cheering from the crowd had reached its peak, the band came running back onstage.

CJ waited until Brandon looked away, then he unplugged one of the drum cables from channel 17 in the soundboard.

"Brandon, we have a problem!"

"What?"

"You need to go backstage." CJ raised the volume slider on channel 17, then took it back down, then he moved the slider up and down several times. "This line is dead." CJ leaned over the soundboard, pretending to inspect the connections. "Channel 17 must have come unplugged. Go check the SNAKE," he said. "Quick! Hurry!"

Brandon sprung from his chair and bolted across the sky-high catwalk. CJ watched, waiting until Brandon had run through the door by Steve's office. When CJ turned back to the stage, he saw Clarise standing patiently at stage right. She had a soft florescent glow about her, like a dimly lit statue.

CJ blinded E with a spotlight. He wasn't ready for E to see her yet.

But Clarise was ready, and she suddenly took the lead by gently stepping into view. Every head in the arena turned her way as she moseyed in between the guitar player and the audience. She then strolled across the stage in a slow, sexual stride, her white hair flowing behind her. The fact that she was radiant seemed to captivate the audience, and if that didn't do it, the way she moved with grace in her bare feet, her arms by her side, revealing a slight glimpse of her breasts ... was enough to make the crowd go wild.

The women were envious of the beautiful girl in the simple sundress. The men were aroused by the striking and luscious Clarise.

One of the security guards spotted Clarise and leapt onstage. He stooped down low and ran toward her, thinking she was a fan that had somehow sneaked up there. The muscle man reached out for Clarise, but his hand swished through her white arm.

Clarise kept walking toward E.

The bouncer tried to grab Clarise's shoulders from behind, but his hands passed through her body again and again. The crowd saw it all and they went nuts, screaming and cheering. The guard put his hands to his face and studied them—as if they were the problem. Then he turned to the audience. People were pointing his way, roaring with laughter. He seemed embarrassed, and then angry, and then he soared into a tackling dive. The security guard sailed right through Clarise. This time he landed on his belly and bounced off the front of the stage. The audience leapt to their feet, cheering loud enough to drown out the music.

Unaffected by the roaring crowd, Clarise kept her stride until she'd come within a few steps of E. She smiled and leaned her head to the side, gazing into his eyes.

Instead of being alarmed by her sudden appearance,

E made the best of the situation; he turned the song into a rock serenade, addressed to the white woman standing beside him. He got down on one knee and played the role well, keeping the microphone to his mouth while his other hand reached for the sky.

As with any crooning performance, an act of passion is required, at least facially, and so it was with E. So much so, that he began to chuckle, then he bowed his head to hide his laughter.

That was the opportunity CJ had been waiting for, the very reason he'd kept his finger resting on the slider, the perfect timing for a total black out. With one flick of his finger, CJ killed the stage lights.

E lost his balance and his arm went to the floor. Without the visual connection to the music, the loud notes and drumbeats blasted through the darkness with a menacing force. His knees trembled when he stood, unable to see anything besides the glowing lights from a few amplifiers onstage. But that was enough light to see a dark red image of Clarise, still gazing into his eyes.

E took a step back.

Clarise took a step forward, and then another, and without slowing down she walked into his body, entering his core with a ghostly wane. In less than half a beat, she'd stepped back out, passing through E like an open door.

"…one thousand three, one thousand four …" CJ raised the master slider and brought the stage lights back up.

Clarise was walking toward the drums, then came to a halt about ten steps behind E. She turned around to face the crowd, and with a deceptively calm presence, she lowered her head and stood motionless in the center of the giant stage.

E broke out in a shiver. He spread his arms wide open, then flung his head forward and hunched his back. His arms fell to his side and he pranced in one spot, tossing his head from side to side.

As the anomalous female energy began to subside, E gripped the microphone stand with both hands and placed his head in the bend of his arm.

It wasn't usual for a rock singer to stand quiet, not for too long anyway, and it could have been seen as a drunken stupor, but as the shock wore off, E started coming around. He let go of the mic stand and stood up straight, peering at the crowd through wavering strands of long blond hair. He brushed his hair back with both hands and ran his fingers down the sides of his neck, then down his chest, and then even lower, rubbing his hands across his groin.

The ladies screamed with ecstasy.

E lifted his arms and spread them wide, once again reaching for the sky. But this time he threw his head back and stood frozen in an unyielding stance.

Behind E, Clarise crimped her sundress and did a gentle curtsey.

That was a cue for CJ.

She was ready.

CJ lowered the stage lights to a soft glow. Then he wheeled his chair to the spotlights and projected two amber-colored circles against the ceiling, both enormous in size, one slightly darker than the other, imitating the two moons of Artha. With the stage lights lowered, the faux moons placed an unearthly glow in the showroom. The sea of heads became a sea of faces, each looking up at the circles of light.

Brandon noticed the drop in lights, even from backstage, where he'd found no problems with the SNAKE, or any cables connected to it. He peeked out from behind the wing and saw the two circles in the ceiling. His gaze went to the sound booth next, squinting to find it. It was dark up there, but he still stared, wondering what CJ was up to.

It didn't take long for the band to notice a change in the song, either, specifically that the lead singer had stopped singing. The musicians kicked into autopilot and started playing a four-measure loop of an upbeat rhythm, just to keep the music alive.

Without wasting a beat, CJ started blasting smoke onto the stage, filling the airspace above the band with a colossal cloud of fog.

With that, Clarise took gentle steps left and right, spreading her feet farther apart until she had secured a good stance. Then she, too, threw her head back and slowly raised her arms. She bent her knees in a slight crouch. Then she bent her wrists backward and exposed her palms, and from nowhere, a strange wind began to blow against E's back—a gentle breeze, subtle enough to barely lift a few strands of hair from E's shoulder.

But as she swayed her fingers and spun her hands, the tender wind became stronger, sending long strands of E's hair flailing toward the audience. As she lifted her arms even higher, the smoke above the stage began to stir.

With her hands above her head, Clarise went into a smooth and gentle dance. She began crossing the stage with delicate spins, and magical sways, twirling her silky arms in a ghostly ballet that was surely intended to stimulate the floating cloud above.

And her mission was a hit, as the mass of smoke began to separate in places, torn apart by the wafts of wind coming from below, coming from Clarise, coming from beyond.

By the time the guitar and violin started trading instrumental solos, the cloud above had broken into thirty or forty smaller clouds, spreading across the entire stage and drifting into the showroom where they hovered above the first ten rows of seats. Like colored rays of sunshine, the stage lights sent gentle streaks of light beaming down through the breaks in the clouds.

E remained motionless with his arms held high. He seemed unaware of the dreamy light show, and even more clueless about the sea of clouds floating ten feet above his head.

Clarise danced her way behind E, and there she brought her arms down and lowered her head. As though a stage light had been lowered, Clarise slowly vanished.

The audience started whistling and hollering, shouting their approval of the spectacle.

So far the plan was right on track, and CJ wasn't about to stop now. He grabbed the 3-PIN cord by his feet and placed the Hayson against the open cavities. After probing the catwalks for any stray techies, he pressed the side-switch on the Hayson.

The blue lights soared into the 3-PIN cord and sent the ghostly energy straight into the mainframe of the lighting system, where the wraith-like force rattled the dimmer-pack, surmounting the metal box of wires. Glimmering rays of blue light streamed throughout the sound booth, leaking from every screw hole and seam in the metal casing.

The unearthly life force suddenly jetted from the mainframe at an explosive speed, traveling through the cables in the ceiling, racing to the overhead grid.

When the fathomless energy reached the lattice of stage lights, streaks of brilliant blue light surged from every light fixture, crackling down like bolts of lightning toward the little clouds of smoke. The arena flashed with a captivating brightness, as though a giant electrical claw had appeared above the stage.

But the audience wasn't so receptive this time, and the excessive amount of light frightened a few fans.

Some covered their eyes. Others ducked in their seats.

"CJ, what the bloody hell is going on up there?" Dean barked through the headset. "What are those—" CJ muted Dean's microphone.

While the mysterious streaks of light were electrifying the small clouds, another stream of blue energy beamed down from the lighting grid. This ray of light was focused on E, and in the blink of an eye a hazy image of Fredrick traveled down through the beam of light. As Frederick got closer to the stage, he lunged into E's body with a surge of ghostly force.

CJ blacked out the stage lights and pulled the Hayson away from the adapter; then he brought the lights back up.

E had bent over forward, as if he'd been punched in the stomach.

The other streaks of light had gone away, but the hovering clouds now had a lime-green hue about them, and they seemed to be stirring from within.

E straightened out and held the microphone above his head. Then he spun in circles until he stopped on a dime. And there he stood, unable to move anything but his wandering eyes. After a motionless measure, E came out of the pose and maneuvered across the stage the same way Frederick had frolicked in front of the mirror the night before, presenting some Gatsby-style dance moves that hadn't been seen in eighty-five years.

The audience broke out with applause as Frederick became Clarise's partner in crime, controlling E's stage persona so the transformation above E could continue.

Inspired by the cheering of the crowd, E began to sing.

"Take me back to the days I treasure.
So many things that money ... money couldn't buy.
I'm forever home on Quitman Highway.
Another lonely breath, another lonesome drive."

Out of nowhere, an enormous image of Clarise emerged behind the stage. With her torso rising forty feet in the air, and her hair swaying to the far corners of the showroom, she created an atmosphere of magical fascination for the audience.

The energy of the crowd shifted into a frenzied madness.

The band, however, seemed to shy away. They were unable to see the same images as the crowd. The musicians only knew something foggy and green had appeared above their heads, and the audience had gone bonkers. They continued to play their instruments, though somewhat apprehensive.

From high above the stage, Clarise reached down and swayed her hand across the little green clouds, gently caressing them. As she pulled her hand away, tiny plant stems began to sprout from the clouds, twisting and winding upward in a time-lapsed, hasty pace. At the same time, thin needles started emerging from the cork-screw-looking trunks, covering the plants in a light-green fur.

The audience went silent. Watching. Waiting.

It was then that white arms started reaching out from within the lime-green clouds. Then cloudy bodies began to emerge, and chalky torsos began to rise, some rolling on their knees while others sat up straight. The semblances grabbed the twisted trunks and stood, old and young, thick and thin, all milky white in color and each projecting a luminescent glow.

The band went into a half-beat bridge as the audience went insane, thinking holograms had just been projected onto the stage.

CJ placed a soft glow of light around E, then lowered the stage lights even more. E stood at the edge of the stage and sang with true conviction while the semblances above his head continued to rise.

"When the sun goes down, my spirit comes alive.
For so many years, you've taken me,
to the other side.
Engines revving on an open road.
I've got to find her—she's got to know.
I'm all alone on Quitman Highway."

Alan's voice came over the monitor. "CJ, what the hell? What are those—" CJ muted Alan's channel.

Clarise smiled and reached down again, this time cupping her hands and scooping one of the phantoms in her palms. Then she softly flung her hands toward the moons in the ceiling, thrusting the ghost toward the amber-colored circles. It didn't take long for the rest of the spirits to catch on, and soon the ghostly men and women began to rise and float upward in a waiflike, transcending haze, migrating to the amber-colored moons in the ceiling. One by one, the semblances reached the ceiling and vanished into the spheres.

Some audience members sparked lighters and swayed them in the air, others shook their fists and screamed out loud.

With the end of the song fast approaching, the band started taking it down a notch, but apparently Frederick hadn't had enough fun, evident by the way E's feet suddenly revved into another dance routine. The musicians followed the cue and the fading tempo suddenly accelerated with some heavy guitar arpeggios, coinciding with E's fancy sidestepping. E shuffled his feet and twisted his body, tossing the microphone from hand to hand as he riveted across the stage in the old-time shuffle. The legendary footwork did nothing but complement the rock-n-roll music, and strangely enough, E seemed to be watching his feet, instead of controlling his moves, all the while losing the look of arrogance he was known for. E apparently felt different tonight—and it showed on his face.

The spirits continued to drift upward while the band played on, bringing the cheering of the crowd to a frightening level. The concertgoers went crazy, tossing drinking cups and pamphlets in the air; they swirled baseball hats and T-shirts above their heads.

E appeared somewhat detached, but not enough to consider the cheering wasn't for him. All he could do was gloat and do what he did best: entertain.

As the last few semblances vanished into the moons above, the corkscrew-looking brush began to swirl downward, and Clarise began to fade, and the green clouds above E's head seemed to melt into a sprinkling, glittery haze. CJ lowered the spotlight on E even more, placing him in a soft shadow.

The final image of the concert was E standing in front of a dazzling shower, slightly illuminated by the moons in the ceiling.

"Good night, New Orleans!" E shouted, as CJ faded the stage lights all the way.

A man named Jonan stood by the door, studying the band, watching the strange lights, impressed by the overwhelming response from the rock-n-roll audience. He held his cell phone above the heads of the patrons to capture the performance, then he left the showroom and entered the lobby. As he approached the bar, he punched a digit on his phone.

"Hey, Cavanaugh," Jonan said. "You're taking a trip."

"You paying my way?"

"You know, you are one cheap fuck."

"That's not the point, Jonan. You run a major record

company, one of the biggest in the country."

"So?"

"So the point is I ain't financin' your operation."

"This is the thanks I get for hiring you? No one will touch you after the St. Louie' fiasco. I'm the only one who halfway wants to know you. Let's show a little gratitude here, can we?"

"Jonan, I didn't steal nothin' in St. Louis. I'm telling you now—this minute."

"My heart bleeds for you. Now … tell me, was that Dean Autry that shit-canned you? The British cowboy? The jerk that owns Intertwine—right? He's the one. Am I right?"

"Yeah, that was him. I worked my ass off for the sour fish, and then he accuses me of stealing money. I ain't seen him in years."

"Well, Cav, the money *did* disappear. You can't expect someone to look the other way when an entire night of sales goes missing."

"I'm telling you, I was robbed! There was a police report and everything. It was real, what happened to me."

Jonan burst out laughing. "Didn't you get that new condo right about then? I bet that cost a pretty penny … say … one night's ring of a major concert?"

"I proved everything. I don't know why nobody believes me. Why you bringing this up? Why'd you call?"

"No one believes you 'cause you're a slimy piece of shit, Cav. You know it, and I know it. That's why I love you. Now … I need your ass in Savannah. You're gonna snoop on this guy, CJ. I want details on the stage gear he's using for Nathan Juju. He's got some kinda hologram thing goin' on."

"Stage gear? Are you outta your head? I know nothin' about stage gear."

"Then you're about to learn. I need to know his gimmick—you hear me? Get inside. Get to know him. Be his bitch for all I care; I want details. That's what I want. You got me?"

"You might want to find another mole for this one, Jonan. Why don't you do it?"

"A, because I'm telling you to. And B, because I'm leaving this bayou in the morning, back to New York. Now ... I need you there Wednesday night."

"All right, all right, but I need some cash, Jonan. Send me some cash."

"You know the rules. Expense report when you're done. Otherwise you're gonna spend *my* money on hookers and juicy steaks, or the other way around. Now ... call me when you get to Savannah."

By the end of the night every piece of merchandise had been sold, even more by the looks of the shirtless sales crew. The launch of the tour had been a success and everyone on board took a big breath—a collective sigh of relief.

Dean was ecstatic about the sales, and that took precedence over any odd type of light show. Still, he was curious about the advents onstage, as was everyone else. CJ told Dean he'd projected an old movie across the stage, thinking it would add a touch of mystery to the show. Dean accepted the explanation because nothing launches a tour like the ringing of a cash register, which was Dean's signal that the months of behind-the-scenes work had paid off. Even more exciting were the six voice messages from various reporters, wanting interviews for the local newspapers. And with that, Dean was officially ready to tour the United States.

While the road crew was packing the stage gear, CJ went backstage and approached a trunk full of Profiles. It appeared he was helping the crew pack lights. No one questioned his presence, or gave a second thought to him lending a hand, and no one saw him wrap the dagger in a towel and hide it in trunk number eleven. Afterwards, he secured the trunk with a padlock from his tool bag. The keys were in his briefcase, and he knew the keychain had a red anchor on it, so that's what he drew on the trunk; an anchor made of florescent orange tape.

New Orleans proved to be a first for CJ. He'd never juggled two ghosts before. Now his wheels were spinning with ideas for a new show, in a new town.

The Landlers

Brandon went out the back door just as Reynolds, one of the roadies, closed the double doors on the road truck. Reynolds secured the latch and turned to Brandon.

"You have an answer for me, right?" Reynolds said, leaning against the truck.

"Of course I do. I just … didn't get the name of the movie."

"That's all I wanted, pretty boy. How am I gonna place wagers without the name of the film? I guess you don't want your cut."

"Wait for me," Brandon told him, taking a few steps back. "Okay? Just wait. I'll be right back."

"No. There's no time. Obviously you didn't play a part in the light show cause you don't have a clue. So it must be true—what everyone's saying, I mean. You *are* CJ's bitch."

"Hey, pig fucker. I'm nobody's bitch. I just want to make sure—"

"Yeah, yeah, yeah … whatever. If we're gonna stay

on schedule, we need to hit the road. We still need to get the band's luggage from the hotel. C'mon. Let's go."

"Just wait, okay," Brandon told him, jogging backward. "I'll get the name from CJ."

"No, Brandon. We're leaving now."

Brandon ran to Reynolds and snatched the keys from his hand, then bolted inside The Resurrection.

Brandon approached CJ in the sound booth, whirling the truck keys around his finger. "Why don't I travel with you, CJ? That show was amazing. I mean … wow. I've never worked with equipment like that. I'd like to learn some more. I didn't see what movie you played, though."

"We'll have time to talk, Brandon. Let's catch up in Savannah."

"But if I go with you, it'll save us a training session down the road. I'll be running the shows in a few days without you. If you tell me how to use the gear, I can get a jump-start."

"That would be great," said CJ, sitting at the soundboard, packing his backpack. "But you have to stay with the truck, and I have to leave tonight."

"Why don't you let me study your notes while I'm traveling. That'll help me *learn from the master*, right?"

CJ paused for a beat, then zipped up his backpack. "You should catch some shut-eye, Brandon. Never kick off a tour with no sleep. You'll be worn out soon enough. Get some rest and we'll talk tomorrow." He plopped his backpack on the floor and stood from the chair. "I need to get something from backstage. I'll see you in Savannah."

Brandon rubbed his chin as CJ crossed the catwalk. Something was off key. The guys in the road crew wanted to know about the bizarre stage show they'd just seen. They had questions, and Brandon was supposed to be the go-to for answers. Instead, he was placed in line with the others; maybe the front of the line, but in line still the same. He suspected more was going on than met the eye, something strange, and CJ's bullshit story about old movies didn't make any sense—not to a soundman anyway.

Forget about the crew, now his own curiosity was boiling under his skin. He wasn't accustomed to being left out, and CJ had just dissed him like an old pizza.

This just couldn't happen.

CJ kept a low profile at the back door, waiting for the road crew to hit the asphalt. The minute the trucks rolled out of the parking lot, he went back to the sound booth and grabbed the Hayson with Bob Dustin inside. His backpack with the empty Hayson was nowhere to be found.

After searching the booth, he called Brandon. Turns out Brandon had grabbed his backpack and taken it to the hotel, as a favor to CJ.

"Dammit."

CJ still had some issues to deal with before he left New Orleans, though. The toughest quandary at the moment was Clarise. Oddly enough, she had become somewhat of a companion. But Clarise and Milo were a package deal, and he wanted nothing to do with vampires. Clarise might be missed, but Milo could stay in New Orleans with the rest of the legendary bloodsuckers.

Then there were the Haysons. He wasn't thinking straight when he used the Hayson on Bob Dustin. Stress had definitely impaired his judgment. He'd never intentionally hurt anyone before, and he wasn't about to start now. Feeding Bob Dustin to Milo was out of the question. He did have to release Bob somewhere, though— somewhere far away.

He approached the bricked-up archway in the back of the club. Before he called her name, Clarise appeared just a few feet away, tilting her head and flaunting a delicate, flirtatious smile. She also knew it was time to say goodbye, and like CJ, she had also become attached.

"You know … you are really something else," said CJ, stepping closer. "You must have been a real wildfire back when."

"Wild … fire? Is that good?"

"It's great! Most people just go with the flow, or sit quiet and never speak their minds, but you … you have spunk … and stubborn! Wow, it's been great to be around."

"Great? You almost killed us … well …" She teased him. "… you almost killed you."

"No, no. Not me. You were the one who took us back and forth. Now we're here. Now we're there. Now we're—"

"Thank you, CJ, for bringing Father back to me. No danger could ever replace such a victory." She reached for CJ's hand. "You are unlike anyone I have met as well. At first I believed you would only bring harm. After seeing how you fill hearts with magic ... I am wiser."

The gaze between them became intense, and they stared into each other's eyes with a heated passion.

CJ took a deep breath. "If there was a way—"

"There is no way," she told him.

He grinned, accepting the truth; that it was crazy to think a love interest could evolve from this. He kept his eyes on her for another beat, then said, "So tell me ... how long can someone like me, a human, survive in Artha?"

"Not for very long. There are no safe places in Artha for the living. Why do you ask?"

"What about temporarily?"

"No, CJ. Artha does not exist for the living. If one should meet with death in Artha, they will leave the living through a horrible dream."

"Okay, not good." CJ raised his eyebrows. "Well, I've done something terrible, and ... and I don't know how to fix it."

"What have you done?"

"I have someone trapped inside a Hayson. I don't want to hurt him, but I can't just let him out. He'll tell everyone what he's seen."

"Someone from the *living*?"

"Wow … yeah, he's a soundman."

"Why, CJ? Why did you do that?"

"I didn't mean to. It … it just happened. I think he saw Frederick, and he was about to see you, and I'm sure he would have told others. I just used the Hayson without thinking. I screwed up, I know, but—"

"He is from the living, CJ. He cannot survive inside the Hayson for very long."

"How long is very long?"

"Before the sun may touch the moon."

CJ held the cylinder to his face. "He's in there right now." CJ cocked his head, curious. "Can he hear us?"

"No, he is waiting for—" She turned away, like she'd done before, like she'd done each time she wanted to spare CJ some kind of ugliness.

"For what? Where is he?"

"CJ, you mustn't use the Hayson any longer. You do not understand how dangerous it is—do you? It is evil and it should never be used—not by anyone. Do you not know about the Landlers?"

"The Landlers? What's that?"

"Not what. Who."

"Okay … *who* is that?"

"I am surprised you have not seen them. They search for the Haysons, but they are not of the living."

"Wait, are they the guys in dark hoods, the ones you mentioned?"

Clarise squinted, suddenly skeptical. "You are certain someone mysterious has not approached you?"

"Yes, no, I don't know. I have strange things happen all the time. I've had a few run-ins with some creepy guys, but I left one of 'em trapped somewhere. He won't be coming around."

Clarise stepped back, frightened. "You did not bring them to Artha, did you? CJ? Please, no, tell me you did not."

"No, no, I didn't bring them, *him*, here. But who are these guys, Clarise? What do they want?"

Her voice shook and she balled her hands into fists. "I cannot talk about the Landlers. They are more evil than demons. It is said the Landlers even harm creatures." Her eyes narrowed, beaming at the Hayson in his hand. "The Hayson is more evil than anything."

"Is that why you have guards in there?" CJ asked, nodding at the brick wall.

"The guards protect the essence."

"*Essence?*"

Clarise gazed at the floor, and with a softer tone, she said, "Some are wounded when they leave the living. They have seen much harm and no longer look the same. The essence comes from the Artha trees. It will heal them."

"Sleeping in the roots," said CJ, as the light came on.

"Some of the essence was taken, though. Long ago. It was believed the Landlers took it from us. That is why the guards protect Artha."

"Wait, Milo said, well … he mentioned the essence, and Octo Mom, or something like that."

"Octogeni. The eighty-eight constellations, CJ. Father knows nothing of them," said Clarise, with a bulldozer gaze, a look that suggested he forget that conversation.

And CJ got the hint full steam.

Clarise grabbed his hands and looked him in the eyes. "The Landlers will appear somewhere and they will be cruel. If they take the Hayson from you, it would change any peace we have."

"How do you know all this? How can I find out more?"

"Only those who have left the living can know this." Clarise placed her hand on CJ's cheek, then said, "You have climbed aboard a ship you do not know how to sail. You must be careful of the Landlers, CJ."

"I will … I promise …" CJ shook the Hayson, getting back to Bob. "Will you tell me what to do with this guy, though? Can you help me? If I let him out, can you take him far away?"

"You do not want to hurt him … you are certain?"

"Yes. I mean *no*! I don't want to hurt him—just confuse him so he won't remember anything. Can you help me, Clarise … please?"

"I cannot take him to Artha."

"How about another place? Can you keep him somewhere for a little while?"

"I can help him forget this day. But I do not know how long it will last. In time he will learn the difference between his memory, and his dreams." She stood quiet, thinking. "I will help you upon one condition," Clarise told him, getting soft-eyed again. "You must come back and visit me."

CJ grinned from ear to ear. "Are you serious? Just keep me away from Milo, okay? He wants my head on a platter."

"Leave the person here and I will help him home. What is his name?"

"His name is Bob. Keep him away from Milo, too, okay?"

They laughed and then got quiet, staring boldly once again.

"I have the feeling I'll see you again, Clarise."

CJ let go of her hands and reached for the cylinder. He pressed down on the side-switch. After the blue web had faded, Bob Dustin was lying on the floor, sleeping like a baby. CJ turned and walked away.

"CJ ..."

He turned around just as Clarise flung her hand from her lips, blowing him a kiss.

And with that, The Resurrection in New Orleans had come to a close.

It's a Boy

The next stop on the tour was the breathtaking city of Savannah. CJ hadn't been there in over a year, but he'd heard about the ongoing renovations with the older buildings downtown. If there was one thing certain about Savannah, it was ghosts, and they were known to come out of the woodwork on just about every corner.

CJ caught the last flight to Savannah from New Orleans. He'd never stepped foot in the hotel in New Orleans, but spending the night in an empty club was nothing new. That's why he always carried a toothbrush and razor in his briefcase, but since Brandon had taken CJ's backpack to the hotel, he wasn't able to change clothes.

As a precaution, he called Mark and asked him to personally toss his backpack in the truck, along with the band's luggage. That would keep his backpack out of Brandon's greedy hands until it arrived in Savannah the next day.

It was late when CJ got to the hotel in Savannah. He sweet-talked the manager into opening the gift shop for five minutes—just long enough to grab a green T-shirt and a new leather bag. A little more schmoozing and he'd finagled two mini-bottles of Jack Daniels from the honey-eyed girl. CJ placed the Hayson in the new bag, along with the few tools he still had, then he headed upstairs to his room.

He ran the shower, then flipped the bathroom trashcan upside down for a makeshift table. He took the radio from the bedside table and brought it in the bathroom. A local DJ named Buzz was broadcasting "Tommy", the rock musical, performed by the London Festival Orchestra.

After a few scoops of ice from down the hall, he set the drinks on the trashcan and gave the hot water valve a few more spins. Before he climbed into the old French-clawed tub, he placed a few towels against the sloped porcelain as a neck rest.

While the hot water beat down on his aching body, he held one cold drink at a time against his face, rolling each frosty glass across the tiny cuts in his cheeks. By the time the song "It's a boy!" was over, the tension in his muscles was withering away.

He started thinking about Clarise, wondering if he'd ever have such an esteemed adventure again. Even though the underwater scenario scared the living shit out of him—almost ended his life, meeting her gave him a sense of hope; that he could get better at this ghost stuff. Never before had he developed such a bittersweet friendship with a spirit. And how could anyone be so damn beautiful? So appealing? So strangely reminiscent?

At least he was on the right track with the stage shows. He knew it. But he had to create these stage fantasisms without provoking fear, and the sooner that could happen ... the better. It came down to bargaining. That was the lesson learned.

People had said some great things after the show, "*what a concert*" ... "*your technical skills are amazing*" ... "*I've never seen a show like that*" ... but deep down he knew the nice words belonged to Clarise, and the Hayson. Okay, maybe a few technical skills of his own, but there was no way he could have anticipated such a mind-blowing spectacle. It was Clarise that pulled that off. It was Clarise that had blown everyone away.

And speaking of shows, another concert was right around the corner. He had to bring more mystery to the table. Having great sound was a no brainer, but the visuals seemed to be the real attention grabber. If he wanted to top the images in New Orleans, then he had to keep exploring with the unknown and dig deeper than ever before, and he had to do it fast. Even Clarise knew more about the Hayson than he did, and that meant other spirits did, too.

And who were these Landlers she mentioned? Was the Suit he'd captured in Boston a Landler? Could these guys track down the Hayson he'd stashed in his apart-ment?

He saw a shadow on the shower curtain just then. Someone was on the other side.

He flung the curtain open and saw an old woman staring straight ahead. He covered his junk with a towel and sat up, suddenly shy as he faced the door, as if there could be more people close by, as if maybe he was the one in the wrong bathroom, sitting in the wrong bathtub.

But he wasn't.

"Hey. You're in the wrong room," CJ told her. "You need to leave." He waved his hand, shooing her toward the door. "Let's go. I'll call someone to come get you, but you need to get out of my bathroom, okay?"

She turned her head to look his way. Her eyes were nothing but black empty holes.

It would have been easy to shut the curtain, but he stared instead, at her soiled brown dress, at the chunks of mud sliding down her legs, at the wet strands of silver hair that fused with her crusty arms. Sludge dripped from her hands when she pressed them together to pray. She leaned her head to the right, offering a bizarre, tiny hint of a smile, and then she parted her weather-beaten lips and bared an orchestra of decomposed teeth.

"Some rest for the day is in motion.
Though the song in your heart,
may be in your favor.
Those in the soil,
will soon be your neighbor.
It has been many years
since the leaves of the trees,
have been swept by the breeze.
When the old Earth is defeated,
a new generation will arise.
Until that day,
the afterlife shall not be spared."

"What the fuck?" CJ rubbed his eyes with his knuckles and pulled them away.

She was gone.

He sat in the tub a while longer, the curtain halfway open and the water streaming down, wondering why the spirits were getting so damn weird. Around 3:00 A.M. his skin started resembling the old woman's, and since he had a wake up call scheduled for 8:00 A.M., he turned off the shower and crawled into bed.

White Limousine

The next morning CJ woke to the ringing of the hotel phone. Still asleep, he fumbled to answer the call, placing his hand on something softer than a receiver. He jerked his hand back and rose to one elbow. Two blinks, maybe three, and he'd focused. The old woman from his shower the night before was perched beside his bed, one hand resting on the phone.

"I'd say welcome back but that would be a lie," CJ said.

Her eyelids were shut, but even so, she held a look of contentment on her face, and she seemed a touch livelier. And there it was; that tiny hint of a smile. "You haven't much time," she said.

He glanced at the nightstand.

"Not that time," she said, as she gripped her legs and stood. "Your time. You will see the future today."

CJ yawned. "Whaddaya got … another poem for me?" He scratched his head, trying to belittle her presence. "And let's bring the creepy scale down a few notches, capisce?"

The woman turned away and took slow, methodical steps toward the door. With her hands on her hips, she faced the wall and said,

"Today is truly a special day,
it will be like no other.
As you will see so very soon,
you cannot run for cover."

"You blind bitch. I'm over here, and what I'm gonna *see* … is *you*—outta my face." He sat up, eyeballing his tool bag at the foot of the bed. "And speaking of see, keep those nasty eyes closed." He quietly inched toward the Hayson.

She bellowed a sinister laugh and spun around in a time-lapsed twirl, her long hair lingering to catch up with her spin. One hand left her hip to point at the bed, and with her arm extended she twirled her finger in spinning circles, rolling the blankets to the foot of the bed. Then she flicked her wrist and the bedding flew to the window.

She kept her finger pointed at the blankets, using some kind of magical force to hold them against the window.

CJ looked at the blankets, and then faced her. "S'that it?"

She crooked her finger and the bedding slid down the wall. Then she started whispering and chanting, stirring up a breeze.

The woman turned and faced CJ, her eyelids still closed. She put her hands to her thighs and spread her knees, then she slowly leaned forward, creeping her wrinkled eyelids closer to his face. As though a shutter string had been pulled—she opened her eyes and thrust her bony finger at CJ's chest.

CJ dove to the foot of the bed.

The old woman lunged at CJ and landed on his back, sending them both tumbling across the bed and on the floor. CJ threw her aside and crawled to the foot of the bed, where he snatched the Hayson from his bag. He rolled over and took aim. She knocked the Hayson from his hand, slamming it against the wall. She then shriveled and vanished before the Hayson had stopped bouncing.

Still unseen, the old woman screeched out another haunting laugh and filled the air with the gagging stench of dead animal. CJ grabbed a bedsheet from the floor and covered his face, but it was yanked from his hands.

"Go ahead you chicken shit, disappear. That's real brave," said CJ, as he backed into a corner with the Hayson.

A blanket rose from the floor and covered his body, pressing him into the corner like a vacuum-sealed toy. "I don't need to see you," his muffled voice said as he pressed the side-switch.

The Hayson seared through the blanket and shot into the wall, then bounced through the room searching for the semblance.

The sound of a slamming door echoed out loud. The blanket fell to the floor.

CJ came out of the corner with the Hayson at his waist, aimed, ready to fire. The slamming door could have easily been a trick, meant to make him drop his guard. He stepped on the blanket, snuffing the smoldering edges as he scoped out the room.

The phone rang and he ran around the bed to answer it.

"That was your wake-up call," the old woman shrieked through the receiver.

He slammed the phone down and flung his briefcase on the bed, looking for his itinerary.

The crew had a 10:00 A.M. load-in at a club called The Interlude, a venue built in the twenties on the edge of the Savannah River, a place known for strange happenings and rickety equipment, or one causing the other. For whatever reason, The Interlude was high maintenance.

"Oh shit."

He dug through his briefcase for his black pouch full of keys. It wasn't there. He grabbed his cell phone. "Hey, DeBussey? CJ. I need you to look in the key cabinet. Look for a keychain with a boat anchor on it—a red anchor with one key attached. I need you to call me ASAP if you see it, okay? Call me yesterday. It's real important." CJ gripped the phone, about to plead more. He hung up instead.

CJ arrived at The Interlude just before 10:00 A.M.. The faded canopy still hung over the door, as it had for about twenty years, which was about ten years too long from the looks of it. The rest of the neighborhood, however, had drastically changed. The older buildings that once surrounded The Interlude had been demolished. The streets were now lined with barn-like wooden walkways that ran along blue plywood walls.

But the door he needed was in the back of the club; the same door he'd once had keys to. As he turned the corner of the building, a strong river wind slammed against his body. The chatter of screeching seagulls filtered through the rustling breeze as he walked along the outside wall of the club. Closer to the back, he heard waves splashing against the cement barrier that kept the beautiful Savannah River at bay, the same eighteen-foot wall that protected River Street from the elements, year after year. A string of ferryboats had lined up in the water below, ready to pull in and dock. Other boats were departing, filled with tourists.

He beat on the back door with his fist.

There was a loud click and a squeaking sound. A teenage girl peeked through a thin crack in the door.

"Hi." CJ waved his hand, trying to peek through the tiny opening. "I'm working here today."

She opened the door an inch or so.

"I'm a little early, but I was hoping to come in and

get a jump start." CJ could see a vague image of her face as he reached for the papers in his pocket. "Is Manny here?"

"Manny isn't here. I can't let you in."

A blast of river wind came from nowhere and forced the door open. The young girl struggled with the door, screaming "Come back when Manny is here!" before slamming the door in his face.

"Wait! I have keys but I left them at the hotel. Manny gave them to me! I've worked here before." After a pause, he spoke to the door again. "I won't bother you. I won't get in your way."

The door clicked and moved in slightly, giving CJ a chance to continue.

"We have a concert here tonight ... and since I've worked here before, I was hoping I could get a few things done before the crew arrives. Can I please come in?"

"You're not with the press?"

"No, no. I'm a soundman. I work with the band."

She stuck her hand through the thin opening and wiggled her fingers. CJ brushed her hand with his notes. She snatched the papers with one quick move, then slammed the door.

He waited until the deadbolt made the slick-click sound, followed by an inward sway.

"Thanks." He stepped inside.

"I'm not supposed to let anyone in." she said, as she handed back his paperwork. "Don't get me in trouble, all right?"

"No, no. I won't say a word. I promise. Thank you."

CJ was in.

When he turned around to lock the door, she yanked the bag from his shoulder. He caught the strap and spun to face her.

She was gone.

Footsteps scurried nearby, scattering away in the darkness. CJ held his bag tight.

The backstage lights hadn't been turned on yet, so he pulled out his Maglite and shined it around. Memories of past jobs started rushing through his mind. It had been about a year since his last visit, but he knew the layout of The Interlude pretty well.

To the right, through an archway of murky red bricks, was an old plantation-style kitchen, with the green room at the far end. The entry was dark enough to merit motion-detector lights, installed just inside the kitchen.

To the left was a sizeable open area, a designated place to stack empty coffins and trunks during a show. Being right beside the back door, the road crews could load in, and load out, with ease. Since the trucks hadn't arrived yet, that area sat empty behind the huge back wall of the stage.

Straight ahead, a set of half stairs led to a small platform on the side of the stage, kept hidden from the crowd by a massive stage curtain. Band members would linger there, unseen, ready to hit the stage when announced.

From the audience's perspective, the stage was a sixty-foot platform with massive curtains on both sides. From the backstage view, there were stacks of electronics piled on shelves behind the curtains, there were mounds of coiled cables hanging from rods in the walls.

With the stage about five feet above the floor, the area underneath was mostly visible through the steps on the half-stairs. It could have been used for storage, but the space had always been nothing more than a dark and endless pit—dusty and unused, probably because the opening next to the stairs was hardly big enough for a person to pass through, much less any trunks or coffins.

In between the kitchen and the half stairs, a thin hallway led to the showroom some twenty feet away. Built with ancient red bricks, the walls were now smooth to the touch from the decades of wear and tear. The old hallway sat gloomy and uninviting.

With his flashlight to guide the way, CJ went up the half stairs and across the stage, knowing the electrical panel was behind the curtain on the other side of the stage. Then he remembered: the circuit breakers in this place were shabby and worn out to the extent of blowing fuses during shows. In a perfect world the breakers would have been replaced since last year. But he knew most club owners refused expensive repairs, and that forced technicians to jerry-rig the gear. The stages at these arenas needed juice, and plenty of it—every night. And like most of these clubs, The Interlude also needed new breakers to handle the extreme voltage, it needed a hundred new cables in the lighting system, and it needed to have been done long ago.

Given the history of The Interlude, he decided to leave the breakers alone.

He felt a forward shove just then, followed by another yank on his bag, and just as before, he heard footsteps running away.

"Hey. Who's there?" CJ said.

No one answered, but the kitchen light came on.

He went down the half stairs and toward the kitchen when he heard a key slide into the back door lock. The kitchen light went out and the back door flung open, leaving CJ to dodge the swinging door in the dark.

A heavy-set, sluggish man slid a brick across the floor with his foot. He propped the door open and shoved some keys in his pocket. "Hey, CJ! Been a long time, buddy. I thought you was supposed to be here yesterday. Welcome back."

"Manny, you've looked the same for the last fifteen years, do you know that? Or maybe it's been fifteen years since I've seen an Afro like yours. Does Jerry Garcia know he has a clone?"

"Is Jerry Garcia a redneck, like me? How'd ya get in?"

"I kinda snuck in. Somebody must have been taking out the trash. Good to see you, Manny. Place looks the same."

"Yeah … you know my boss ain't gonna spend no money less'n he's gotta."

"Well, that goes for every club in the country. Is anyone else here? I thought I heard someone a minute ago."

"Oh, you did—did'ja?" Manny chuckled. "Well, I done learned not to ask nooo questions ... then I don't get no answers. Always good to have ya here, CJ," said Manny, kicking his foot at the kitchen entrance. The light came on. He grabbed two wires from the baseboard, then lifted them level at his chest. Manny shoved his fists together and the backstage area became bright as day. He turned to CJ and said, "You still chasin' them spirits around?"

"Seen a few odd things, just like you. I'm not chasing any spirits, though."

"Now I'm hearin' you got some kind o' little silver thang."

"What?" '*Holy shit.*' "Where did? Oh ... that." CJ rubbed his chin. "Hey, the women love it."

"C'mon, CJ ... I know you got some kinda weird thing goin' on with them spooks and goblins. That's half the reason I like you bein' here ... 'cause you ain't afraid." Manny shook his head and went up the half stairs, a roll of cable in his hand. "Some o' these other techies, well, they come in here all snooty 'n' shit. But they end up runnin' away like a flea-bitten dawg." Manny tossed the roll of cable on a dowel and came back down the stairs. "Hell ..." he said, pausing on the last step. "One of 'em tore outta here a few months ago, and he ain't been seen since."

"Hate to disappoint you, Manny, but all I have are

tools. Everything looks strange when stage lights are flashing. You know that."

"Okay," said Manny, as he shuffled down the thin hallway. "If you says so."

CJ stood quiet, wondering how Manny could possibly know about the silver thing. He heard the trucks honking outside.

The road crew had arrived. It was time to get to work.

Dean and E had flown into Savannah with the band that morning. Sara had reserved a Cadillac SUV and Dean was behind the wheel, driving the troupe to the hotel.

"Hey Dean," E commented. "Did you see the way the crowd ate it up last night? That show was amazing. I still got it, Dean. In fact, I think it's better than it ever was ... my performance, I mean."

Dean focused on the map.

"I've seen the girl that jumped onstage last night," E went on, "Yeah ... she must be another groupie. God, they're everywhere."

"What bloody bridge?" Dean asked the map.

"Can you hear me, Dean? Don't you think we're gonna make some major money with this tour?"

"I'm sorry, E; I wasn't listening. What did you say?"

E bursted out laughing. "Well, you have a built-in radar, then, because every time you hear the word *money* ... you come to life."

"I was studying the road, E. Would you rather we—"

"Money money money! You heard that, right?"

"E … I'm—" Dean grinned and tossed the map on the seat. "Well, it's a good thing CJ was there to pull that room together. I must say I've never heard of a sound-man repairing pipes before a concert. You have to admit, the boy's got the right stuff."

"Yeah … he's got the stuff all right, but he's weird, Dean, ya know? He has this strange thing about him. Gives me the creeps. But as long as he does the job *and* keeps his pack of freaks under control, I'm cool." E stopped petting his hair and faced Dean. "Hey … we're not paying all those people, are we?"

CJ trailed Manny down the thin hallway. Manny must have taken a turn somewhere in the showroom, so CJ went up the main aisle, passing hundreds of seats on his way to the lobby. Just inside the lounge, he took a left and went upstairs to the crow's-nest.

He ducked his head and entered the sound booth. Unlike others who'd never been there before, he didn't accidentally raise his head once inside. He couldn't. The ceiling was a mere five feet high. CJ plopped his tool bag on the floor and eyeballed the gear. He recognized the dilapidated equipment right away, but even more familiar were the notes he'd taped to certain pieces of gear, in-structions for other techies about which knobs would shock the living bejiggers out of someone.

Then he saw it, the scratched out name on the wall spelling *Zwie*. Only then did he remember her, a ghost that had chosen The Interlude as her eternal hangout. She'd been a real nuisance last time he was here, nothing short of nasty. He couldn't remember why she was so furious, or maybe he never knew to begin with, but all of a sudden he was back on her stomping grounds, her domain, her set of rules.

Or was he?

Maybe he was too inexperienced with ghosts at the time, or maybe Zwie was that talented at haunting, but he never got a clear view of her. She could appear as anyone, or anything, she wanted. She was tricky, but then, he'd learned a lot since last year.

"It was you." CJ rubbed his hand over the carving. "You can tug on my bag all you want, but I'm here for the night. Don't mess with me and I won't mess with you."

Brandon hopped out of the road truck and stretched his legs after pulling an all-nighter. The crew had driven six hundred and fifty miles to arrive on time for the load-in, giving them a luxurious four hours to set up the stage.

The road crew unpacked the sound equipment and stacked the empty coffins behind the giant stage wall. Manny and CJ had rigged the stage with plenty of juice, and in a few short hours the sound check was underway.

Brandon joined CJ in the crow's-nest to set the

sound levels, starting with Mark, who hit the tom and bass drums in a steady, four-count beat. As CJ was mapping the soundboard, he heard a distorted after-tone resonating from somewhere in the showroom. He popped his trouble-shooter CD in the player and went down the stairs.

Brandon followed, staying on CJ's heels like a puppy dog, eager to soak up his knowledge. CJ stopped under a speaker in the showroom. He raised his hand in the air.

"Listen to that, Brandon. Hear that hiss?"

"Umm …" Brandon tilted his head. "No, CJ. Not really."

"Good. There's not one. Just seeing if you were gonna kiss my ass all day." He held out a wrench. "But … we do have to get the vibration outta that puppy over there." CJ pointed to a speaker some fifty feet away. "You wanna get it, or should I?"

Brandon snatched the wrench from CJ's hand. "Another test?"

"No, no. That speaker has a rattle. Either it's touching the wall and vibrating, or some bolts are loose in the mounting. Hear it?"

"No."

CJ dragged an oversized ladder under the speaker. "Take this wrench and go up there. Find out what's loose. If everything seems tight, you might have to wrap some foam around the hardware. Worst-case scenario, you'll have to gasket the bolts in the mounting."

Brandon climbed up the ladder while listening to Patrice O'Neal talk about tits. Only halfway up the ladder he said, "Damn, CJ! You're right! How did you hear that from over there?"

"Just take care of it … okay? We need to get rolling."

The bridge to Hutchinson Island wasn't on the way to downtown Savannah, but Dean had somehow managed to drive over it several times before finding the hotel.

The band dropped off their luggage with the concierge, then went on to The Interlude for the sound check.

Dean and E checked in and went to find their rooms. When the elevator opened on their floor, an old woman with scraggly gray hair was standing at the door, blocking the exit. Dean slid past her first, then E followed and they walked down the hall. She trailed them, staying ten steps behind.

"Don't look now," said Dean, under his breath. "But I think we're being shadowed."

E turned around anyway, stopping on the whim he'd get lucky.

After a few steps, Dean stopped and turned back, too.

"It's one of your groupies, E," Dean chuckled, then squinted his beady eyes and said, "It seems your demographics are expanding, my dear boy. Yes, yes, I'd say you still have it."

E threw his head back and caught up with Dean.

The old woman lingered a few feet behind until E went to unlock his door, then she nudged up against him. "I know a secret," she whispered.

"I know lots of secrets, you muddy old hag." E swiped the card and the door clicked. He reached for the handle and said, "And one of them is ... you're barking up the wrong tree. In fact ..." E faced her. "You ..."

She had vanished.

E looked down the other end of the hall. She hadn't gone that way, either.

"Aww ... man. *Dean*!"

E nudged the door open with his foot and peeked inside—not because of the old woman, but because he'd entered hundreds of hotel rooms, and sometimes he hadn't been invited. Guests could be, and very often were, still lingering in the rooms. Even worse, some hotel employees might be using the empty room as a love nest, and barging in on the bone dance would only embarrass all parties involved.

What E saw in his room did surprise him, though, but in a good way. A beautiful woman in a skin-tight red dress was standing only ten feet away. She had long blonde hair, and she was licking her lips, curling her finger, insinuating E should come closer.

"Never mind, Dean." E walked inside and let the door close behind him.

Brandon repaired the rattling speaker, then wrapped up the sound check with CJ and the band. The vocal check with E could happen anytime, but most likely it would be a while before he showed up. Otherwise, the stage had been prepped and everything was ready for Nathan Juju.

"Brandon!" CJ called out from the back door. "Let's get a slice!"

Brandon hollered from backstage: "Go without me, CJ, I'm gonna hang in the sound booth!"

"Don't change anything, ok? Everything is mapped out, capisce?"

"Yeah, yeah … capisce."

CJ grabbed his tool bag and went out the back door. A white limousine had parked by the curb. The driver stepped out of the limousine and walked toward the back. He opened the passenger door for CJ.

CJ laughed. "Thanks, man, but I don't think that's mine. I'm just going to lunch."

"Are you CJ?" he asked.

"Yeah, but—"

"Allow me," said the driver, motioning CJ inside.

CJ peeked in and saw a blonde-haired woman in a skin-tight red dress.

CJ smiled. "Hi," he said as he got in the limo.

The woman sat quiet while the driver closed the door.

"I guess lunch is on the house?" CJ joked.

She gave CJ a small hint of a smile. "Yes. Lunch is on the house."

CJ recognized the smile right away; the same odd smile as the old woman in his hotel room.

"Dammit!"

He lunged for the door handle, but the limousine power-slammed into reverse and tossed CJ into the seat facing him. The limousine kept racing backward. CJ saw a brick wall through the back window, only ten feet away.

"Holy shit!"

He'd barely covered his head when the limousine busted through the wall, sending bricks tumbling across the roof. The limo then flew through the air and landed trunk first in the Savannah River. After bobbing up and down a few times, the back end of the limousine started sinking.

CJ grabbed the door handle and tugged. It wouldn't open. He yanked harder with no success. He turned to the woman in the red dress. She had vanished.

"Shit—shit! SHIT! Stupid!"

He kicked the window with the back of his heel. The glass wouldn't break, and as the water rose higher, he started losing his footing. He dove under and grabbed his tool bag, hoping the Hayson could break the window. The limo kept sinking, though, and that left him only a small pocket of air when he surfaced at the partition window. Even through the dark windows, he could tell he was surrounded by water, that the limousine had been swallowed by the waterway, that he was being dragged to the bottom of the river.

He slammed the Hayson against the partition window and the glass shattered, but that caused a sudden vacuum and the air pocket was sucked away in a bubbling flash. The limousine started sinking even faster.

E secured a leather band around his ponytail, then went to the sexy woman with open arms. Not missing a beat, he moved in close and slipped his hand to the small of her back, when out of nowhere, a flood of water came blasting down through the ceiling.

E tried to jump away, but he went the wrong way. He slammed straight into the wall. After the surge of water had stopped, he was drenched.

The woman did a slow sashay toward E, taking advantage of his state of shock. She clutched his throat with one hand and grabbed his ponytail with the other, then yanked E's head back with one quick tug, forcing him to look her in the eyes. She squeezed his neck and leaned in close—real close, planting her face only two inches from his. The beautiful woman then opened her mouth and sunk her teeth into his cheek.

E hollered and struggled to break free. He gouged his thumbs in her shoulders, trying to push her away, but she was in control, proving so when she pulled away from his face and opened her bloody mouth, showing E the chunk of flesh on her tongue.

"*Deeean!*" E screamed for his life and gave the woman a sturdy shove. She still had a grip on his hair, though, and her fall pulled him down on top of her. He rolled sideways and spun around on his butt, then he shuffled backward in a panic. When his back hit the closed door, he put his hand to his face to feel the bite mark. He glanced at his hand, and then at the woman.

She was gone.

E flew out of his room. "Dean!" he yelled, running down the hall. "What the hell kinda place is this? *Deeean!*"

Other guests flew out of their rooms to check out the commotion. Dean bolted out of his room, too, and there he saw E, whimpering in the hallway, his hands to his face.

"What the bloody hell is going on, E?" Dean asked, tugging on E's forearms. "Are you okay?"

E was hysterical, his body shaking something fierce. He took deep breaths, then moaned, then shivered, then trembled some more.

Dean grabbed E at the shoulders. "E! Talk to me!"

"How could she bite me in the face?" E cried. "Not the *face*, man ... damn!"

"Ol'right. Ol'right," Dean said. "There's nothing on your face." Dean looked up and down the hall.

The guests had started going back in their rooms.

Dean tried to escort E back into his room. E

squirmed and jerked away. Dean grabbed his shoulders and guided him to his own room, next door.

He sat E on the corner of the bed. "What the hell, mate? You're scaring the shit out of me! What's going on, E? Who were you with?" Dean slapped his hands together and wiped them on his pants. "And why are you all wet?"

E jumped up and ran to the bathroom mirror, where he stroked his cheeks and moved his head in circles, viewing every angle of his face. Then he bolted out of Dean's room and ran next door to his room, stopping at the doorframe, afraid to go inside.

Dean came up behind E and moved him away from the door. He went inside E's room and sloshed around the bed, the desk, and the bathroom. Minus the water on the floor, everything seemed okay.

"E, what the bloody hell is going on? Has this crew lost the plot? I'm bloody miffed with all the water leaks."

E stood motionless in the doorframe, his eyes hazy and glazed over. He looked as though he could pass out any minute.

Dean put his hands to his hips. "This is bloody naff, E! You promised me—*no drugs*. It's in your contract, for fuck's sake!"

Dean stormed past E and went to his room.

A loud slam echoed through the hallway.

Savannah

CJ tried his best to squeeze through the partition window, but the narrow opening had snagged him at his stomach. He kicked and squirmed, running out of air.

'*No way. Not again.*'

"CJ!" someone called out.

CJ spun around, but his head seemed to spin in slow motion, as if the water was sucking him in the direction of the voice.

"Hey … CJ!" he heard once more.

In a split-second flash of light, the mind-bending horror ended. CJ was lying on the floor just inside the back door of The Interlude. Manny was beside him, perched down on one knee, poking CJ in the stomach.

"Hey, buddy," said Manny, hands at his belly, roaring with laughter. "Maaan … you is out there! She plum shook the doo-doo outta you—din't she?"

CJ jumped up and bolted out the back door to see for himself. There was no white limousine, no sexy lady in red, no damaged brick wall—nothing. Everything was gone, except for his anxiety.

CJ had been sliced.

Manny was still laughing when he stood and said, "I thought you's used to that stuff, CJ. Damn, Son ... you been away too long."

CJ got angry with himself for not paying attention, for being stupid enough to think this wouldn't happen again. He may as well have just handed Zwie the opportunity to slice him, on a silver platter, with a *Thank You* card.

But something else was going on here, and that's what really frightened him, and that something was his fear of drowning. It had somehow become known by the spirits. It had to be. The recent string of water episodes was too coincidental. He also knew once a ghost detected a weak spot, it would go in for the kill. He had to keep the fear of drowning out of his head.

"You ain't gonna ketch 'er, CJ. But I ain't seen her around this much in a long while. You piss 'er off?" said Manny, still chuckling as he walked out the back door.

CJ reached in his bag and gripped the Hayson. He wanted to pull it out right there, too angry to be concerned with anything besides capturing Zwie. But he had just played dumb when Manny asked him about the silver thing. He had to eat this one. He had to keep the Hayson hidden, and he had to let Zwie get away ... for now.

Manny stepped back in the club. "What's the name o' your singer, tonight?"

"His name is E. He should be here anytime."

"Looks like he's pullin' up. I see you guys are usin'

limos these days. Well, all right."

CJ peeked out the back door and saw a white limousine parking by the curb. He turned back to Manny, who was standing in front of the kitchen, a few strands of hair sticking straight up above his head.

CJ started losing it, and he knew he had to put Zwie in her place. He pulled the Hayson from his tool bag and aimed it toward Manny.

Manny's hair dropped flat, then Manny said, "I told you!" He rushed over to CJ. "You got a silver thang. Show it to me CJ! C'mon … lemme see it! What is it? Give it here!"

Shooting the Hayson without knowing where Zwie had run off to would be a sloppy move. He knew that. She could be anywhere, and even worse, he could have easily captured Manny by mistake. Once again, he lost his chance to capture Zwie.

"Dammit!"

"I'll show you later, Manny," said CJ, peeking out the back door. He gripped the Hayson. "Right now I need to take care of something."

Manny bolted, saying, "I is not waitin' 'round fer that."

CJ stood patient by the back door of The Interlude, watching from the edge of the doorframe as the driver got out and went to the back of the limo. The driver opened the passenger door and a silky-smooth leg sprung out, followed by another leg, and then both luscious limbs squeezed together as a dainty hand reached for the driver, who helped a woman in a red dress rise from the car.

He watched her walk to a plywood-covered construction site, next door, stepping through a maze of wooden street-guards to get there. The sexy woman seemed out of place next to the piles of supplies, but she maneuvered around them with ease and zigzagged her way deep into the work area.

CJ went out the back door to follow her.

"CJ! You ready for me?" he heard from behind.

'*Shit!*'

E was walking along the outside wall of the club, and he looked like he was in a terrible mood.

"Not much sleep, E?" CJ slipped the Hayson in his bag. "A sexy woman just went inside looking for you. I can wait a few minutes if you want."

"I've had my share of babes today. I don't have time for that shit. And speaking of shit … you look like hell, CJ. Take a bath—will you?" E stopped and sighed, like he almost realized he was being an ass. "Can we just get to me and my vocals? I need some rest."

Dean walked up behind E, lugging CJ's backpack.

E pointed to the limousine and faced Dean. "We're not paying for this, are we?" E stormed inside the club.

"Hey, Dean," CJ said.

"Now then." Dean plopped CJ's bag on the ground.

"You all right?"

"Don't ask."

And CJ didn't. He could tell something was wrong.

This wasn't the same happy Dean he'd last seen in New Orleans. He wasn't sure what had happened, but whatever it was, he had enough to think about. Zwie was all over him and it didn't look like she'd ease up anytime soon.

E ignored the green room and went straight to work, even walked past the mirrors as he bounced up the half stairs and went onstage. He yanked the microphone from the stand and snarled, "Check! *Check*! The mic's not even turned on, CJ! Did you do anything today?"

"Give us a minute, E," said a voice through a stage monitor.

E heard the voice and went to the monitor, staring down at it. "Bob? Bob, is that you?"

"It's Brandon, E. CJ's coming up. We're gonna set your levels."

E looked up toward the crow's-nest and shielded his eyes. "What happened to Bob, anyway? Did anyone hear from Bob?"

"Bob who?" Brandon asked, still speaking through the monitors.

"*Bob Dustin* …" E looked down again, as though a man were hiding in the black speaker. "From the city," E said to the monitor. "He was coming down to check out the show in New Orleans." E threw his hands up. "Why are all of you soundmen so fucking flaky? Can you tell me that … huh? Do you see me acting all weird and shit?

What the fuck is with you soundmen?"

Dean chose to stay outside, to avoid the tension inside. This tour had already begun to rattle his nerves—after only one show, no less. He wasn't used to traveling with the talent, and he had a hard time understanding why artists were such a handful.

Having never been to Savannah, he was leisurely strolling across the asphalt, taking in the salty air on River Street when he approached a cart full of seafood. He cupped his hands behind his back and studied the various sea animals piled in baskets. After another look at the Savannah River, he leaned in close and gave the crabs another glance, intrigued by the tiny air bubbles rising from their mouths. He pointed at the half-live crabs and asked the vendor, "Did you pull these creatures from the river?"

"Caught them just this morning," the vendor answered. "Best on the coast, my dear man. How many would you like? You can eat 'em raw if you want. They're pretty good that way, too."

"I've suddenly lost my desire for seafood." Dean said and turned away from the wagon. That's when he noticed a beautiful woman in a skin-tight red dress. She was standing by a blue wall at the construction site across the street, next door to The Interlude.

"Bloody hell. Miss!" Dean called out. He crossed the street and approached her. "Are you lost? Can I be of assistance?"

She seemed comfortable resting her hand on a stack of boards, twirling her blonde hair with one finger.

"You should be on the cover of a magazine," Dean said. "Not dallying over a construction site." He extended his hand. "Shall we get you out of there?"

"Where are you from?" she asked him. "I don't believe I recognize that accent of yours."

Her Southern drawl pulled Dean in. His beady eyes lit up. "Why ... I'm from London."

"Oh, a Limey. We already have too many of them down here. Y'all should just go on home with the Yankees." She turned and walked away.

"Well bite me raw," Dean mumbled.

Dean watched her enter an area that seemed dangerous, and even though she had just snubbed him, he still felt the need to help her.

"Miss, let me help you. It's not safe over there. Come, now. I insist." Dean approached her again, stopping at the pile of boards and extending his hand once more. "Please ... allow me to help you."

"Well, I suppose even a Limey can pretend to be a gentleman."

Dean guided her through the unstable gravel and piles of wood, releasing her hand only after they'd reached the firm pavement. "Do you need a ride anywhere?"

"I have a ride," she said with a small hint of a smile. "But I suppose one could ask you the same thing."

Dean perked up and tugged on his lapels. "I actually have a bit of free time—if you do. Why don't we grab some lunch and chat for a short spell?"

"I'm sorry, but if anybody found out I had lunch with the likes of a Limey, why … I'd be run outta town." She walked away, but then she stopped and turned her head back toward Dean. She dropped her chin to her shoulder and said, "You are kinda cute, though."

Up in the crow's-nest, CJ and Brandon were setting E's vocal levels when a cell phone with an unfamiliar ringtone resonated through the sound booth. Although somewhat muffled, the song was unmistakable, as "The Boys Are Back in Town", by Thin Lizzy, started a repetitious cycle from inside Brandon's backpack.

"What the…" Brandon muttered, then leaned back and unzipped the side pocket. He felt around for the phone, but he couldn't seem to find it. Brandon rose back up to the soundboard, leaving the side pocket wide open. The phone kept ringing, and with the pocket unzipped, it rang twice as loud.

E heard the ringtone coming through the stage monitors, bleeding through the VOG mic. He grabbed the microphone and shielded his eyes, as if there were any chance in hell he could see the crow's-nest. "Hey, I know that phone. Bob Dustin! You made it, man. I knew you'd show up. Did you see the show last night? Gimme a minute and we'll talk, okay?"

"Could you get that, CJ?" Brandon asked. "I found that phone in the green room last night. It's probably the owner calling. I forgot to turn it in before we left New Orleans."

CJ grabbed Bob's phone and turned it off. He tossed it back in Brandon's bag and zipped the side pocket. "Later, Brandon, let's take care of E. The more we make him happy, the more he can talk down to us."

"C'mon, CJ!" E shouted into the microphone. "Give me what we had last night. That was some great sound. If you can do it once, you can do it every night—if you try. Bob can tell you what you're missing, okay?"

Brandon put his mouth to the VOG mic, then said, "There's no Bob up here. Only Brandon and CJ."

"Can we just finish this fucking sound check? *Thank you!*"

E's comment seemed to take Brandon over the edge, but it wasn't just E; it was the broken down sound booth, it was the strange happenings, it was not having a grasp on sound design—even though he considered himself a proficient soundman. But more than anything else, it was being second in command. He clutched his hands behind his head and sat back, putting up a wall.

CJ could tell Brandon needed a few minutes to himself. Since CJ did, too, the timing was perfect.

CJ made a few adjustments to the sound system, such as manipulating the power distribution, and redirecting sub-channels to allow for the damaged elements in the gear. As soon as the soundboard was back on track, CJ said, "Hey, Brandon. I'm gonna get a drink of water. Stay in the crow's-nest and keep your eye on E, okay?"

Squatting behind Brandon's chair, CJ removed the Hayson from the backpack Dean had just delivered. He had the cylinder in his hand when Brandon asked, "So why is this sound booth called a crow's *nest*? I mean, what the fuck is that about?"

"That's because ..." said CJ—his eyes locked on Brandon. "It sits so high in the sky, that it resembles a crow's nest on a ship." He slowly unzipped one corner of his tool bag, careful not to draw attention. "Just a nick-name." He said as he slipped the second Hayson in his tool bag. "I'll be right back."

CJ zipped his bag and stood—ready for any trick Zwie had up her sleeve, armed with two Haysons now, instead of only one.

The last thing CJ wanted to hear was more of E's bitching, so he bypassed the stage and went out the front door, then he walked along the outside wall of the ware-house-sized club. When he came around the corner, he saw Dean talking to the blonde in the red dress. Both were standing beside a white limousine.

Dean raised his foot to step in the limo.

"Dean! Stop!" CJ shouted.

Dean turned to see CJ running toward him. He stood waiting, one foot resting on the floorboard of the limo.

CJ kept his eyes planted on the woman. "Zwie! You need to back off!" he said, shaking his tool bag, referencing what was inside.

Zwie threw her odd smile at CJ and laughed.

Dean rubbed his forehead. "I presume you two know each other?"

CJ stared at Zwie. "I need to speak with her alone, Dean. Could we have a minute?"

Zwie pinched Dean on the cheek. "Seems you gentlemen have some business to discuss. I guess we'll have that lunch some other time."

Dean backed away and Zwie slipped inside the limo.

As the driver closed the door behind Zwie, Dean turned to CJ. "What's the deal, mate? Aren't I allowed any free time?"

"Dean, you don't know her. She's bad news. Getting in that car would have been the worst thing you've ever done."

"We were simply going to lunch." Dean glared at the black window while the driver got behind the wheel. "I take it you two have a history."

The limo slowly pulled away.

"Trust me, Dean. It's not what you think; besides, E was calling for you inside."

"Bloody hell! What now?" Dean stormed in the club.

CJ bolted after the limo and caught up to the driver's window. He pounded on the glass, yelling for the driver to stop. The limo kept moving. He grabbed the passenger door handle and flung it open, then ran alongside the limo while he pulled a Hayson from his bag. As soon as he aimed the cylinder inside the limo, it stopped. CJ slammed into the open door. Before CJ could fall, the limousine screeched into reverse and the door whacked CJ again, this time knocking him to the ground.

The limousine backed up far enough to smash into the cart full of seafood. Fish, and ice, and broken crates tumbled across the trunk. Baskets of crabs poured onto the street.

CJ rolled across the pavement and came to rest on his stomach. He gripped the Hayson and crawled to his tool bag, and he'd barely had it by the strap when some-one stepped on his hand, then someone grabbed his hair and shoved his face into the street. He tried to get up, but a foot stomped his spine and pushed him back down. He hugged the cylinder to his chest and struggled, trying to break free.

"Get offa' me!" CJ yelled, flinging his arm behind his back, trying to strike his opponent. At the same time, an arm was reaching under his chest, trying to take the Hayson. Then he felt the amulet press against his throat as the string was pulled from behind. It only took a few tries to realize he couldn't reach behind, so he rocked his body back and forth, trying to roll over.

A rock-solid thump hit his head, though, pressing him to the pavement. Someone started jumping on his back with even more fury, bouncing the wind from his lungs, scoring the Hayson into his chest.

As if it couldn't get worse, he heard laughing, a big-winded snarl that sounded happy about causing him pain.

He turned his head just enough to see Zwie as her

true self. No fleeting fly-by's, no glowing eyes from a dark corner, just Zwie—a mean and mighty black woman weighing in around two hundred fifty pounds. She was mad, and she wanted the Hayson.

Should Eartha Kitt ever speak with a demonic twist, Zwie nailed it. Her incantation was downright creepy, and with an undertone that made his skin crawl she said, "It doesssn't belong to you. I will take it to themmm and trade yourrrr life … for miiine."

"Not a chance in hell, Zwie," said CJ—his cheek mashed to the pavement. "You won't get the—"

"*Today you die!*" Zwie shouted, then grabbed CJ by the heels and drug him to the back of the limousine, and there she handled him like a rag doll. She seized a fistful of CJ's hair and thrust his head into the rear bumper. Then she straddled his neck and pinned his face behind the exhaust pipe.

Twenty men couldn't break her grip, much less one CJ. She was much tougher and her moves came too fast. Sheer strength on her part kept him from moving a muscle. Exhaust from the tailpipe began to burn, first his eyes, then his nose. He squeezed his eyes and puffed his cheeks, holding his breath.

Zwie roared with laughter as she bent over and snapped the amulet from CJ's neck, but her smile became a scowl when she saw his ballooned cheeks. Her sledgehammer fist came down on his back, forcing him to gasp for air. As she repositioned her grip, he broke away.

CJ spun around and slammed her in the head with the cylinder. Zwie took a few lopsided steps and waggled her head, then she rocked back and forth and dropped the amulet.

CJ scooped the amulet from the pavement and shoved it in his pocket.

He aimed the Hayson and fired, but his eyes were like waterfalls and his aim was off center. The blue lights seized a basket of crabs. Through one twitching eye, he saw he couldn't have captured Zwie, because she was running toward the back door of The Interlude. He pressed the opposite side-switch—to stop the Hayson— but he hadn't given the lights much time to withdraw. The web drew inward only briefly, before flying out again, but this time ... his aim was dead on.

The blue lights caught up with Zwie and sent her tumbling across the pavement, along with a dozen or so crabs still trapped in the web.

Zwie became violent, kicking and punching, whacking the crustaceans and scratching at the blue web. Waning images of the muddy old woman, and the sexy babe in the red dress, and even a few other characters appeared until the blue lights started retracting, pulling Zwie and all her buddies into the Hayson. With the sun glistening off the lights, the flash of the spectacle was tenfold its normal brightness.

The vendor had been under his truck when Zwie was

captured, rushing to catch his scattering crabs before any could plunge back in the river. Even though he'd witnessed the entire battle from the beginning, he hadn't seen the blue lights attack Zwie, and he wasn't aware of the spectacular, blinding flash that confiscated a portion of his inventory.

He finally stood and tossed a few crabs in the bed of his truck, then he wiped his hands across his jeans. With the tip of his foot, he sifted through the broken crates on the street, searching for salvageable goods. That's when he saw CJ crouched on the pavement with his head hung low.

The vendor ran to CJ and said, "I think she's gone. Are you okay?"

CJ raised his head.

The vendor took a step back. Maybe it was the stream of blood running down CJ's forehead that startled him, or the pebbles embedded in CJ's cheeks. It could have been the half-circled slash on his face—starting on the side of his nose and curving down through both lips. Between the oozing tears and the blood on the bridge of his nose, CJ couldn't seem to stop blinking from an apparently painful sting.

"Oh wow ... that's bad," said the vendor. He leaned close to CJ. "Damn, dude ... what did you do to her?" The man squat down and took CJ by the arm. "Let's get you to a doctor." As they stood, CJ flinched and bent over again, tucking the Hayson under one arm. His hands went to his knees.

"My bag," CJ said, catching his breath. "Where—"

The vendor raised his head and looked around. "It's by the railing. I guess you need it, huh?" He patted CJ on the back and said, "I must be a nut-job magnet, I swear." He rambled over his shoulder as he went to the bag, saying, "I know you're in pain, but your little spat cost me a lot of money. I need you to pay me—for wrecking my shit." He scooped up the bag. "Sorry for the double whammy, but you …"

The white limousine was crawling toward CJ, only a foot away from his butt. The vendor dropped the bag and waved his arms in the air. "Hey, man! Move! Jump this way! Now!"

The limo screeched its tires and sped forward. CJ rolled onto the hood, then up against the windshield. The limousine raced to the wooden guardrail and busted through the railing. CJ flew through the air and the limo plunged down to the river.

Landing seemed to take forever, but CJ finally hit the water. The Hayson went hurling through the air and plopped into the river with a tiny splash. With Zwie still trapped inside, the Hayson started sinking to the bottom of the Savannah River.

This time the vendor saw it all from six feet away. As soon as CJ hit the water, he called 9-1-1.

CJ's body stiffened, and he began to aimlessly bob up and down. Blood from his wounds soon mixed with the sizzling air bubbles, creating a light brown hue on the surface of the water. Just before he went unconscious, a small boat pulled up next to him. Waves splashed him in the face, and before he knew it, somebody had grabbed him by his underarms. CJ was yanked into the tiny boat and it sped away.

"Brandon here."

"Hey, Brandon. My name is DeBussey. I work with CJ in New York. I'm sorry to call you, but he's not answering his phone. I need to get in touch with him. Have you seen him, or can you get a message to him?"

"He's here somewhere. I'm up in the crow's-nest wrapping up a sound check. Can you call back in a few minutes?"

"Just tell him there's no red anchor, and no black pouch. I'm sure about that. I looked everywhere this morning."

"There's a what ... where?"

"He'll know what I'm talking about. Just tell him, okay? And tell him Chris quit his job at the Dark Star. Since I'm already covering for CJ, I need someone to cover for me, cause now I gotta cover for Chris. Or someone else can cover for Chris while I cover for CJ."

"Yeah ... I'll get him to call you."

"I'm starting to wonder what he got me involved in," DeBussey said.

Brandon peered out across the empty arena. "You and me both."

Mr. 5008

Dean hauled treacherous E back to the hotel after sound check. The road crew followed, except for Brandon, who chose to stay and prep the stage for the opening act.

A band called The Blue Collies was scheduled to open for Nathan Juju that night in Savannah. They'd had a small amount of radio exposure with a few catchy tunes, and seemed to be on their way to a great career. Their promo-package plugged them as a straight-ahead, British rock-n-roll band. Brandon was eager to run their sound.

While he made adjustments to the stage, he began to think about the next three months, about the rest of the tour. It seemed he was low man on the totem pole when CJ was around. He pondered over how to change that, maybe even swap positions with CJ. There was no shortage of tricks up his sleeve, and he would no doubt pull a rabbit out of his hat at some point. Things would be smoother if he were in charge. He knew so, but the truth was he needed CJ to keep things neutral with E, or at least keep E off his back while he figured out a plan.

Now that the stage was ready for the Blue Collies, Brandon decided to look for CJ. He went out the back door of the club, and there he saw a street vendor tossing mangled baskets in the bed of a truck. CJ's tool bag was sitting by a busted guardrail across the street. He went to the bag and picked it up, only then catching eye of the skid marks on the pavement, noticing they went the wrong way—across the flow of traffic—and how the tire marks disappeared at the edge of River Street where a guardrail once stood. Brandon crept to the wall and leaned over the edge for a peek down below. All he could see was a peaceful river.

"Hey," Brandon called out to the vendor. "Have you seen the guy that goes with this?" He raised CJ's bag in the air. "Taller than me, brown hair; jeans and boots?"

"If you mean the asshole that wrecked my cart ... then yeah ... I saw him."

"Okay, then ..." Brandon let the bag drop. "Did you see where the asshole went?"

"He was thrown in the river," said the vendor, flinging debris in the back of his truck. "Then some boat picked him up. I guess he's at the hospital."

Brandon gyrated his jaw, then said, "Ex ... excuse me?"

The vendor stopped tossing boards and faced Brandon. "Well, first, he had a fight with some lady out here, I guess it was his girlfriend. She pretty much kicked his ass. Then this limousine just pushed him into the river." He flung a basket over his shoulder. "They destroyed my cart and disappeared. Thank them for me ... will ya?"

Brandon pointed down to the river. "He went ... in *there?*"

"Yep, you missed it all by about two seconds. He just flew into the river. Him first, then the limo. It was something right out of a movie, man, I'm tellin' ya."

Brandon stayed quiet, trying to wrap his brain around this story as he went closer to the vendor.

"I called the police," the vendor went on, "but when I looked down to see if the guy was okay, I saw a boat pull up and snatch him out of the water. Look ..." He stopped and faced Brandon again. "... I did all I could do to help the poor guy before he went into the river. When I saw the boat, I figured he'd been rescued." The vendor raised the tailgate and slammed it shut. "If you go to the marina, you can probably find out who the guys in the boat were. They were wearing suits—dark suits and hats ... which seems a little outta place, come to think of it. Heh, they looked like men who'd be dropping somebody *in* the river ... not taking somebody out."

"What did the boat look like?"

The vendor snarled, "It was a *boat*, man ... a small dinghy! It wasn't a police boat or a rescue team; it was a plain little boat. You want the driver's name, too?"

As farfetched as this story seemed, Brandon still became alarmed. He stared at CJ's bag before squatting down and digging through it. Inside were copies of *Wired* magazine and several CDs, along with a cell phone, a few tools, a 3-PIN lighting cord, and one shiny, gleaming, silver cylinder.

Brandon froze when he saw the cylinder, spellbound by its brilliant shine. He pulled the silver object from the bag, then held it to his face as he went back in the club with CJ's bag.

"Hey, Jonan. It's Cavanaugh. I'm driving as we speak. Just a few hours away."

"Good man. Good man. Now listen to me—listen good. Dean ain't no rookie. You're gonna have to get around him. He's not gonna want you hangin' around his crew, especially since you stole money from him."

"You are too much, Jonan. I tell you the truth and you diss me anyway. You're a piece of work. A real—"

"*Watch it*, Cav. Unless you wanna sell ties for Raphy Loran, your employment options are limited. Now listen to me. You got a camera, right? I mean a good one, not some pocket piece of shit—right?"

Cavanaugh hit the steering wheel. "You should 'a told me to bring a camera, Jonan. No … I don't have a camera."

"Get one."

"What's so special about this band? You got me on some 007 mission … driving across country … chasing some tech geek. I don't get it."

"It ain't for you to get. But if you must know, I want his gimmick. I saw what he does with a stage show, and it's hot. I mean … this is a new era, Cav. A whole new dimension. With my money, and *brains* mind you, we can triple the action and slap this gimmick on every band we own. We'll make zillions—but even better—we'll leave Dean and his group of B flats in the dust, you got me? That's why this band is so special. Cause they have something I don't, and believe you me—on my sweet mother's grave, nobody outdoes me, you got me? *Nobody*."

Manny was backstage rolling cables when Brandon walked through the back door with a silver cylinder close to his face. Manny tossed the wires on the floor and went to Brandon.

"You got one, too? Damn if everybody ain't got one 'a them but me."

"What is it, Manny?"

"You don't know?" Manny stood quiet for a beat, then he scratched his head and confessed, "well … I don't know, either." He noticed Brandon's fascination with the shiny object and jealousy reared its ugly head. He made a fast nip at the cylinder. "Lemme have it!"

Brandon pulled the cylinder to his stomach and spun away. Manny reached around Brandon several times, trying his best to grab the cylinder. The struggling started at the back door, but they'd soon wrestled their way to the half stairs.

Brandon noticed someone from the corner of his eye. He stopped struggling and said, "Ma-Manny."

Manny tugged a few more times with no luck. He looked at Brandon's face, then in the direction Brandon was staring. Then he, too, froze.

There was a woman standing next to the railing, just in front of the thin hallway. She stood about four feet tall, chalky white from head to toe, wearing a wide, puffy dress that covered her feet and scraped the floor. Her hair was hidden under a small bonnet, neatly tied under her chin, and she had a ruffled apron wrapped around the front of her big, flowing dress. The little woman looked like she had just climbed off the Mayflower.

"Fuck me runnin' up a tree ..." Manny whispered.

The woman took a step forward. They took a step back. She noticed their fear, but didn't seem to understand why they were frightened. She placed her hands on her stomach and intertwined her fingers, then she tilted her head and gave them a warm smile.

Brandon and Manny lost it. They bounced off each other, scattering to get away. Manny shoved Brandon to the ground and ran out the back door. Brandon bolted for the space underneath the stage, but he wasn't watching too closely. He whacked his head on the platform and fell to the ground. Before he could feel the pain, he scratched his way under the stage and hid under the half stairs.

The woman went to the back door and stopped, as though she were taking in a long overdue, outside view. After an eyeful, she turned around and faced Brandon. But she was interested in someone above Brandon, as in high in the catwalks above Brandon. She waved gestures to someone, suggesting they come to her.

A cloud of white haze appeared next to her, and within a few seconds the haze had transformed into the shape of a man—an older man, wearing white overalls and sporting a long white beard.

A man in a Confederate soldier uniform came out of nowhere and walked right by Brandon, leaving the darkness under the stage behind as he strolled to the back door.

A small boy in knickers emerged on the platform behind the stage curtain. He hopped down the half stairs on both feet, one step at a time, and then ran to the others at the door. No more than a few feet tall, he took hold of the soldier's hand, then looked back and forth at the older ghosts, as if he were waiting for directions from the grown-ups.

An older lady in a sundress and slippers stepped out of the kitchen just then. She wore a bandana with twisted knots above her forehead. She seemed cheery standing in front of the kitchen, greeting semblances as they walked by, drying her hands on a towel that hung from her dress pocket.

Brandon stayed hidden under the stairs, watching from in-between the steps. Parts of his body started twitching. He stayed quiet, hoping the spirits would soon be gone. The semblance activity did anything but slow down, though, as one ghost after the other kept appearing. Within a few minutes, ten or so spirits had strolled toward the back door. Strangely enough, the apparitions stood motionless when they left the building, hesitant to go any farther. The group of ghosts stood just outside the back door, staring at the river.

The sun was on the way down, and the river mist had begun to float above the surface of the water, yet the vapor seemed to be alive tonight. Instead of peacefully floating in the air, the mist seemed to roll up the river wall and slither across River Street. As the mist came closer to The Interlude, the see-through, smoky fog pushed against the back door, sending small billows of mist inside the club.

One particular section of the mist began to swirl around at the back door, flowing in a peculiar, ethereal way, spinning and twisting in front of the ghosts until it became a lingering mass of much thicker fog.

Brandon thumped his palm to his forehead again and again, trying to correct his vision. But then a milky-white figure began to surface within the swirling mist, slowly transforming into an oversized frog ... only five feet away from the group of ghosts. The frog was three feet tall sitting flat on its stomach, with eyes the size of coffee cups on a face the size of a tire. The semi-transparent frog then wobbled to the ghosts and stopped.

Like passengers at a bus stop, the ghosts bundled together, taking baby steps toward the frog so they could reach out and touch its head. The pack of phantoms thinned as the last few spirits touched the frog and vanished.

The frog turned and hobbled its way back across

River Street, where it eased over the wall with one quick roll, and suddenly the frog was gone, as were all the ghosts from the club.

Brandon had no doubt he'd taken a good blow to the noggin. He muttered as he staggered to the back door, leaning against the door after it had been shut.

The light in the kitchen came on and an outlined shadow of Brandon's head appeared on the back door.

Afraid to turn around, Brandon stood facing the door, holding his breath.

"Is she gone?" someone asked from behind.

Brandon spun around to see a man in the entrance of the kitchen, a sharp dressed man, wearing a classic, pin-striped suit. His hat resembled something from the Humphrey Bogart era. The man stepped out of the kitchen.

Brandon yanked the door open too fast. It whacked him in the head and bounced closed again. He spun around and backed up against the door.

The mobster-looking man went to Brandon and said, "Listen here ... is she gone?"

Brandon hooked one arm around his face and tried to slide down the door, but the strange man grabbed his elbow and kept him standing. Brandon flopped around like a cat on a leash, trying to break free while the man drug him in the kitchen and shoved him against the sink.

"Now listen here ... I'm asking you, is she gone?"

Brandon stopped struggling, somewhat, one arm still curled around his face. The man eyeballed the kitchen and sniffed the air a few times before finally loosening his grip.

"I don't feel her," he said. "I think she *is* gone."

"Wh-who?" Brandon stuttered, taking quick peeks at the man.

"The mean one … the Dame who runs this joint," he said. "She's been keeping us here for a long time." He faced Brandon. "Where's the rest of your pals?"

Brandon could only stare back.

"I saw them talking to her. They looked like me, but them guys didn't look so nice. All black. No sense of style, I'll tell you that much. Where'd they go?"

Brandon's face twitched.

He looked Brandon up and down. "I get it. Mama's boy—eh?" The man put his finger to his lips. "Shh …" He took off his hat and slowly poked his head out of the kitchen. "Lo and behold …" he turned back to Brandon. "I think the Dame is gone." He tucked in his shirt and pranced out of the kitchen.

Dean sat at the desk in his hotel room, huddled over a laptop. His thoughts were a bit scattered as he scrolled through the plethora of incoming emails, most of which he forwarded to Sara. From the coat rack across the room his phone chimed a Caribbean jingle. Dean marched to his jacket and pulled a bottle of pills from the inside pocket, pressing the lid to his palm as he went to the mini bar. He placed a small bottle of whiskey on the desk, then shook the pill bottle, dropping one of mother's little helpers in the palm of his hand. The phone rang and he put the pill by the whiskey, the phone to his ear.

"New Orleans is reconciled, Dean. You came out on top. Did the additional merchandise arrive in Savannah?"

"I bloody hope so. We certainly paid enough for handling. I'll pop in early and have a look-see." Dean scribbled something down. "How are the numbers for … well bloody hell, Sara. Tell me where we're appearing next, will you?"

"Next stop is Charleston, South Carolina."

"Ah, yes …"

"We have nineteen radio spots scheduled day of. Print's been running for ten days, and E has two interviews lined up, both radio. One of them is a double hit; we're doing a live broadcast in Charleston, for Richmond. It's a sister station."

"Excellent. Two birds, one stone. What are the numbers, Sara?"

"I won't get an update until midnight, but yesterday's report showed a definite increase."

"And tonight, here in Savannah? Are we flush?"

"You have definitely met the contract. We've sold twenty-three eighty-one, and you were required to sell …" Sara paused, quietly reading. "Twenty-two hundred. You're good."

"Splendid. Back to Charleston. Shall we beef up the press?"

"Let's wait for an update, Dean. Whatever you did in

New Orleans, you did it well."

"That may be, but this midnight report may not be so appealing," said Dean, rolling the pill in his fingers. "I don't enjoy gambling with numbers."

"As a matter of fact, ticket sales in other cities have almost doubled in the last few days. Did you read the New Orleans review?"

Dean glanced at his desk where the newspaper sat folded. "It was bloody brilliant. E seemed pleased and I received several messages from the press. I've sent them your way. Did you get them?"

"Got 'em. We couldn't buy advertising this good. A few more reviews like this and the press will start selling tickets for us. Tell me … did CJ have something to do with that? I'm hearing he has some kind of device, or gimmick, like hologram lights or … all I have are second hand reports and they seem, well …"

"It's a combination of all players, Sara. It's certainly unusual, but it's going quite well, and I want mileage from the reviews. I'll leave that in your hands. Now back to Charleston." Dean tossed the pill in his mouth and threw his head back, draining the bottle of whiskey.

"We still have three days on ticket sales, and that includes a night off in Charleston. Actually," Sara corrected herself, "you're going to Hilton Head to put your feet up."

"Why a night off so soon? We're just getting rolling."

"The only contract available was Columbus and the

numbers didn't pan out. It's cheaper to stop for one night."

"I suppose one night may be good for E." Dean pitched the mini bottle in the trash and wiped his lips. "He's a bit rattled, that one."

"How about CJ?" Sara asked again. "Personally, I mean. Anything out of the norm going on?"

"Odd you should ask, Sara."

"Because," Sara cut in, "E called and said he had some issues with CJ, but something tells me E has issues with everyone. Or … maybe the light show got more press than he did, and it didn't rub too well. He says CJ brought his family with him. Who are they? Have you met them? Is something unusual going on?"

"As a matter of fact, yes, which reminds me; review the contract, will you? We may need to bully up on security. Find out who pays for that, and where."

"Will do," Sara said, "Good to hear CJ's working out."

"Yes, he seems quite dependable, though somewhat capricious, that one. A bit headstrong as well, but the boy knows his wires. I can assure you of that. So I must pick my battles … and if the light show is our wooden spoon, then let us stir the stew."

"Keep it up, guys. The press is on fire."

"Then you … must carry gasoline."

"Night, Dean."

The Blue Collies arrived at The Interlude, instruments in hand, ready to go. They were held up outside, though, as was everyone else. The police had blocked the back door. No one was allowed inside, until they'd answered a few questions outside. As the vendor drove away with his truckload of damaged goods, a team of scuba divers was suiting up to search the river.

The ghost tipped his hat and winked at Brandon. "Well, I guess I'm 5008," he said, kicking into a spinning dance backstage. He smiled and laughed out loud, shouting, "I'm a singer!" The gangster-looking ghost dashed up the half stairs and ran across the stage, where he held his arms out and took a big breath of air.

Eager to entertain, he held the microphone stand at his waist—Bon Jovi style—then he shimmied across the stage flaunting some Chuck Berry footwork. He kicked in to a twirling waltz and held the mic stand upright, as if it were a beautiful lady, even caressing her imaginary hair. After a few minutes of circling and twirling across the stage, he spun toward Brandon and stopped. He put his hat to his chest and bowed his head, saying, "That's *Mister* ... 5008, to you."

Mr. 5008 seemed to be right at home, humming in the same manner as a Tommy Dorsey band member would have done, keeping it bouncy and fun. He placed the mic stand in the middle of the stage, snapping his fingers and swaying his shoulders. Once he'd established a beat of his own, he started singing to the empty show-room.

"Who's that,
knocking on the back door?
What's it for?
No more.
No more.
I see a small boat,
lying on the river floor.
Won't float,
no more.
No more.

Another sad tale.
The story isn't very kind.
Left behind,
with no sunshine in your sail.
Used to be we never failed.
Do you think that you can summon me,
to come back,
come back?
I'm looking deep inside.
Come back,
Come back.
Give me a reason why."

Brandon stood motionless backstage, better yet, in a state of shock. The more he watched Mr. 5008, the more he resisted, telling his eyes and ears not to accept what he was seeing and hearing.

Had he bumped his head that hard? Why couldn't he wake from this dream? He struggled to find a sense of balance, to feel the ground below his feet as he walked through the thin hallway and into the showroom.

His footsteps were slow and cautious as he went up the seating aisle. He kept his head down, afraid to look at the empty seats, afraid of facing the stage, terrified he wouldn't make it to the lobby. He'd only got fifteen feet up the aisle when he heard, "Hey, you! I'm over here!"

Every muscle in Brandon's body twitched. He spun his head around in slow motion.

Mr. 5008 was prancing around onstage, tipping his hat to the empty seats and smiling from ear to ear. "Looks like you got your wish," Mr. 5008 hollered out.

Brandon tried to speak, but hardly a stutter came from his lips.

"*In charge*, boy. You're in charge now," Mr. 5008 told him. "Ain't that what you wanted?" The ghost shimmied his way to the microphone, where he once again embraced his re-claimed desire for the stage.

As Brandon watched the ghost command the stage, he realized everything he'd ever known about spirits could fit in a single sheet of paper, and that sheet of paper had just gone up in a blaze, taking his world of reality with it.

He knew when he took this job he'd be leaving his safety zone; that he'd have to walk the wire without a net, but he had no idea he'd be faced with something that would obliterate his senses in a matter of minutes, something that could wipe the slate clean of any preconceived notion that spirits were no more than a bump in the night, or rumors of some dead Sea Captain that frequented a foggy lighthouse.

He also found it strange that within a few hours, and without lifting a finger, he'd suddenly moved up in the ranks. Was this another trick?

"It's just you and me now, kid," said Mr. 5008.

Brandon stared at the ghost.

"Say … I'm real sorry for your bad luck, but don't look so sad. You're gonna like it here … now that the Dame's gone, that is. We can sing all we want."

Brandon turned to leave, but his muscles seemed frozen. He felt himself pushing and straining with everything he had, trying to move away. His feet wouldn't budge.

Mr. 5008 bursted out laughing, tilting his head back as he pointed at Brandon. He put his hands to his hips and said, "Well don't just stand there. I'm ready to sing! What time do I go on?"

to be continued …

Acknowledgements

Special thanks to:

Adrienne Cazier / Alison Lynch
Anita Haddad
Dr. B's Academy
James Harris / Jennifer Sims
Jeanne Washington
Jeffrey Banks
Jheri Miller / Jim Kennedy
Joseph Dino Galindez
John David Kudrick
Judith Fourzan Rice
Julie Alexander / Marina Corbi
Michael Palitz
Peter Jones / Michelle L. Slaton
Randy Hall
Ricardo Fernandez
Sherry Mazzocchi / Stephen Moramarco
Sara McCaslin / Travis Segretto
Ted Stafford

Very Special Thanks to Tim Thompson,
Co-writer of lyrics to "Quitman Highway"

Cover art: Josefhanus /Hypermania37 /CIC Publishing

Photography: Mona Zubair

About the Author

Originally from the Southwest, Johnny graduated with honors in orchestra throughout grade school and high school, winning state competitions in both Violin & Cello. After high school he went on the road as a hired musician, performing five to six nights per week, year-round. After basing himself in New York City in the late eighties, he worked as a professional sound designer in the live music scene and theater community, while traveling abroad with various artists and sound design projects.

Johnny studied music with the *French Conservatory of Music* at Carnegie Hall and performed throughout various studios in the building, raising money for children to receive musical training.

He has written songs for himself and others for twenty-five years, racking up two *Billboard Song Writing Citations* from a CD he produced in the early nineties. He spent two years working on the Media Services team with *Ralph Lauren,* where the team designed the music and sound production for the seasonal, runway shows, held at the world headquarters on Madison Avenue. As an author, Johnny has had short stories, reviews, and articles published in various books and magazines around the globe. He currently resides in New York City where he enjoys the arts, music, outdoor activities, animals, and writing about everything related. Johnny currently pens EKKO Mysteries from his home in NYC.

What people are saying...

EKKO—Book I: White Limousine

"Johnny Walker's new book, *EKKO*, is a journey into the spiritual world using a mysterious device that CJ really doesn't really understand but has, by trial and error, learned to use. These excursions are not without danger, or suspense, as CJ discovers. The spirits CJ meets are interesting characters to say the least, but the most intriguing is the hauntingly beautiful Clarise. *EKKO* is a departure from the usual as far as sci-fi goes, and Walker's mixing of two worlds, the now and the past, is flawlessly done. Great reading. Sci-fi fans will love *EKKO*."

—Ron Watson, Editor2 New Book Reviews

"WOW!!!! I got the book and read every page of it on the beach in one weekend, and I loved it. I need another one, or at least a real quick short story. I gotta know what happened to CJ. By far one of the best books I've ever read! BRAVO!!!"

—R. Coates, Reader from Columbia, MS

"There is so much atmosphere and description. It's so fully realized, man. When the Savannah ghosts come together, it felt like Spielberg. This is such a friggin' smash, man. I haven't been so awed in years by fiction ... or is it? Brav-fuckin'-o."

—J. Kennedy, Reader from New York City

"Johnny Walker has written a fun novel in an episodic style similar to that of Patricia Highsmith. The narrative is linear, following the adventures of roguish protagonist CJ and his encounters with the supernatural. The story has the cliffhanger feeling of an old television serial with a modern approach to the subject matter. This is a great start to a series, which should prove to be very entertaining. An accessible novel for readers who enjoy Orson Scott Card, Anne Rice, and Christopher Moore."

—D. Craven, Reader from Atlanta, GA

"Loved this book from start to finish. It's a long time since I read a ghost story book, and this was brill better than expectations. CJ is a character, and the ghosts he meets are really interesting. Cannot wait to find out how CJ gets on and what's happened to him."

S. Murray, Reader from Dumfriesshire, Great Britain

The EKKO Trilogy

Book I:

White Limousine

Book II:

Black Coffee

Book III:

Blue Violin

Music by Nathan Juju

www.NathanJuju.com

For information on books and music, please visit:

www.EkkoMysteries.com

Books and Music Published by CIC Publishing. NY, NY.

www.CICPublishing.com

Excerpt beginning of Book II:

EKKO

Black Coffee

After thirty years of promoting rock concerts, Dean proved he still had it when it came to making decisions. By hiring CJ, he'd secured one of the top soundmen in the country for his latest tour, and despite the unusual light show, or holograms, or whatever they were, last night's show had been a hit. The arena in New Orleans was close to full, and every piece of merchandise had been swapped for cash, notably good news for a band like Nathan Juju who hadn't toured in a while.

Even better, the press junkies were calling. They'd left messages requesting interviews, wanting to know more about the holograms, asking the name of the movie CJ had projected across the stage.

Dean couldn't think of a better way to launch a tour, except, he was just as mystified.

The stage show in New Orleans was nothing short of mind-blowing, fantastical, out of this world, but rumors of witchcraft had already gone full circle with the band

and crew, then they were passed on to Dean. The subject of strange lights was tapping on his brain, crying for attention. Dean fought it. As the backbone of the tour he saw no reason to question CJ's behind-the-scenes activity, and he'd invested too much money to get involved with hearsay and speculations. That was a recipe for disaster. Plain and simple.

And yet, there could be no mistaking the signs.

Dean had never traveled alongside the talent before—never experienced the nitty-gritty of touring, nor the logistics of how it all came down. The road turned out to be quite different than flying across the pond every few days. In less than a week, he'd been presented with enough road sagas to last a lifetime. Maybe it was a sign of the times changing before his very eyes. Maybe it was the result of a particularly great band, exceeding the boundaries of normalcy. Maybe it was hogwash and he needed to crack the whip.

He had no clue about the history of semblances in the Savannah rock club, much less that they'd been stirred up earlier in the day. And he was light years away from knowing his brief encounter with the beautiful blonde stemmed from the evil phantom searching for CJ. Even so, Dean was no idiot. Maybe he couldn't pinpoint the ominous presence in the air, but questionable behavior wasn't anything new; he'd seen plenty of it over the years, and he didn't intend for this batch of nonsense to get in his way.

With the next concert only a few hours away, he

suddenly remembered his gut feeling about this gig—way back, when he first saw it on the list of potential contracts. The Interlude in Savannah. The phrase alone seemed to welcome the unknown. Still, he thought it best to keep an eye on the business end of things, which meant he had to get to the club.

Dean had driven plenty of times in America, but he still wasn't used to driving on the wrong side of the road, much less maneuvering a gigantic SUV across the city. He left the hotel before the band, claiming he needed some extra time with the bulky vehicle. Truth be told, he was eager to get a jump-start on the merchandising.

The minute the dust had settled in New Orleans, Dean got on the horn, attempting to have more merchandise brought in for the show in Savannah. All he could do was borrow from a drop shipment sitting in Charleston. He'd arranged to have the merchandise shipped overnight, but there was no guarantee it would make it in time. On the slight chance it did, he wanted to be the first to rip the boxes open.

The sales in New Orleans had surpassed everyone's expectations, and Dean knew he got caught with his pants down. If the crowd in Savannah happened to buy merchandise at the same furious rate, he planned on giving them something to buy.

Unsure about many things, he barreled through the streets of Savannah, heading for The Interlude.

The back door of The Interlude slammed shut.

Brandon's eyes popped open. The first thing he saw was Manny, The Interlude's house technician, kicking his leg into the kitchen to activate the motion detectors. The light came on and Manny went in through the arched entrance.

Brandon rubbed his head. He examined his surroundings, then crawled out from behind the half stairs.

Manny came out of the kitchen and saw Brandon standing a few feet away, and since he'd been in the kitchen for all of two seconds, he seemed to think Brandon had appeared from thin air. He stood frozen, bug-eyed, still troubled by the ghost activity he'd witnessed earlier.

Brandon stared back.

The look they shared said it all; that nothing had really happened earlier, that it was business as usual, that this would stay between them ... whatever *this* was.

"You got people outside," Manny said, then went down the thin hallway and into the showroom.

The setting sun was blinding when Dean pulled into the parking lot. He snatched his briefcase from the passenger seat, then flung the door open and hopped out of the SUV. As he closed the door, he noticed the flashing lights of a squad car in the side-view mirror. He turned around to see a small crowd gathered around a wooden guardrail, the only thing separating River Street from the mighty Savannah River, eighteen feet below. A police van pulled up as Dean approached the crowd. One policeman stood by the railing, scribbling in his notebook.

"Something happen here, mate?" Dean asked him.

"Just an accident," the cop said, his face in a notebook. "Nothing to see."

Dean went closer and noticed a set of black tire marks running against the flow of traffic. The tire tracks disappeared at the edge of River Street, bookended by broken guardrails.

Dean patted the damaged railing. "Looks like some wanker drove through the bloody thing."

"Ya think?" the policeman said, still not raising his head.

"Dean!" someone hollered.

Dean turned around to see Brandon running toward him.

"Dean, I gotta talk to you!" said Brandon, coming to a halt. "Something strange is going on here. I think—" Brandon saw the policeman standing next to Dean and he paused. He spun Dean away from the policeman's view, then leaned in close and said, "I heard CJ was involved in this."

"CJ?" Dean scoffed. "Why, that's ridiculous. What would CJ have to do with an automobile … crashing through the …" Dean turned to the policeman, who'd already stepped closer to eavesdrop. "What kind of automobile was it?" Dean asked the cop.

"Some guy in a white limo," the officer told him. "A

witness said he had a fight with his girlfriend. Then she drove him over the edge." He scratched his eyebrow, and with a slight chuckle he said, "*Literally.*"

"Bloody naff." Dean turned to Brandon. "CJ warned me about her …" He put a hand to his chin. "Although I believe he …"

The policeman came closer. "Do you know the suspect?"

"Suspect?" Dean argued. "Sounds more like a victim to me, wouldn't you say?"

The cop folded his pad and tucked it in the back of his pants. "Boy, if I had a dime …" He threw a wary look at Dean, and then faced Brandon. "How about you? Do you know the … *victim*?"

"I … I came outside afterward. Some guy—a vendor, I think—told me what happened. I didn't really … I didn't see anything."

"Which guy was that? Do you see him in this crowd?"

Brandon probed the crowd for the vendor. "I don't see him now. He was loading a … a truck … an old green truck." Brandon pointed to his left. "Over there. He was pissed off."

"What was he loading?"

"Looked like a bunch of wood scraps … I guess. Baskets and wooden crates. I didn't look at his stuff. I was …" Brandon slipped his hands in his pockets. "I was listening more than looking."

The policeman saw some shards of wood scattered

on the street where Brandon had pointed. He went and gathered a few, then held them up to his face for a down-home examination. "How long ago was that?" he asked, walking back to the guardrails. He held the splinters next to the broken railing. After spotting the blatant differences in the two types of wood, he looked at Brandon from the corner of his eye. "I'm gonna need a way to reach you." He pulled a business card from his shirt pocket and offered it to Brandon, purposely holding it a foot higher than Brandon's hand.

Brandon lowered his eyelids.

The policeman grinned, then lowered the card and said, "I'm Officer Travis. Do you live in Savannah?"

Brandon nipped the card from his hand.

"I'll need you to come to the police station and fill out a report."

"Like I was trying to say, I have a show in a few minutes. Can I—" Brandon's eyes popped out of his head when he realized what he'd just said. He faced Dean.

Dean met Brandon's stare, his face also brimming with anxiety. "Flat out! *The show!*" Dean grabbed Brandon by the shoulders and stared him down. "Brandon ... where's CJ?"

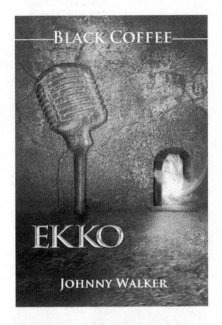

Nathan Juju

Meet *Nathan Juju*, the band that lives in the books.

Now that you've read a bit about the band and road crew, who babysit E on tour, we welcome you to experience the songs on Nathan Juju in full format, uncut and uninterrupted by semblances and strange lights.

The songs vary from southwestern rock to melodic instrumentals, featuring male and female vocals. Some tunes are straight and narrow, while others take a road less traveled. Their signature sound comes from the twinning of electric violin and electric guitar throughout the songs, adding a smooth edge to the rock beat.

There are live snippets in the electronic multimedia books, and samples on the EKKO Mysteries web site. This is not an Audio book; it's a CD of songs from within the story.

To learn more about Nathan Juju, please visit the band's web site @ Nathan_Juju.com

We thank you for your support and hope you enjoyed the adventures of CJ, as well as the good 'ol rock-n-roll of Nathan Juju.